TRIPLE CROWN PUBLICATIONS PRESENTS

GRIMEY
By
Ka Shamba Williams

Compilation and Introduction copyright © 2004 by
Triple Crown Publications
PO Box 247378
Columbus, Ohio 43224
www.TripleCrownPublications.com

Library of Congress Control Number: 2004102057
ISBN# 0-9747895-1-8
ISBN 13: 978-0-9747895-1-4
Editor: Kathleen Jackson
Consulting: Vickie M. Stringer

First Trade Paperback Edition Printing February
2004

10 9 8 7 6 5

Printed in the United States of America

Dedication

This book no doubt is dedicated to my sweet angel watching over me, my first born, Robert Ross, Jr. aka Lil' Bobby. Even though you're gone, you manage to still make your presence known. Thank you for comforting me on those tear-jerking sleepless nights. I know that you are with me forever...

To my daughter, Mya, I am so proud of you. You are growing into a very mature pre-teen ☺. If you were to grant me one wish, my wish would be that you'd join me in the literary world. Some talents, you just can't hide. You'll find it in your heart one day to pen stories. I know it. It's already in you. Dreams can be reality, always remember that.

To my daughter, Mecca, anyone who looks into those beautiful eyes can see the sparkle that's behind them. You have the natural ability to take over any room you enter with your presence. If you use that ability in a positive way, you are destined to be a media magnet.

To my son, Mehki, the honorable Rev. will say this over and over again, "Be careful what you pray for!" Baby boy, you are a handsome handful, but the most loving child of them all. Thank you for constantly reminding me that after you, there will be no more!!

To my husband, Lamotte, thank you once again for the unceasing support. Holding it down while I'm on tour, signings, meetings, photo shoots, filming, writing late nights, all that stuff! I realize that you have your own career but sacrifice many times, just to balance the family all out. You've been there for me when I was down and out and now when I'm... oh, I guess I got a little above myself ☺. Anyway, you know how much you're appreciated!

This book is also dedicated to the grimey individuals on the streets and those hiding behind masked faces, you know who you are and I do too! It's written all over your face and you don't even realize it.

Acknowledgements

I must give praise to God for everything that has evolved in me. Without Him, I am nothing.

Thank you to all the readers that sometimes sacrifice ends to buy a book and to the real readers who express their true feelings, after reading a book. If it weren't for you, there would be no us. Thank you!

In less than twelve months, I was blessed to put out two Urban Tales. Words can't describe the way I feel. Thank you so much, Triple Crown Publications. You've allowed me to flourish with this company. I am humbly grateful for the opportunity. Vickie and Shannon, the vital information that you provide me with on a daily basis, I will never turn a deaf ear to. For giving so freely, both of you will be blessed three-fold! Specials thanks goes out to the entire TCP staff, Lauren for sharing your honest opinion, Leah for holding me down in Blinded, to Keith Saunders for the outstanding book covers and to the models, shout out to Barbara on the Blinded cover, I can't tell you how many compliments you've received, girl you are getting much play! Although, I have to admit, I had to take the credit sometimes LOL!

To all my family and friends, Mom-Mom, Mom, Kenyatta, Angie, Kenny, RIP Aunt Alice, RIP Mom, Aunt Charlotte, Aunt Darlene and Aunt Delores, Granddad, Dad, Dee, Grandmom Portia, Pop-Pop, Leslie, Alexis, Bonita, Brian, Kashamba, RIP MJ and Tanya, Malik, Aunt Paulette, Uncle Saint, Steven, Kim, Teali, Michael, Lois Moore, Jasmine, Lamotte, Shontai, Donald,

Glenn, Poppy, RIP, Grandmom Florene, Shana, Shay, Janice, Cory, Tracy, Richard, Prentiss, Sam, Dawn, Pete, Uncle Mike, Uncle Edward, Uncle David, Buddha, Randy, Brian, Chalary, Rhonda, Renee, Theresa, Robin, Armelvis Booker, Cindy, Donza, Selma, Tara, Nieka, Cheryl, Tiffany, Shawn, Nicole, Tammy, Charmaine, Melissa, Kiana, Will, Cabrella, Russell, Ada, Jimae, Kiesha, Terrance, Red, Mrs. Lois, Ronnie, Gale, Sheen, Karen, Kevin, Dee-Dee, Shawn, Demar, Deartis, Shell, Bryon, LaRae, Tilla, Tracy, Kelly, Parry, Marcy, Jay, Troy, Black, Sondra, Melanie, Kitty, Ms. Linda, Kita, Helen, Mr. Larry, Leondre Prince, Keith, Spoony, Chuck, Dawn, Andre Harris, Nee-Nee, Jackie, Tiny and family, Devon, Bryon, Chittum, Rob Berry, Yo-Yo, Joanie, Tameeka, Donna, Marie, Sia, Wink, Simone, Tony, Sabrina, Dona, UL, Brian, Shannon, Wilbur, Tara, Danielle, Dwayne, Linda, Camena, Mesa, Derrick, Dennis, Milford Revival Center, Shiloh Worship Center, Francine, Timmy, Ronnie, Kendell, Mira, Roslyn, Tigger, Joanie out of Jersey, Brian, Nicole, Shiela, Leo, Michelle, Terrace Bowman, Adrienne Bey, Camp Defy, Hope Rose, (DPI, Inc.), Ken-do Photography, Anthony, Ebony, Urban Anthony. A special shout out to Mil Dirty for supporting me in anyway you could. Thanks for the honest criticism. I respect you for that! Kevin Carr (ourcityjammin.com), thank you for shining the lights on my website, you always come through for a sista. People if you need a website, graphic designs, contact him kcarr78@comcast.net. Corry Burris (Picture That Productions), whether it was blistering cold or a warm and sunny day, you always made time to film. I told you, the sky is the limit – keep sticking around me and we are bound to blow! Just wait to hear the whistle sound. Ray Woods aka Cho Woods, author of "Brotherly Love, Sisterly Affection," your talents can never go unnoticed. Trust and believe it will come to pass. Thank you for helping out with my C.D.'s. John Williams (Save The Seed, Inc.), thank you for always believing in me, not a day goes by I don't appreciate it. Let's continue to save those seeds! It's tough, but somebody has to do it. To my Aberdeen family, Mrs. Connie, Ms. Chandler, Mr. Green, Bobby, Duvowel, James, Mrs. Pauline, Mrs. Brenda, the Housing Authority staff, Autumn, Ella, Pam, Theresa, Alphonso, Rayford, Malcom, Badger, Ayatta, Mike, Vick, everybody down there, Lill, Shereese, Cherita, Mary Hurdle, Linda, Monica, Amanda, Kim, Professor Mayfield. To my brothas on lock down, Devon Gardner, Keith Watson, Mike Reynolds, Coley Hobson, Marc Briggs, D. Jamison, Nyerere Bey, Corey Bridgeforth and William. Keep your head!! To everybody, Westside, 22nd Street, Riverside, Market, everybody holding me down! If I forgot anybody, you are in that "to everybody" shout out ☺!

To all my nieces and nephews, I love you and continue to strive hard in school. You need that education.

To the TCP family, Nikki Turner, I'm happy for you. Tracy Brown, keep doing your thang! K'wan, you motivate me to write like none other. Joylynn, stay on your hustle, I like your style. T.N. Baker, good luck to you. Kane and Abel, much respect to you. To all the new authors coming up on TCP, just stay focused and be humble, the rest will come. That's the best advice I can give you.

To all the authors who looked out and shined on Precioustymes Entertainment's web site. Marni Williams, Crystal Baynard (Girl, we're doing big things together!), K'wan, Tracy Brown, Mark Anthony, Al-Saadiq Banks, Author of No Exit and Block Party, I'm telling everyone, it's a must they cop both. To aspiring authors on the come up, if you need someone to blast out about your book, visit www.precioustymesentertainment.com and to all those still waiting to get posted, it will happen soon, I promise.

To all the bookstores that keep my books on the shelves, thank you for supporting me. Mejah Bookstore, thank you so much Emelyn and Marilyn, Ninth Street Bookstore, Waldenbooks, Shrine of the Black Madonna, Truth Bookstore, Tru Bookstore, Karibu Bookstore, Tooks Book Cart, Black Images Book Bazaar, Jokaes African American Books, Borders, Cush City, A&B Bookstore, The Literary Boutique, Hue-man Bookstore, Masomba, Liquorius Bookstore, African American Images, Nubian Bookstore, Haneef's Bookstore, Oasis, African Spectrum and special thanks to the street vendors holding both the books down, to many more, thank you for helping one of my dreams come to life.

To all the book clubs, thank you for the hot reviews, Rawsistazs, Mahogany Bookclub, Ebony Expressions, Sister2Sister Bookclub, No Baggage Bookclub. I can't forget all those who posted comments on my website and those who spread the word about my book by mouth, thank you! Thank you for everyone who invited me to set up at an event. Thanks for helping me support my children!!

To all the African-American Film makers, especially the Hip-Hop moguls – Ice Cube, Master P, Dame Dash, Hype Williams, would you holla at a sista ☺.

Prologue

On one of the busiest days of the week, the United States Parcel warehouse was overstocked on the gurneys with outgoing boxes. Rather than gripe about the overload, the crew members laughed and joked as they normally did everyday. Everyone dressed in brown uniforms, slightly dusted by the shifting of the shipment. It was an ordinary day at the job. Clerks pulled orders from overtop, underneath, in between and stuck in corners, trying to load all of the packages on the respective United States Parcels delivery trucks. Truck #10, bound for Wilmington, Delaware, was fully loaded and ready to go. Russell, the driver, spent late hours the night before getting his drink on, his mouth twisted, loosely hanging as if the world owed him something for working a nine to five. Had he known that he would be called into work at 5:00 a.m., he may have reconsidered going out, putting the partying as a lingered thought.

The night before he was tired as hell, but when his boss rang out time and a half for his day off, he was down for the ride, even with the smell of alcohol seeping from his pores. Russell's route was going so smoothly, the sun shined brightly and the clouds apparatus separated blossoming beautiful shapes. It was soothing the music at a bare minimum as he enjoyed the scenery. So much, he decided a little power nap on the road was needed. Instead of pulling over to the side, or at a rest stop, he dozed while driving on the Delaware Memorial Bridge, just 10 minutes short from reaching his final destination. His eyelids were very heavy as he fought to keep them open. His eyelids dropping every few seconds, finally won the battle.

They were now completely closed. The truck glided from one side of the bridge to the other. Even the constant horn honking didn't wake this hung over driver out of his much-needed rest. Drivers intently watched, stopping their cars to avoid being in the collision that was to come. The truck hit the solid side railings going at a high speed of 93 miles per hour. The impact wobbled the truck causing it to skid on two wheels. The weight of the vehicle was too much for it to handle. On the freeway this day, was disorder, mayhem from the beginning of the bridge to the sadistic end.

While the truck couldn't stay steady on two wheels, it slammed against the blacktop flipping over three to four times. Russell, unacquainted with his fate, flew over to one side of the window to the next, shattering glass every time his head smashed against it. Blood was forming from the skull pouring out like a fire hydrant gaped opened. The accident was so bad that Russell was pronounced dead at the scene. The remains from Truck #10 spread across the highway, sprawled out like a dump truck had spilled its remnants. A towing company wheeled away the cargo and the decapitated truck to the tow yard, holding traffic up at least two hours. To release the remains from the USP truck, an authorized personnel person from USP had to personally claim that the packages collected were, in fact, in the possession of Truck #10 bound for Wilmington, Delaware from New York City on that day. It took the lazy ass officials two months before they would travel to Delaware to verify the contents. Inside the remains were the answers to many questions the Foster family hadn't resolved.

Rightfully so, the boxes were beat up but none damaged or torn from the impact. Finally, they were gathered together and taken to the Delaware USP shipyard for examination. Recipients were given courtesy calls to let them know they had packages waiting for them at the Ruthar Drive office location. Most of the packages were delivered due to the lapse in time. The packages addressed to Ms. Rhonda, Mona's mother were two of them.

On the flip side, the beauty of Granny's estate stood out amid the other estates miles away. The gated house, with a driveway that even the celebrity red carpet couldn't extend the length of, was outlined with steel electrical lights that enhanced the beauty of the black asphalt. Prince parked his SUV outside of the gate, and for the first time,

walked holding his hand to his face to avoid
the horrid sun glare, onto the pavement that
led to Granny's house instead of pulling
around in the horseshoe driveway in front of
the house. Fed up with all the pretending and
foul company he kept, he made up in his mind
this was the final straw. Not another day
could he remain pretending like he was living
the life deserving to him. This reality hit
close to home when he found out Mona was
murdered.

Had he known sooner, he would have
graced the funeral with his presence, at least
to pay his last respects. Instead, he found out
weeks after. Though Mona misbehaved in his
presence on a number of occasions, he was
still fond of her style. He didn't like the bad
girl image she tried to portray cuz he had seen
the gentler side of her. With the realization
that Cam would soon be out to confront him,
he wouldn't allow defeat to conquer him. He
isolated himself from everyone, including
Cam, trying to piece together a plan that
would set him and his daughter, Mya, free.

Nikki, his baby's mother, updated him
on all the talk being said underground. He
pleaded with her to leave Kiesha's trick house,
the one Cam sent her to for being disloyal to
him, and try to start over new by admitting
herself into a rehabilitation center. She
denied his request. This day would be the last
time Granny would set eyes on Mya. It was
already bad enough that Nikki was known to

the addict world as "Peaches," Now, Hitting the pipe convinced her that she had given up hope for her life. She didn't want any parts of Mya at all. Mya was someone else's problem, not hers. Drugs enthralled her life and it was no turning back.

Prince went over to Kiesha's whorehouse one last time to convince Nikki to leave trickin' for crack, for Mya's sake. Nikki refused the invitation once more, and instead told him this time to take care of Mya the best way he knew fit. Her life of happiness was taken years ago by the murder of her husband and the birth of a child with a father that constantly was concealed to everyone except for four people: the mother, the father, the mother's grandmother and Mona, an acquaintance, who stumbled upon the information while living in Nikki's grandmother's house snooping in the woman's personal belongings.

However, Mona never had the chance to tell anyone before her death. She took that secret to her grave. Now the only chance Nikki had to relive her former happiness was to make her memories come to life, by getting high smoking on that glass dick. The drugs gave her the illusion that things were okay, nothing hurt, all the pain was gone. The drugs kept her happy and that's the only feeling she needed.

Prince's palms were sweaty, and even though this was the normal routine for Friday, this Friday would be much different. He'd talked to Granny a few weeks ago and told her how he really felt about the ordeal. Their conversation never left the two of them, for the bond was too great for Granny to deceive him. Even when Granny opened the door things seemed very strange.

The door crackled, making squeaking noises that a spray of WD40 lubricant would take care of. She greeted him very exuberating hoping to receive the same response in return. Prince asked Granny if it was okay if he took Mya by herself this time, instead of them going out together. She never opposed and never thought twice about it, because she knew Mya was safe in Prince's custody. They had a spiritual bond between them. She handed him two bags of money and asked him to deposit it in the account as usual.

When Prince left with Mya that early Friday morning, he had his mother clean out the account that she co-owned with Mya and got on I-95 South, never turning back. Prince had a lot of explaining to do on the ride. Mya was shielded from the truth all of this time, thinking Cam, her mother's boyfriend, was her father. Prince was really her biological father, and played the role as her father without Mya knowing the real truth. He spent more time with Mya on a weekly basis than her alleged father, Cam and her mother, Nikki did on a monthly basis. When Mya didn't return that evening, Granny knew in her heart that Prince finally did what she'd been praying for all these years, take his daughter away from the drama she was in the middle of. She knew neither Nikki nor Cam were capable of providing a decent lifestyle for her. Prince was the only one she trusted anyway. She knew Mya was in good hands.

Chapter One
Flashback...

Camron and Kenny sat staring, astonished by the thrill of darkness, experiencing emotions associated with death, swallowing up what appeared to be the apartment walls. Black clouds of fear filled the room instead of the normal puff of gray smoke from the foot long 'ew whop, *three blunts rolled into one thick ass blunt,* pearly perfected earlier by Kenny. After each man sucked in the feigned mind altering drug... *"Purple Haze,"* the room closed in, unbalanced from the movement of a single tractor-trailer agitating the bedroom windows. Minds now racing in anxiety, analyzing each occurrence in their lives that could've been handled differently, without a blink.

The game changed and all the insane killings, fornicators, crack addicts, snitches and deceiving *"Ghetto celebrities,"* proved it time and time again. Kenny and Cam sat in silence, listening only to the sounds of city life, until one decided to speak. The droplets of water that fell against the window had a crashing sound, plopping one drip at a time. They could hear each droplet as if they were sitting directly by the window. The only thoughts that clouded their minds were that of Mona, Cam's former girlfriend that he murdered months ago. The memory of Mona's funeral haunted both of them, haunting their minds. Camron's heart had been shattered into small, bite size pieces.

Smoking out was not his forte, but recently smoking weed eased his mind, helped him think clearer. They were on hiatus from everyone, for a minute, until things got back to normal. They didn't hustle or show their faces, both stayed strictly on the low. Mona seemed to be the topic of conversation that kept popping up each time they conversed. Kenny's heart was bruised by his younger brother's ego. His facial expression was overly animated, exaggerating his displeasure of his brother but knowing damn well, he was just as guilty, withholding information on a murder.

"Damn Cam, what would make you do some stupid shit like that?" Kenny asked, his eyebrows raised with his back humped over in position.

"That girl didn't deserve that man. How could you be so in love with her but hate her at the same time?" His back, now straighten from his body stiffening, giving off mixed signals like he truly cared. "Her moms couldn't even view her body. She had to pay her last respects with a closed casket."

The unconscious manifestation of his words was an attempt to hide his own guilt.

"You know it was even wrong to attend the funeral knowing you were the cause of her death. After all these years, I thought you would at least show some type of humility. At least in the name of our mother. Word to life! I can't believe you man." Kenny knew his brother was a cold-blooded murderer with a vendetta against anyone who had nerve enough to cross him.

The murder of Mona Foster, his last girlfriend, once again confirmed his evil being. Kenny didn't agree with how his brother ended her life, simply because she cheated on him with Brooklyn's Rap mogul, "Controversy." It wasn't like they had kids together. They were basically screwing partners, wasn't no real love there. Others thought it was, but shit, how could there have been. If he loved her that much, she would still be alive. Actually, the murder wasn't really about her, it was the fact that someone had the audacity to deceive the deceiver. And, Mona did it best. The Artist of Deception himself couldn't handle what he dished out. She played him and he couldn't stomach losing the battle in the war of a relationship. His failure in relationships proved to him, what he refused to believe, that he would never find true love.

Within, Kenny felt convicted knowing that his brother killed again. He often wondered when the murders would stop. Cam left him, not only to morn his two younger brothers, but a younger sister also. Left with little sympathy, he knew the madness had to end. Internally, Kenny hoped he would be the reason that Cam was mandated to stop.

Mona and Cam shared relations for a short period of time. They elevated from a one-night stand to what seemed like a five year run, in reality it was only one year. From the beginning, though from similar backgrounds, they were incompatible and doomed for failure.

She excelled in high school, beating the high school drop out status. Maintained an apartment and drove a nice little car for a teenager. She fed off of taking naïve individuals pride. It wasn't until she coupled up with Cam that the layers of strength began to peel away from her. After hooking up with him, she began to realize that she wasn't ready for the fast street mentality of Brooklyn, New York. The street life in Delaware was no where near comparison to that of Brooklyn and she soon found that out.

Camron was a Brownsville native, growing up on the seventeen hundred block of Prospect Plaza, surrounded by three huge housing complexes standing fifty-some stories tall. His childhood, wilted and full of abuse, created an unsympathetic path for a young boy growing up as a young man. His stepfather Jab was a discrete heroin addict of thirty-seven years. Kenny, the eldest of five children, became accustomed to the psychological and physical abuse.

Cam, the second oldest, thought of his brother as a coward, a sissy even. He hated Jab with ferocity and contemplated his death many times in his dreams. He studied his stepfather closely. The point being to learn his moves, it could make or break him if he didn't follow closely. Time was an essential factor when it came to this matter. It never failed when Mrs. Shug, their mother, left for church, Jab would begin to search through the room trying to find her money stash. After searching for fifteen minutes and coming up with nothing, he would start on the kids. Since Mrs. Shug only worked part-time, she wasn't able to provide for the kids like she desired to. Jab was unemployed and successful at being unemployed. His desire wasn't to stabilize a job, only his drug addiction.

Once Jab found out what happened to his kids, he left the surroundings afraid of what his crazy ass stepson would do to him, caging his emotions yet allowing them to occupy a space of hate. Little did he know, his bucking attempts to hide would one day surface to loosen the feelings of hatred. He was bound to bump into him someday.

"Look nigga." Cam responded, without biting his tongue, trying relentlessly to make Mona an afterthought in his mind.

"Her slick ass deserved what was coming to her. Of course, I had to attend the funeral services, dumb ass. If I didn't, suspicion would've been directed all at me. Her brother, Yatta, is on the payroll remember. We don't need the heat from him and those trigger happy Forklift niggas he run with. At least not right now."

Not only was Cam angry that he had to keep Yatta close but he was furious at himself for letting Mona convince him to help the Forklift niggas come up in the drug game with major dough. The Forklift niggas started purchasing all types of luxury cars, expensive jewelry and the latest models of guns with the money they made. It was protect and serve on 5th and Forklift, the street where Yatta and his crew hustled. In a matter of minutes, they would be ready to take on a battalion army squad.

Yatta raised the conscious level of everyone. He told his crew, everyone was a suspect. If it even appeared like someone was acting shiesty about his sister's death, they were a done deal.

Cam had no idea that Yatta was so level headed, unlike him. His downfall was his cocky, so very arrogant attitude. People hated to be in his company. Everything was always about him or for him. He wanted to control his every situation and everyone else's. Most of his peers only put up with him because they needed him for something, other than that, they didn't give a damn about him. He was bloody meat on the cylinder cutter, a second away from getting sliced up. What he really needed was a reality check. A straight, gut check and only God could give him that.

"I heard you stepped up for prayer. What was up with you?" Kenny asked, trying to ponder his brother's actions.

"That's right playa. A thug needs love, too." Radiated Cam, laughing on the inside as if it were a joke. Circumventing the question altogether, Cam refused to answer Kenny, brushing the question off with a bullshit response.

"You on some unrighteous shit, man! Playing with God is like playing Russian roulette. You ready to die? Cause if not, stop playing son." Kenny was heated, standing stiff as a board, hands tucked inside her pockets with his fists clenched. He hated the very essence of his brother's being.

"That's alright." He thought outloud to himself. "He'll get his one day."

"Now, what would it look like if I didn't show my spiritual support?" Cam asked, reflecting back to the day Mona was laid to rest.

The death registered in Kenny's mind over and over again. Thinking about it, he lowered his head and allowed two soft tears to trickle from his eyes. She may have played his brother but she was al'ight with him. He got plenty of trim on the strength of her. She was like his little sister. Cam would have never exposed his sympathetic side; but Kenny was known to shed a tear or two. Ignoring his brother's depressing spirit, Cam finally responded to the question, trying to come up with the right answers. He took a minute to respond. If Kenny could read the signs that Cam was lying, he would have caught on but he didn't.

"Yo bro, I was a little crazed going up there wasn't I? Come to think of it, what the hell was I thinking? Don't you get like seven times worse or some shit like that when you backslide after repenting? I really got saved that day. I can't believe it. I must be out my goddamn mind. You know what though playa, I felt a little lighter after the Rev. prayed for me, on the real!" Kenny was still in thought and ignored him as he continued to speak.

"Hey man, don't you hear me?" Cam's vocal cords tightened under all this stress, changing his raspy voice to a higher pitch. Taking his position on the plush leather sofa, Kenny finally gave him feedback. His stomach was bubbling with hatred and he was ready to express his hatred aggressively. Cam was his only living sibling and he hated him so much. How could they share the same mother and father when they were like black and white, so very different? They never knew their biological father, he died when both of them were very young.

15

"You's a cold nigga Bro, and right now, I have some ill feelings fo' ya." Kenny's words garbled and his sentence was barely audible.

"Shut up! You bitch ass sucka, man made *mothafuckaaa*." Cam retorted, elongating his last word, with a serious griddled look of disgust on his face.

"If I gave you a loaded 45, you wouldn't know what to do with it, Pussy! You soft duke! Anger and frustration quickly embarked the room. They weren't feeling the bliss of being high anymore, rather they analyzed one another in this stage of their high. Kenny leapt up from the sofa and grabbed Cam by the collar.

"Listen young'n, you may think I'm a little soft, but please don't ever underestimate me." He pushed Cam back so hard, Cam hit his head against the wall.

"So, a nigga has a little heart." Kenny could almost taste Cam's breath as he spoke. The pictures hanging on the wall shook from the impact. One of them, the picture of Mona that mystified her existence, fell to the floor fracturing the glass.

"I'm glad you're finally stepping up, I was starting to think that time in Riker's State Prison did your ass in." Cam reached down alongside his pant leg and pulled out the small toy he kept hidden, a 32 caliber, and pointed it directly at the temple of his big brother. Kenny's heart was beating fast and the thumping of his chest, you could see raising up and down. Cam smelled the fear that he put into him and was satisfied he made his point. He dropped the gun and stepped away from his brother. Kenny took in deep breaths, relieved that the trigger was never pulled. His second reaction was to pick up the gun and blast off on his only brother, but the love for his mother caused him to think a little clearer. He didn't want to be anything like his younger brother.

"Be easy big brother, I was just testing you. Now for real, we need to raise up out of Philly. This condo is getting really hot. Just the other day, I thought I seen some unusual faces plotting back in the cut. Let's get to packing, we're on our way back to the city, New York." Cam didn't realize the relationship he built with his brother was severed years ago. Kenny would finally demonstrate to his brother that love, especially when it wasn't given unconditionally, was rendered null and void in his eyes.

Chapter Two
Missing You

When the reality of Mona's death finally hit Nee, her best friend, she couldn't stand the loss. She couldn't believe Mona was never coming back. She acted out in ways that were really out of character for her. That sneaky, soft-spoken woman became a wicked, vindictive individual overnight. "No ho's barred," was her philosophy. Meaning, the countless actions of males will, for once, feel that griminess on her behalf. No man was to be spared. In for the dough, out for the ho, the ho's being the men she schemed on.

The lesson to be learned from Mona's death, she wasn't feeling. Her lesson was "get in where you fit in." Whatever needed to be dealt with had to be taken care of right then. Tomorrow is never promised, so while she had today, she had to handle her business no matter what. She kept up an apartment on the East side of town. It was rather small, but it suited the needs of her and her 7-year old daughter, Kenya. Even though after the funeral, she packed up all Kenya's things and sent her to live with her mother so she could live alone.

Nee was woman enough to admit the life she was living, a child should never be exposed to it. She made sure Kenya had everything she needed, paying her Mom every week to help out with the groceries and living expenses. She had a set schedule of visitation as if she'd officially went down to family court and they ordained the order. She never let any man come in between her visitations. Her intentions were almost always good when it came down to her daughter. One would have thought she'd change her life around since her impactful loss, however the loss made her turn just the opposite. She was now very spiteful and bitter. She knew it was get up or lay down and she wasn't ready to lie down.

Nee sat inside her apartment, lying in her plush Teal colored swivel chair. All of her girls clowned her about buying a "retirement" chair at such a young age, but every time they came over to her apartment, they'd be fighting trying to be the first one to put their fat ass in it. That's how comfortable the swivel chair was. Instead of her sleeping in the bedroom, sometimes she'd find herself crashed at night right in the swivel chair, body lounging over in comfort. Her legs were crossed and her hands were folded as she looked at the shrine on her wall of Mona.

As memorabilia, the entire "Won Sumth'n Clique" received a 24 x 36 photo frame with a collage of pictures that they all took together with her. Since the funeral, the "Won Sumth'n Clique" gracefully asked Nee to play the role as the active leader in their clique until they found someone suitable. Humbly, she declined. When Mona was living, Nee rarely hung out with them without Mona being around. The mere thought of them asking her to be an active leader let her know her game stepped up considerably. Though it was a compliment to her come up, it was best that she carried on as she did before, on her solo mission. The center picture on her wall was of Mona and the clique posted up at Delaware's exclusive nightclub, Club Utopian. That night, Delaware's own radio personality, DJ Doc B of Power 99 FM, was spinning in the DJ's booth.

"Now that was a night to remember!" She smiled an unforced smile that spread gleefully on her face, as she reminisced.

"That night we were all blitzed." She said to herself, in a one-sided conversation. Mona had bought the bar out for all her friends. She even went against the rules and paid for the dudes in the club as well that night. Nee couldn't help but smile as she reflected back on that night.

She used all the tools and rules of engagement in the game, her best friend taught her wisely. Mona would surely be proud of her. Countless times she told Nee she needed to step her game up. Nee's game was so tight now, not even the best of the best of hustlers could run that shit on her. A man couldn't do anything for her that she couldn't do for herself. Except, be a warm body when she needed one.

Tears of sadness dropped from her face to her fully extended lips that still formed a smile. Sadly, the last time she met up with Mona was when she and Yatta met up with Cam at Kiesha's trick house to cop drugs. Cam surprised Mona by telling her to meet him at Kiesha's crib, around the same time he was to meet them. He, per say, wasn't really stressing about meeting with her. What he really wanted her for was to visit with her brother and best friend since she hadn't seen them in a minute.

Nee remembers clearly that day. Mona was excited beyond belief that she finally had a lusty affair with one of Brooklyn's hottest rappers around, Controversy. Not wanting to forget one detail of their sex-capade, Mona allowed Controversy to tape every lasting moment.

At the time, Mona wasn't thinking with intelligence, but with lust. She gave the porn tape to Nee, telling her it was mandatory she watch it and how she put her thing down with Controversy, with her "snap back come back" loving.

Nee heeded to Mona's request, taking it home and watching the dreadful tape that had wild sex scenes with Controversy burning hot wax on Mona's body, using a sexual stimulant, nympho cream on her genitals, to keep her wanting more.

They sexed in the common areas of his apartment, the living room couch, the kitchen counter, the dining room table, until he picked her up with his big chocolate muscular arms and took her to the bedroom, pounding inside her hotness, every step of the way.

It was in the bedroom the scene changed. Controversy handcuffed Mona to his bed and blindfolded her eyes with his bondage items that he kept in his bedroom closet. This was spicy, kinky sex for Mona, considering the one thing Cam lacked was spontaneity in the bedroom.

Once Controversy had her in this position, he left the room as if he were going to the bathroom. Nee could see Mona sprawled out on the bed, cuffed and blindfolded, lying on her stomach with her face looking in the direction of the wall. Then all of a sudden, the lights dim to a minimum and you could see a man fully clothed, coming into the room pulling down his pants, creeping up from behind to sex Mona. It was visibly clear that it wasn't Controversy. After the man was done, another came in, and then another and another, they were running a train on her without Mona knowing! Sexual it was, but worth a dear friend or family member watching, not! Nee hid that tape in a safe location, hoping no one would ever discover it, at least, not in Delaware. That's what most rappers who film girls do, sell the tapes to the public, maximizing off the groupies. She prayed that Controversy would only toss the tape around in New York and not filter it in her hometown.

She was determined to get back at Kenny and Cam's ass for what happened to Mona. She looked at the time and remembered she was expecting some mail from her cousin, Unique, in the Pen. He said he had some very important information that should help her out. She raised the chair to lift up her butt that was wrapped in cotton by a soft teal color Victoria Secret's summer pajama bottom.

Teal was her favorite color. It represented her "use to be" personality, soft and humble, that's how she *used* to be. Before she could make her way into the kitchen to grab a cold brew, her doorbell rang.

"Ding, dong! Ding, dong!" The bell sung, interrupting her afternoon.

"Who the hell is it?" She yelled out, startled from the bell, mad that someone was bothering her reminiscing moments.

A faint voice of a frail elderly woman on the opposite side of the door answered, "It's the United States Postal Service, Ma'am."

Nee unlocked her door and opened it with her pajamas on. It was three o'clock in the afternoon and she was still loafing around with nothing to do. She stared at the little old lady, cutting her eyes at her.

"It should be a crime against this shit." She said, speaking directly to the postal worker.

The elderly lady was a little confused about what point Nee was trying to make. Inquisitive, so she asked her.

"What should be a crime dear?" Nee waved her hand with the gesture of "never mind" but the woman insisted she tell her what she was talking about.

"I'm just saying, the Post Office knows damn well they should have you working on the inside. No pun intended, but you are an elderly woman barely making it up these steps and it's only four of them. How do they expect you to deliver mail up and down the streets?" Nee played right into the sympathetic role that the elderly woman hoped for.

"They do M'am, but at least one day out of the week I like to come out and get my exercise in." The woman may have given the impression of being a frail woman, but she was in tiptop shape to be 60 years old.

"Anyway, I didn't want to leave this package at your front door, being this is a bad neighborhood and all. I didn't want nobody to steal it from you." Her innocent eyes darted at Nee with a charming slant. Nee started feeling very compassionate for this elderly woman for taking the time to personally see to it that she received her package. The gratitude that she felt for her kindness could be seen visually by her facial expression.

"I appreciate this very much." Nee said to the elderly woman, letting off a half smile.

"Not a problem dear. I see it must be important. I read on the package it was from someone in jail." Nee sharply cut her eyes at the woman, overrating the woman's kindness.

"Nosey, ass." She said to herself. Just that quick, her thought of the woman changed.

"Here, let me take that." Nee said, reaching over to get her mail. The postal lady stood there like she was waiting on something, a tip preferably. Nee stood there just looking at her.

"Okay, thank you lady." She said with one hand on her hip, getting ready to close the door. The elderly woman reached out, took one step inside the doorway to avoid the door from closing in her face. She spoke freely and frankly.

"Well, like I said, I don't typically do this. I just wanted to make sure." She was persistent as Girl Scouts selling those damn Girl Scout cookies, at your front door, the grocery stores, and churches. She wasn't leaving from in front of Nee's door without receiving a donation for the effort she put in. Nee got the picture.

"Hold tight a minute, damn!" She went into her apartment and pulled out a $5.00 bill from her Fendi bag. She opened the door and the elderly woman was standing right there waiting, patiently tapping her foot. Nee had hoped she'd left to deliver more mail, but nope she was still waiting.

"Have a nice day lady!" She told her.

"And if that's not good enough, too damn bad. Next time, leave my shit at the door. I don't know which is different, getting robbed by my neighbors or getting beat by the person delivering your mail. Exercise, my ass. You knew what you wanted when you came to my front door." The elderly woman was clear down the hall by now, walking with swift motion to set up her next package victim. Nee took the package and sat right back down in her comfy chair.

She was curious to know what information her cousin Unique had for her. He informed her that this kid from New York named C-Lo was his celly, and was down doing a bid on burglary charges. Anyway, the dude said that he knew all about Cam and that he knew for sure that Cam killed Mona. He said that he was the one who drove the car to Delaware waiting patiently for Mona to come back home.

Cam knew the only place she would go after getting away from him was home. So, they waited between the train station and the bus station. After a few hours went past, Cam went inside the bus station to ask them if they had a rider who purchased a ticket named Mona Foster from the Manhattan station. When they told him no, he went over to the train station, who confirmed she purchased a ticket and what time the train was arriving. Knowing that information, they waited at the train station until the train came in. Cam supposedly got out the car and left C-Lo in the car, telling him to stay put in the parking lot until he came back. Dude said he knew something was wrong when he heard all the gunfire and saw Cam come running back to the car hollering,

"Floor this mothafucka!" He said Cam's clothes were all bloody and shit. The dude couldn't have been lying. How did he know so much information and the streets weren't talking details of the murder?

I asked him why he was telling me all of this. He said because he was mad that Cam didn't pay up like he was suppose to and he wasn't even looking out for him while he was on the inside. Anyway, the nigga told me that he got this cousin that is "bout it, bout it" that just got out of Riker's named El'san. He's a thoroughbred from the Kingsborough Projects in Brooklyn, New York that's off the damn flip.

Dude is not a hustler, his hustle is the hustlers. He robs them for their "already made money." C-Lo saying a sho 'nuff way to get back at Cam is to hook up with this dude.

He said El'san would strip him of every penny he got. All you would need to do is let Yatta know, let him and the Forklift niggas handle the rest. He left El'san's telephone number and his address. The word revenge showed all over Nee's face, she didn't need anything else.

"Yeah, Mr. Camron, your day is coming!" Were the exact words that came out of her mouth, while she rocked back and forth in the chair, holding the letter tight.

Chapter Three
The Payoff...

Yatta moved carefully up the block watching the surrounding and his every move. This wasn't the first time he coped in New York but things had changed. He headed up solo on this trip and the nervousness began to dominate his senses.

Everyone was out today. It was almost a hundred people walking on either side of the street. Females were taxing as usual, but this time, using their kids to con money from the hustlers. Yatta blended well with the masses, his public image was equivalent to the current trends and styles of a New Yorker.

Standing at 5'11, bubbling brown skin with a close dark taper, he was a cutie. However, today he was determined to wear his game face. There was a lesson to be learned for disseminating the Foster Family.

Cam's grimey ways were at an all time high. Everyone back home was talking about how Yatta was going out like a sucker, still coping from a man who is a suspect in his sister's murder. They didn't understand, the prices were right. If Yatta cut off his connection, then his partners would be making noise because of the decrease.

He already planned to cut Cam and Kenny off, it was only a matter of time. Actually, it was sooner than later. Since his sister's death, life was chaotic. He tried everyday to console his mother, trying to convince her it wasn't her fault. But she continued to reinforce that her lack of parenting skills was the reason. Mona watched her mother closely, just as a cub learns from its mother. Emulating every simulation of enthusiasm, sexual pleasure, jilting, full cooperation with others or people with like minds, interested in fulfilling a man's every want and desire. She imitated her mother and every rendition about a weak woman, stupid enough to let a man use her and get nothing in return. It was pure idiotic and noise to her ears.

Only negative presumptions actually distinguished the truth between man and woman, boy and girl. It was true, chastisement in the Foster household early on, was not to bring a man home or introduce him to your friends if he didn't have money. It didn't matter his methods of producing the money, he just needed to be in position to either have or get the money.

Mona learned early from overheard conversations about how her mom had been with this man and that man, and about how much money she was able to swindle them for. Ranting and raving all the time about the many material items she had, because of a man. This misinformation imparted Mona's mind.

It made her think, reality was only obtaining a high school diploma and getting a man with money to support her every need. Ms. Rhonda was accurate in her choice of words, she was a major component in her daughter's conduct on the streets. If she indeed assessed the path that lie ahead for her daughter, the unpromising and unnecessary baggage would have been tossed to the wayside earlier on. Had she not waited so late to provide nurture and unconditional love, maybe her daughter would still be alive.

He still questioned his mother's reason for getting saved in the first place. Had it not been for one of her best friends getting murdered by a man she was trying to pimp, would she have gotten saved? Or, did she fear she would end up the same way?

Rhonda's version of her accepting God in her life was that it was time, and though her words sounded convincing coming out her mouth each time she confessed, even with Christ, she still had an addiction that was yet to be dealt with. She wasn't getting high, but was reservation of getting high still in her mind? Satan knew her weakness.

The vibration from his cellular phone surprised Yatta as he walked, with caution, over to the Prospect Plaza building, hoping to bump into Cam or Kenny before climbing the filthy stairwell since the elevators were down.

Earl, Richey and Slowdown, Cam's boys, were posted up against the wall engaging in a dice game of 7-11. People surrounded them, hoping for the chance to dib in on all the cash that lay on the ground.

"Hold up, that's seven right there, four to the right and three to left on the dice! Come on baby, my baby mama want a pair of stiletto boots, and with that $700 on the roll, I can buy her a spiky pair, bay-beee!" Slowdown continued to stress his point to those in on the roll. His gold and diamond initial necklace benchmarked the dollar sign. With his black faded State Property jeans sagging, exposing his burgundy Polo boxers, Slowdown reached down to grab the money in the pot.

"Nigga, put that money down! How can that be a seven when the right dice is on four and the left dice is on four? Nigga, that's an eight. Can't you count? Now, stop playing with my loot Slowdown." Earl spoke loud and clear, knowing how Slowdown played people on the roll, trying to catch them slip'n.

"You need to get your vision checked cause today, you sure ain't seeing 20/20. Your vision is blurred son. Now come up off my goddamn money." Slowdown wasn't about to give the stash up that he already placed in his pockets.

"Richey, would you tell this joker that's a four and a four, not a four and a three on the dice roll." Earl said, trying to convince those watching.

"Man, Slowdown can see that's four and four. Nigga playing with your mental state, that's all. It's the money talking. The freshness of those $100 bills that's calling him, and that trick ass woman he keeps calling his baby mama is chomping him for another pair of those boots." Richey knew if he kerm shot, came at Slowdown sideways, he would get his attention to help Earl out, maybe get his money back.

All the others with money in the pot, dared not to come against Slowdown. He chumped the dudes into putting in money for the game he knew they didn't have a chance of winning anyway. Richey knew if Earl won the roll, he would peel off some of it to him, but if Slowdown won, that whore of a woman he had would get all the dough.

"Shit, Slowdown ain't even sure if the baby is his, talking 'bout she's his baby momma. I told his dumb ass to get a blood test. A few other brothas from the 'Borough was hitting that at the same time he was. He too scared. Talking about, 'What if my daughter is another joker's?' Like, a bitch! Acting like he don't know what his next move would be if the child wasn't his. You better beat that ass, her playing you like that. Then you'd better bounce before the Po-Po gets there. Man, I'm telling you, I'll beat a bitch ass if she plays me like that."

"You're telling me, what Richey man?" Slowdown asked, seeking answers to the point Richey was trying to make.

"There you go again, flashing back to the situation with your 'wanna be baby mama'." Slowdown laughed, as he reflected on Richey's drama.

"It was your fault she played you like that. You knew she was a 'ho' before you met her, and even more so after we set her up, but you believed that whore before your own boys. Money over bitches, niggas stick to the script." Slowdown said, bopping his head in rhythm.

"Richey, I'm telling you this is your baby." Shawna sounded so convincing trying to prove it to him.

"*After all these years we've been together, I mean it was off and on, but you know you were the only man hitting this pussy. Why do we need the white man interceding for us regarding 'our' daughter? These people don't know a damn thing and don't care about us. Look at our beautiful baby girl. She has your eyes and those full lips of yours. When she gets older, I bet she has your wide smile, showing all her teeth. Just like you! Can't you see that already? Anyway, your Momma already gave you the approval that she is your daughter. Why do we need to take it further? Don't she look like your youngest daughter, Mi-Mi? They could almost pass for twins.*"

Richey was taking in all her claims. "*Shawna, if you're so convinced this is my daughter, why the hell are you trying to plead your case? The blood test will prove whether or not she is my child. I don't give a damn about what my Momma said. She told me your son was mine too, and during that time I wasn't even hitting, so why would I consider her opinion this time? Just be prepared for the results. If Richesha don't come out to be my daughter, you better pray to God that I don't kill your ass. You done already hit me for more than eight thousand, and the little girl ain't nearly six months old yet! Clothes, pampers, strollers, cribs, sneakers, sandals, an automobile, security deposit, 1st month's rent, last month's rent, this month's rent! You taxing me for what others should've been helping you with. In 'your' apartment and with 'your' five kids by five different men; somebody else should be getting taxed. None of those kids are mine, and this one is questionable.*"

"You shouldn't be so frustrated, boo. Don't let it get to you. Once you find out Richesha is your baby, you will love me even more. I just can't believe you gonna let them stick a needle in your little girl's arm, for them to take some blood samples for a paternity test."

Shawna began to caress his head, slowly planting kisses on him.

"Do you feel it's really necessary to go through with this?" She laid her head softly on the backside of his shoulder and continued to kiss his neck.

"Hell yeah, Shawna." He replied.

"Now stop trying to use sex as a weapon. Every time you're pushed against the wall, you use sex as a tool. This time it's not going to work, so get your hands off of me. You too damn slick for me. Don't think I didn't see you last night posted up in another man's face. Slowdown and I were sitting in the parking lot watching you all over the next man. His hands were rubbing your body down all over, damn near undressing you outside. Slowdown told me to leave your scandalous ass alone ten months ago. Why didn't I listen, I would've never been put in this predicament."

"Oh I see Slowdown has a nerve! I bet you he didn't tell you he was trying to push up on me, did he? Yeah, all the times you left him over the crib, he used that as an opportunity to hit this." She said, patting her ass.

"Go 'head, I guess it's now time to pull all the tricks out your bag. My part'na never had interest in you. I told him to gut check you, to see if you would give him play. And, you did! What, didn't you think he told me about you hitting him *off and asking him for $500 a month to keep quiet about it? He gave you the money because he felt sorry for all those damn kids having a mother using modern prostitution to support her lustful ways. If you can remember clearly, that's when I stopped coming over on the regular and the money stopped. Then you decided it was time to protect your assets by blaming me as Richesha's father. For all I know, Slowdown is a candidate. That's exactly why he's meeting us up here. He wants his named cleared, in the event you try to blame Richesha on him next."*

About two weeks later, Richey found out Richesha couldn't possibly be his daughter. The test was 99.9% sure that the baby was not his. There wasn't a chance in hell that he was the father. Slowdown's paternity test indicated he was closer at 67.6%, but was ruled out as the father. Both of them were relieved.

Richey dropped Shawna after that, only after giving her a one-time ass kicking, courtesy of Richesha. A little girl that had to live with being named after a man that had no ties to her. He told her not to the name the baby that anyway!

Yatta flipped out his cell, not yet noticing Earl, Richey and Slowdown, cause he was to busy paying attention to some touters sitting in the car watching his every move. The good thing was they didn't notice Yatta either. They continued to argue until Earl, who was known for being the least confrontational of them all, finally gave up on the $700. It wasn't the money but the principle that his man was trying to dick him around.

"Yo, this is Yatta, what's up?" He answered, in the norm for him.

"Hey baby, this is your mother." The voice on the other end gracefully responded, thankful that she still had one child to talk to.

"What's going on Mom, you alright?" Yatta said, very concerned about his mother's well being.

"Yeah, baby I'm fine. I need to talk with you. Do you have a minute?" She asked, firmly with the butt of the phone muffling her voice.

"Of course, maybe two for you darling." He answered, pausing on the block for a second.

"I received a package today from your sister." She said, as her voice started breaking. It was prime time for her to breakdown, yet another time, as she did this often over the last two months.

The puzzled look on Yatta's face made him turn around and walk facing the opposite direction of the building.

"Mom, what do you mean you received a package from my sister? Mom, Mona is dead. We buried her, remember?" Oh, Mom please don't tell me, you have lost your damn mind! They say the death of a child is hard to deal with, but please don't do this to yourself. How can I tell her that Mona's existence is NO MORE! His thoughts wandered.

Ms. Rhonda huddled in the corner holding one of the packages, with tissue near for every dropping tear. Her red sweat suit was wrinkled, and desperately calling out to the iron to smooth the wrinkles out.

"No baby, I'm serious. The United States Parcel Company called me to inform me that they had back dated packages from two months ago addressed to me. The truck that was to deliver the packages had been in a bad accident, resulting in the driver's death. (The call was from the shift supervisor to claim the packages from the tow yard that the truck was in that long, but finally they did.)

The kind USP man came today and delivered two packages that were addressed to me with Mona's handwriting on it. The same day she died. Now, I know my baby girl's handwriting. She was calling out for help." Rhonda's thoughts drifted off.

"Word. What was in it?" Yatta asked, pryingly. (Now, either Mom is telling the truth or that evil Camron had something to do with this. Either way, it's my duty to find out what's going on.) The position his mother was in would be enough for him to hit the highway had he known, but when he heard of the packages, he knew the trip to New York would be cut short.

"You may want to come home for this. How far are you from home?"

"I'm a minute away, well more like a few hours away. I'm in the City and please don't start that preaching shit. I'm sorry, I forgot you don't want me to curse anymore, I mean 'stuff' with me. Everything is under control."

Here we go again, it's time for testimony. Every time I give her gateway she wants to start on how I need to transition my life into spirituality. What if I'm not ready to turn my life over to God? I never suggested or pressured her about her previous life. All those devious acts of sin she committed. If God saved her from all her mess, I'm sure he will do the same for me and anyone else in a fight to claim the victory over sinful nature. She's no different than these Preachers today. They forget where they come from. Now she's all holy and pure. What she needs to do is keep it real with me. If you're going to come at me trying to convert my spirit, you need a sho' nuff testimony to win me over. Right now, I'm not feeling that mediocre shit. When you've been in my shoes, walked down my paths, that's when you can come at me. Until then, save that shit!

"Son, how do you feel in control under the Master of Deception himself?" That's what he would like for you to believe, that you're in control. And, just when you think you've made out, BOOM! Here comes the drama. Stop being so slow minded about what's going on in the spiritual world. You were born to lead, born to build, and born to protect those around you. How can you conceivably do this under Satan's wings?

The entrapment of your mind, the enslavement of your heart must be loosened. I'm not telling you that conversion from sinning to holiness happens over night, it doesn't. Let me ask you a question: have you ever read the Bible? I mean, really taken time to read some of the powerful stories in the book of rules and regulations? In the Bible, Jesus speaks out how he's coming like a thief in the night to devour our souls. You know many Christians get this scripture misunderstood.

When He says He's coming like a thief in the night, He doesn't mean He's coming down from heaven on a cloud, crackling the sky like a thunderstorm bolt while you're sleeping. I mean really, imagine that, Jesus on a boatload of clouds, crackling the sky, calling us by name. That's a little "fu-gazy" as you would put it. That's unreal!

The word needs to be dissected, studied and researched because for many, it continues to be miscommunicated to believers and non-believers. When he comes like a thief in the night, he means that with his power He will snatch those evil tendencies, deliver you from them and recreate a new creature on the inside. The transformation will be so quick that not even you will understand his movement.

One day you will arise and the spirit that once was dead will now be alive. You start to think different, you start to speak different, you start to lose 'so-called' friends that you've had for years, your walk will be different and your conscience mind will now be awakened. And, when that day comes, I want to be right there. Judge me not by my past son, but how God has bestowed mercy and grace upon your mother's soul.

What I'm merely saying is that one way or another, you need to invite spirituality in your life, whether you accept the Lord Jesus Christ as your Savior or join a Mosque and convert to Muslim beliefs. Whichever you select, you need to do it quickly. Remember, your sister died in sin. Yes, and I know it's no doubt in my mind that she called upon Jesus to intercede to God for her. I feel that in my spirit, she did. But God knows, I'm not ready to bury another one of my children behind this insane underground world of narcotics! Do you hear me son?

It's a struggle everyday trying to cope with the death of my baby girl. Remember God gives you enough trials to keep you strong, enough sorrow to keep you human, enough hope to keep you happy, enough failure to keep you humble during a struggle, enough success to keep you eager from taking a loss in your venture, enough wealth to meet your current needs, enough faith to drive out depression and enough determination to make each day a better day than yesterday. Praise God!"

Yatta remained quiet until his mother finished speaking her mind. Had he given room for her to go on, he most likely would be on the phone for hours.

"Yes, Mom I hear you. Getting back to Mona's letter though, what did it say?" His mind was on what was in the packages.

"When you get here we'll go over it. Until then, don't let it bother you. I'll be here waiting and try to get here as soon as you can." She dared not to tell him about the money over the phone.

Trying to get back to Delaware in a rush, he would be inclined to pick up a speeding ticket, maybe catch more than a speeding ticket if stopped, since he was an unlicensed driver. Seemed like most of the hustlers had suspended licenses. Why is that? He asked himself.

"Alright, one Mom."

"One what, son?"

41

"Mom come on now, you ain't been saved that long, all the streets that you've been through. I know you've heard this saying more than a hundred times. One meaning, I'll check you later, peace, goodbye. Got it? One!

"Yeah, alright. Two."

He smiled as he disconnected the call. The change was ever so present in his mother's characteristics. Her spirituality was at levels unseen by those living in the flesh. This was finally her time to shine in the Lord and Yatta knew first hand how she used to be. To witness the transformation of her spirit was more than he ever desired, though his gut feeling was that something was going on. He wasn't sure what, but what he was feeling, it didn't feel right.

Before making the decision of seeing Cam, Yatta found it necessary to take heed to his mother's phone call and head home, especially since this package was undoubtedly the last he would hear or feel of his sister. The ride home was troubling as his mind wondered what the package contained. What could it be? His sister always was a mystery while living, now in death, she still maintained being mysterious. He recalled the last time he conversed with her. She was so high spirited and adventurous during her time spent in the City.

He remembered the first time she informed him about Cam and chuckled. Yatta rotated his head thinking about why his sister had to die. What had she done that caused another to assassinate her? Was she really in that deep? Did she hook up with someone else while up there? Did Cam take her out? So many questions came to mind. Whoever did it, they had to pay, regardless!

Crossing the Delaware Bridge, his pain inside became reality when his stomach muscles knotted, as the anger built inside of him. He would never see his sister again. He knew he was losing his mind, traveling two hours to New York for nothing, just to get right back on the road to head home. That was over four hours wasted on g.p. - general purpose. It was definitely poor time management on his part. He pulled out his cell phone, dialed his mother's telephone number and waited patiently for her to answer. The phone rang two times before she answered.

"Praise the Lord!"

"All praise due! What's popping Mommy?"

"Mommy? Boy you haven't called me that in years. You must really be going through something. Where are you?"

"I'm coming down Route 13 North, headed in your direction. Now can you tell me what is in the package? I'm eager to know what my crazy little sister is up to."

"What she was up to, remember my baby's life was taken. She was viciously gunned down." Her voice began to crack and her breathing became heavy on the receiving end. The telephone slid down her face to the side of her wet cheek. Beating the phone against the wall, her body fell down to the floor, right back in the same position she was in when she first talked with her son. At the moment she fell apart, the tears constantly flowed. Sitting with her legs sprawled on the worn carpet, she remembered Mona's first day of kindergarten before crack became her best friend.

"No, Mommy please don't put my hair up in a ponytail like that. My head looks like a cone and the kids are going to laugh at me."

"Now Mona, you're being awful silly! Nobody is going to laugh at you." Just to satisfy her little princess, she submitted to her request.

"Okay, let me take it down. You can wear your hair out." As if that wasn't bending enough.

"No Mommy, don't do that either. The other girls are going to say, "She thinks she's cute with her hair out because she has long hair." She looked at her daughter and smiled.

"But Sweetie you are cute, even with your long hair. So they won't be telling a story, Princess. How about I comb your hair into a style of your choice? What do say about that?" She was confident that this would make her baby girl happy. Mona's frown quickly turned into a wide smile.

"Okay, two ponytails. That's my favorite hairstyle!" Pleasing her baby girl, Ms. Rhonda adhered to her wish.

"Two ponytails it is."

The brief reflection of the past allowed her to vent even more.

"Why did they do my baby like that? Why? She didn't deserve to die. She was so young and naïve, not realizing what she was getting herself into. I have so many mixed feelings." All that preaching she did not less than two hours ago, didn't mean a damn thing, as she sat on the floor with a homemade crack pipe with crumbs of crack inside of it not yet burned as she wrestled with the addiction demon inside her, not to spark the matches.

In her lowest moments, the demons rose inside of her. She fought hard battling her addiction. The church walls protected her from this demon that followed her everywhere. She had to fight him alone, not with the saints of the church or her pastor, but by herself. Her body trembled from the urge to get high, rocking back and forth. The longing of the instant rush from the cooked cocaine impeded her mind. She started reciting the Lord's Prayer. *The Lord is my Shepard, I shall not want...*

Her strength built, raising the conqueror inside of her to life, Yatta was waiting for her to reply. She got up from the floor, throwing the homemade pipe clear across the room, hoping it smashed to pieces, dusted her sweatpants and resumed her conversation like she wasn't a second away from relapsing and backsliding. What she had to realize was that, she would fight this demon everyday until she sought out treatment to deal with her issues that she continued to conceal.

"Didn't you see her that day? She said, finally coming around.

"Yes Mom, I did." Yatta came back with.

"Well, what did she say?" Ms. Rhonda wanted answers.

"Nothing out of the ordinary. She was chill'n." He wasn't trying to pacify her pain. He told her the truth.

"Was Cam around?"

"Yeah, that's who I went to see. Why?" Yatta asked, inquiringly.

"Was he acting suspicious at all?" Ms. Rhonda asked, knowing from the letter Mona sent, he was the first person they should focus in on.

"He was tight that day because Mona was late, as usual. I thought it was odd that he was mad at her for being a few minutes late, that's all." Yatta responded, without hesitating.

"That's ironic because when I talked to him after the funeral, he mentioned that the day of her murder. Mona was upset with him for some unknown reason." Ms. Rhonda countered, letting Yatta know the real.

"Funny, she didn't appear mad to me. Actually, she was in good spirits. Even wanted us to go cop a meal together but Cam had other plans." Yatta said with pride, thinking his sister always had something up her sleeve. Ms. Rhonda became silent as she listened attentively to her son.

"Mom, are you there?" He thought he'd lost his connection.

"Yes son, I'm here. I hate to make an accusation like this, but I feel strongly that Cam played a major role in Mona's death."

Without hesitation Yatta responded, her words couldn't be more truthful than what he felt already.

"Believe in your intuition. My heart has been telling me the same thing. He'll get his, don't worry."

"No son, 'Vengeance is mine sayeth the Lord'! Leave it alone! God will take care of that young man if he was the cause. Now, how far are you from the house?"

"I'm pulling into a parking spot now."

Nothing about 22ⁿᵈ Street had changed except for a few minor details and the young hustlers on the corner of Pine Street. The location across the street from 22ⁿᵈ and Pine that housed a family of eight was now a vacant lot of dirt and soot. Accidentally, three of the kids decided that playing with matches, watching blue and red flames was rather exciting. However, when the bed caught fire, they didn't find it intriguing anymore.

Panicking, not knowing what to do, they curled up in the closet until the smoke would eventually replace the natural air they breathed. Seven people died in that fire, all the children. While all of this transpired, the mother waited in Walt's Chicken, one of the best chicken spots in Delaware affordable to everyone in the hood. The mother was getting dinner for her and the kids. When the Wilmington Fire Department came flying past Walt's Chicken, her heart dropped. With extremity, she ran out only to see from her current location, the house engulfed in flames. Her body fell limp as the pavement caught her face. If you listen closely at night, you can still hear the cries of the children. What a tragedy.

On another occasion, he remembered Mona and the "Won Sumth'n Clique" held a late night vigil for the family. Mona used to babysit the kids from time to time while in middle school. Nevertheless, they were good kids, all stairsteps. She cried for hours when she heard of their deaths. The funeral was the worst in Parkside history. This was one memory that could never be erased.

Opening the jaded screen door, stepping inside the house, Yatta called out to his mother. He was fifteen minutes shy of seeing his mother in a tempting situation, one that he'd seen her in many times before.

"Mom, I'm here." Yatta yelled out, holding one pant leg with his hand that kept going under his Timberlands because of the length.

"I'm in the kitchen son, frying some chicken." She said, wiping her hands on her apron. To take her mind off things, she called Sweetback over, her neighbor's man, to chat with her while she cooked up a meal for her son.

Yatta sniffed, "Mmmm, sure does smell good up in here!"

The aroma hit the house, as the grease crackled after each piece of chicken was placed in the blazing hot frying pan.

"Grab two of those hot yeast rolls for your chicken." She instructed gleefully, as she was preparing a meal for her son rather than some man. Sweetback was in the bathroom when Yatta came in, so he didn't know Sweetback was there.

"And Mom, to what do I owe this honor? The last time you cooked for me was years and years ago. What's this all about?" He thought it was rather strange, but was thankful she was cooking for him. When Sweetback came waltzing in the kitchen, Yatta's heart skipped a beat.

"What the fuck is this fake ass, cracked out nigga doing here?" If suspicions served him right, something was indeed wrong. His body language changed significantly, showing his discomfort, when Sweetback came into the room. Sweetback was nothing but trouble, in a slick roundabout

way. Everybody in the neighborhood knew that, even Mona.

"Sit, eat first, the questions can come later." Ms. Rhonda said, pulling out a chair for him. She noticed his reaction when Sweetback entered the room and told Sweetback to stop by later.

Yatta took one bite of the buttered yeast rolls trying to ignore the facts that were presented. There was a possibility of his mother getting high again, keeping company with the likes Sweetback.

"Oh my God, these rolls are delicious." He said, with butter shining across his golden lips.

"You ain't seen nothing yet, wait until you bite into that southern fried chicken." She gleamed, breaking into a new era with her son, friendship.

"Hand me the hot sauce Mom, please." He put his hand out to get it as she passed it to him.

"I marinated the chicken in hot sauce, you may not need any hot sauce." She boasted on her home cooked meal.

"Come on Mom, since when you know black folks not to eat hot sauce on their chicken."

She laughed, knowing he was telling the truth.

He finished up four pieces of chicken in less than ten minutes, sucking the bones clean.

"I don't care what they say, even though Walt's has the best chicken in Delaware, their recipe doesn't have anything on you. Your chicken is like that!" Yatta's eyes searched around the house for his grandma.

"Where's Grandma?"

"She's at work as usual." He didn't want to touch a sensitive place but he knew he had to ask.

"Have you been to the apartment lately, Mom?"

"It's been rough since Mona passed away. There are so many memories of her there. I've been staying with your grandmother trying to help her out for a change."

Switching up the conversation she said, "Let's go up stairs, I have something to show you."

They walked up the stretching steps covered with worn out carpet. "What's that on the floor?" Yatta asked, squinting his eyes as he picked it up. A sharp pain ran through his heart, it couldn't be what he thought it was, a crack pipe. Rhonda put her head down in shame and responded in defense.

"It's not what you think son. I'm not getting high." Yatta bit his fingernails, not sure how to respond after finding the pipe. He was shut down. All that preaching she did was in vain, from his viewpoint. As bad as he wanted to believe she was telling the truth, it was then he knew that getting high was on her mind. Once in the back bedroom she said to her son, trying to break the ice from him freezing up.

"Sit down, this may startle you son."

Opening the package, Ms. Rhonda pulled out the letter Mona had written and handed it to her son.

"This is the letter that was inside of the package." She passed it to him, hoping to see a sorrowful reaction.

Yatta reached over as butterflies built intensely inside his stomach walls. He was almost afraid to reveal the words of the pages. He read it with intensity and in pure silence.

Ms. Rhonda broke the silence looking directly in her sons eyes. "Well, I guess five days have passed. Actually, two months have passed. Had the driver not been in that accident, maybe we would have found out sooner." She sat on the futon in the lounge room.

"It's my job to fulfill my daughter's last wishes. The journal inside contains so much information, bad things, good things and things that I'd rather not discuss right now." She shook her head in embarrassment.

"My daughter was something else, just like her mother. She was more than a card, she was a deck with the extras. Anyway, I do believe from reading her journal that Camron was the one who did her in. It was clear that she was on her way home to us. My baby wanted change. She sought out change." Her mind shifted into prayer, something she needed so desperately.

"Oh, God! I know you told us never to question your judgment, but it's hard for me to understand. She was so young and sweet on the inside with so much initiative."

Wiping the tears from his mothers face, Yatta scooted closer to her, laying his head on her shoulder. "Mom, we need to do what's right."

"And what is right?" She questioned, fighting the temptation to coat her feelings.

"Execute Mona's final wishes." Yatta stated, sure of his response.

"This may be a way for us to mourn her death in happiness and not so much in sadness and pain. We can't bring her back." Rhonda followed, in a low and subtle tone.

"We can't bring her back, so we have to move on, right?" As hard as it was to say, he knew it to be the truth.

"Hold on son, you must understand what I'm really saying and take it to heart."

"Even if we fulfill her last and final wishes, we still have other obligations to render." He gazed with a complete loss on his face.

"Mom, what are you talking about?"

"There will be another Mona Foster. As we speak, there are Mona Fosters' stet in training or on the front line. Look at her friends. The only one close to change is that young girl Nieka, Nee, whatever you call her." *That's what she thought.* "The others are still in the grind of things. What would it profit us to ignore these factors? Yes, we can open up a store *Precioustymes Feet Boutique,* like she dreamed of but why not start a foundation? A group home to educate, empower and bring other young people out of their comfort zones, to get the help they need?" She needed to take heed to her own advice and seek help for her addiction.

"If we don't help these young girls, they will fall victim to the same lifestyle as your sister. They might not necessarily be gunned down. Their course may be different, suicide, in a car accident while trying to re-up or maybe life in prison. You understand what I'm saying to you son. I want to do more than set up the trust fund and foundation. I want to open a group home to provide nuturing, unconditional love and undying support that your sister longed for in her life. This is a chance to give youths an opportunity to understand themselves and not blame the world because of their personal situations. Think about it, youths aren't the only ones who've suffered."

The conversation began to turn in another direction. In the bellies of her hurt, she spoke with pain gorging all over her face.

"Mona wasn't the only one who suffered. I'm not making any excuses for the way you two were raised, but I had problems as a youth also. Your grandma will never admit to it, but I suffered from similar situations. Men always came first, I was always second. Hell, I was molested and sexually assaulted by one of her so-called boyfriends. She will never tell you that though. That pervert was never arrested for what he did to me. He never spent one day in jail!" It was a raw moment based on bitter emotions.

"Mom, stop! I don't want to know these things about your past and how grandma raised you. She's not like that now. If I were to dwell on your past we'd never get further than a sour welcome. We'd both be stuck in position. I'm trying to move forward and I thought you were too." He was upset and unsettled from her words and the intensity built second by second.

"No son, I will not stop. In other words you're telling me to shut up. I refuse to hold these feelings back any longer. Until we deal with this past, we can't deal with our wrong. I'm giving you this information because the cycle has to end. It's been abiding in our family for many years now. I can't allow another day to pass until we bust this thing wide open."

Tears of frustration began to peddle down her face. She was now pacing back and forth in the bedroom they were in. This was yet another reason why she needed to seek help for her internal pain. She wouldn't remain clean long, only going to service on Sunday, she needed relief everyday.

Yatta's head was aching and the headache pounded loudly, jarring his temples. Both of them headed downstairs back to the kitchen.

"Only on the strength of Mona, will I sit through this. You waited so late in our lives to change. And I mean change so drastically. How can you expect me to absorb all of this in such a short time? Now, it's like you're this 'Rites of Passage' activist. Just because you've accepted change doesn't mean that everyone else wants the same."

Nee interrupted their heated conversation. It was unlike her to walk in the house unannounced. She walked in greeting both of them. Yatta excused himself from the kitchen and Nee followed after him.

"Yatta, can I talk to you for a moment."

He asked coldy, "What do you want?"

Nee responded, "It's no need to be tight with me. I have some shit I need to get off my chest. This shit is detrimental information for us." Yatta stared, waiting for her to speak.

"Go 'head then, speak what you know." Nee recited word for word what her cousin Unique in the pen, relayed to her about Cam's involvement in Mona's murder, the guy who gave up all the tapes, C-Lo for his vested interest and about C-Lo's cousin, El'san. That would be the link to get sweet revenge from the nigga Cam.

"Give me the number. I'll handle this." Yatta called El'san and introduced himself.

During the introduction, he told El'san about his personal venedetta against Cam. At first El'san wasn't feeling him. Helping a stranger out, that wasn't what he was about, playing the helper role. The only thing that helped Yatta out, was when he told El'san that his cousin put him onto him. He explained the benefits to El'san if he helped him bring Cam down. El'san was down for it under one conditon, Yatta and the rest of his crew stayed away from the city until the job was done. It took a lot for Yatta to succumb to his request, but he agreed. What he didn't tell El'san was that he was a hustler. He knew that would screw up all the plans from what his cousin C-Lo said.

Chapter Four
In Due Time

Yatta laid on the plastic covered couch at his Grandma's house, just thinking about how his sister managed to get her way even in death. He admired her feistiness and courage. She'd left him $200,000, and Kenya, Nee's daughter, $50,000 of the $1,250,000 that she sent home. She made sure the church got their ten percent and her mother was to handle the rest. It was just like her to do something like that. That's how generous and kind she was.

Now all he had to do was find a way to cut Cam off. With the money she'd left him, he was good. Do Good, one of his partners from 5th Street, had managed to get a better deal from a Florida connection. He really didn't want Cam to find out, but he knew sooner or later he would, especially when the money stopped coming his way. He couldn't tell anybody about the money. But he would damn sure tell them about his mission to get at Cam. He knew for sure, from the journals and other information that Mona left behind, that Cam was the murderer. His family had to feel some consolation regarding her murder.

Her case was opened and closed quickly. When the police didn't take the time to do a thorough investigation, the family was devastated.

57

It was closed as an unsolved murder within a month. They claimed they didn't have enough evidence to match DNA. They all knew different. The Police Department was unconcerned because it was just another black on black crime from their perspective. With all the blood left on that scene there should have been enough DNA to test a thousand people. Yatta's job was to take care of the groundwork, revenge for the Foster family. He had to plan this out very carefully cause Cam was no dummy.

Even though he and Nee weren't that tight anymore, he tried to keep her abreast as to what was going on. Ever since Yatta found out that Kenya was his daughter, he was less than thrilled of Nee's very being. His sister never mentioned the possibility of him being Kenya's father. Fact was, Nee was too embarrassed to let her best friend know she slept with four guys in a matter of three days.

One of them was Do Good, whom Mona used to hit off every now and then. She was quite sure that that wouldn't have made the difference in their relationship, the way Mona tossed around men. Coming from a stable home, made it even more embarrassing. She had no reason to recklessly sleep around, she knew better.

Yatta was one of the four possibilities. He never made a big fuss about being the last one informed to take the paternity test, because he thought it was certain that he wasn't the father. The timing though was way off. The night of the funeral, they shared the same bed. She should have told him then. She had ample opportunity. It wasn't till they started planning the revenge on

Cam that she informed him. It was then she told him that it might be a possibility that he was Kenya's father. She let him know the guy that she claimed to be the father Black, was not. Black found that out, only after requesting a paternity test.

His new girlfriend knew about Nee and her history with men. She kept persuading Black to take the test. Really, she was hoping and praying that Kenya wasn't his. To hear her tell it, Kenya didn't look nothing like him. Besides, all the money he was paying in child support was needed at the home front.

For seven years, Black was paying child support and spending a little quality time with Kenya. It wasn't much, but enough for him not to be called a deadbeat and enough to keep Nee off his back. This way he satisfied them both, his woman and his baby momma. When the results came back from the paternity test that Black was not the father, the fall out began. Black thought all along that he should have listened to his girl. She was right about Kenya, she wasn't his daughter.

One by one, other possibilities were tested on different dates, most with a swab of DNA from their mouths. Each of their results came back that they were not the father. Nee had no choice but to tell Yatta, the last man standing, that he needed to be tested. When Yatta went down to take his, he was a little humiliated. He just wanted to know for sure if he was or wasn't the father. Hell, it had already been 7 years. If she was his daughter, the little girl only knew him as Uncle Yatta, not being her daddy. How was he going to explain it to her if he was the father? He never thought twice about being her father. One thing for sure, he wasn't going out like the other suckers taking a swab test. He made them take blood from him. Even though that was a little shady. He didn't even realize that he'd been hitting and missing with Nee for that long.

The notice of paternity determination came a month shy after Mona's funeral. Nee didn't even give him a chance to mourn the loss of his little sister. In fact, she didn't know when they'd be testing him or notifying him for that matter. She was seriously distraught that she had to take him through this. As if she wasn't offended enough about the situation. In less than one week after the test, the clinic forwarded him the results. They were 99.8% sure that he was Kenya's daddy. For that, he let Nee have it. He remembered that day like it happened moments ago.

They were sitting on the porch waiting for Ms. Rhonda to come home so they could pick out Mona's marker for her gravesite. He kept staring at her waiting for her to break the news to him. In an attempt to force the conversation, he initiated without being feeble about it.

"Yo, I just got the results back from the blood test." He said, very heatedly, pulling his fitted hat tightly down on his head.

"I got my letter today but I didn't open it." Nee was more than disgraced she had to take another man through this. It was bad enough Kenya knew her father to be one man, but now the man she called Uncle was actually her father. Looking her dead in her face Yatta said, "Man, say

60

something." He felt like punching her dead in the face. Nee responded by saying in a less than jovial way, "I'm sorry."

"What do you have to say for your sorry self?" He asked her, thoroughly sickened. Up until now, he had no kids. Stepping into a child's life after 7 long years and trying to play daddy was going to be trying. That's if a father and daughter bond could began between the two of them.

"I'm sorry. That's all I can say." She never once looked up at him while apologizing.

"I'd choose another set of words if I were you." Yatta responded bluntly.

"Did my sister know?" Yatta asked.

"No, I never had the courage to tell her." She said, all at once letting him know.

"So, all this damn time, she was calling Kenya her niece and she really was her niece. Even so, you robbed her of the chance of knowing that Kenya shared the same blood with us." In his frustration, he pounded on his chest very hard.

"I don't know if I can forgive you for that. Then to top it off, look how you did yourself in. You took different men into the white man's court system just to prove what they already believe, that most African-American women are blood suckers utilizing the welfare system, not wanting to get ahead."

Nee interjected, "I ain't on any welfare, and I'm not taking you to court for child support if that's what you think." She stared at him in a blur. Her intentions weren't to hurt anyone involved in this ordeal. She felt she deserved every fowl word that came out of this mouth.

"How many dudes participated in your open buffet feast?"

"Huh?" She responded. She acted like she didn't understand what he was asking her.

"Huh, my ass. You heard me! How many dudes had to suffer the humiliation of taking a blood or swab test to determine paternity?"

She didn't realize that each time a man went into the clinic to subject themselves to a paternity test, it mired their intelligence. Just the thought of being in the midst of others in determining the chance of being a father to a child that shared another man's semen, taunted their minds.

"Well, it was three others." She said, in a murmur.

Making sure he heard her correctly, he repeated what she said. "Did you say it was two or three of them?"

"What the fuck does it matter? The damage is done now!" She responded, saying fuck it to herself.

With his lips parched closely he responded, "Yes slut, it does matter. I need to know if I should be taking an HIV test behind this shit."

"Al'ight damn, well altogether it was four dudes, including you." She said it like it wasn't a big deal.

"Fuck all these niggas." She said in her mind. Empathy would last but for long.

Yatta's facial expression changed drastically.

"Yo, you let four dudes run up in you, in the course of three days? I hope at least, you only had sex with me on the day you conceived. Ugh, you a nasty ho! We all had sex with you unprotected, *which means you had four different types of semen up in you. It's a wonder your coochie wasn't stinking, it probably was. I was perhaps too damn high to realize it."* He kept hitting her where it hurt. *"Are you sure it was just four? Or, did I just so happen to be the first one with the same blood type as Kenya. You know that shit can happen, right? The system doesn't give a fuck about who the baby's daddy is, as long as they have one listed down to reimburse them. It's surely hundreds of other men with the same blood type as mine. O positive is very popular.*

The system is just happy that it doesn't have to test anyone else. They are tired of women like you wasting the State's time and money. Then, women wonder why men call them bitches, sluts and whores. You are a prime example of why we do!" He stared at her in aversion and spit on the ground.

"And, who were the other two dudes? I already know about Black. I feel sorry for the man. I hope they make you repay him every dime of the money he put into your sorry ass."

"You don't have to look at me like that!"

She looked at him up and down.

"I'm still human. People make mistakes you know."

"Yes, I do, like I did." He was still very persistent. *"Who were the other dudes?"* He asked again.

"If you really need to know, it was Bird and Do Good. There, I said it." She shrugged her head to the right like she didn't care. For a moment, Yatta's blood pressure boiled on the inside. He

wanted to haul off and smack the daylight out of her when he found out who the other dudes were.

Then after thinking, it was no need to be mad at the fellas he grinded with for fucking her. Hoe's was going to be hoes regardless and a man will take advantage of a woman if she lets him.

"That means you've been over the Forklift acting like you a damn dime piece when all three of us, in the same crew, standing on the same blocks 'den hit it. If my recollection serves me right, I done hit it well over 72 times in the last three years alone and that's just on a humble. I know I hit it at least two or three times a month. So in three days, you hit each of us off, with a fourth man! Damn! I knew you were a little frisky but I didn't know you rolled like a true tramp! I'd hate to know what a seven day stretch is like for you. I'm not convinced we are the only three that hit it around the way. The others must be keeping it on the low. Now, how about that." He reflected.

"All the niggas knew late at night if I didn't catch a prime piece, I'd step up to a sure hit, you! What I didn't know is they did the same thing too. My niggas!" He had to laugh it off to conceal his resentment. It made him feel like all of his boys robbed a bank and he was the only one who got caught. He was like, why me? Why was he the one that got caught up in the bait? He felt like, he was robbed by a whore.

How foolish could he have been to hit that. Without a condom? It was a lesson well learned. At the same time, he had to step up to the plate and take care of his responsibility. It wasn't Nee he was terribly upset over. It was Kenya. She had a whore for a mother. He had to save his daughter from the same lifestyle her mother was in. He'd seen it all before. Hell, he witnessed it in his own household.

"I'm not bitter with you, cause you do what you do best, whore! Just don't whore around my daughter." The thoughts that played in Nee's head was, "This nigga still want me. He's just mad that I boned Do Good and Bird, that's all!"

"When I do shit, know that I'm going to do it on the strength of Kenya." Having enough of the negative one-sided conversation, she replied, "I don't need you to come play daddy to my child. My mom and I take good care of her already." Yatta got all up in her grill.

"Let me tell you something bitch, this is not about you. You've already robbed me of seven years of her life all because of your lying and deceitful whorish ways. I'm not about to let you ruin her life anymore. You created issues in her already. Got that girl thinking Black is her father. How the hell are you going to explain that? You got into this mess and you have to be the one to get out of it. It's your job to tell her the truth about me.

Teach her early on how not to be like her mother. And you can stop the bullshit early on about not wanting me to come around. I'll have your ass up in family court so fast, proving to the white man the unfit mother that you are. You have 72 hours to tell her the truth. You ain't gonna trip on me and this is my only seed too! Bitch please! You picked the wrong damn man to screw if you thought you'd end up with a deadbeat father. I'll be just the opposite. I'll be around so goddamn much, you'll be sick of me. I won't be the only one mad as hell that we went raw, without protection.

I will be a permanent fixture in your household. Word to motha, your ass gonna feel this shit! I don't give a fuck who you are screwing. You could be in another room giving head to a joker and I'll be in the other room with my daughter, not giving a damn." He laughed in her face.

"It will be like you never existed in my life, you trick ass bitch! It's not like my daughter is not familiar with me. Hell, it will be a rough start but we'll make it through. She knows me as Uncle, but damn, a daughter and a niece are two different things." He stroked his chin. *"See what you've done!"*

"You have a right to have your feelings about the circumstances, but can't we just get along? I said I'm sorry. I made a mistake, I openly admit that." She started to change up from being cocky about it. Really, she had no defense, he was right.

"The fact of the matter remains, that you are Kenya's father. I'll make sure she is aware of that, trust me. This situation can really be ugly or we can squash it now and become mutual friends. Deal?"

"Deal my ass! One thing is for sure, two things for certain, she'll be taken care of. Mona had my mother set up a college trust fund for Kenya. All her expenses will be paid for. Later, I'll set up a checking account with both of your names on it. You take out what you need for her. Don't use that money to splurge on yourself. I mean that shit." Why fight over it any longer? He thought.

"Oh yeah, you need to break the news to Rhonda. I'm quite sure she'll get a kick out of this. Tell your mom she better get used to sharing

custody, cause Kenya will be over my mom's house just as much as she'll be over yours."

Nee didn't fuss, she let him have his way.

"Trouble doesn't last always." She thought to herself. The most important part had been handled.

Ms. Rhonda was on a serious mission to start a legacy on the strength of her daughter while the good spirit in her controlled her actions. She made phone calls to the Mayor's office trying to find a location for the group home. She opted for two locations, one on 22nd and Lamotte Street and the other on 5th and Madison Street. The city gave her condemned properties and told her it was her responsibility to get them fixed up to city code. Her church backed her 100% on this endeavor. Thinking about it, she guess they would.

They received $125,000, ten percent of the money Mona made mention of in her final journal entry, even though they knew it was *"blood money"*, made from selling narcotics.

The Pastor knew that Ms. Rhonda paid her tithes and gave generously, so when the group home started receiving governmental grants, the church would benefit tremendously. The pastor made sure the members contributed to helping her make the dream a reality. A few of the men in the congregation were professional carpenters, certified electricians, painters and in general maintenance.

One of the members even worked as a manager at Home Depot. He was able to get her discounted prices on the merchandise needed to reconstruct both houses. The project moved smoothly into transition.

She purchased the furnishings from Ethan Allen. The sales representative picked out the best in the store. The lady couldn't understand why Ms. Rhonda wanted to spend that kind of money on a group home for disadvantaged kids already living in deplorable conditions.

She made comments like, "Aren't you afraid they're going to tear your furniture up? I mean you could get very reasonably priced bunk beds from Value City Furniture Store."

"Who said I wanted to purchase bunk beds young lady?" She responded.

"In fact, I want 50 full size beds with the best Sealy mattresses that you have in the store. Throw in 50 plush comforter sets in different patterns to go along with that. That is, of course, if you have the merchandise in stock. Otherwise, I can take my business elsewhere. I hear that Bombay Furniture Store has a rather large selection." Rhonda could get used to this, talking to store managers as nasty as they did to others, from time to time.

The sales lady responded very quickly, "Oh no, please don't do that Ma'm. We can accommodate your request immediately."

"Then don't make suggestions for me, get what I need fo' I decide not to do business here!"

Ms. Rhonda ignored the young lady's previous comments and purchased only the best for the kids. She figured since, not only did they live in shameful conditions, but also she did too at one time, she believed they all deserved the best.

This was going to be a new experience for them all. An interior decorator had already made an assessment of both buildings and decided she wanted to go with colorful earth tones to liven the place.

A Calico Corner designer picked out the fabrics and had all designs custom made. She selected wood grain vertical blinds for both Bay windows and a huge beautiful gold octagon marker placed on the exterior that read "In Memory of Mona Foster, The Foster Foundation."

After the building was inspected and approved by license and inspection, Ms. Rhonda hired twenty staff members, ten people for each location and one consultant to prepare all the legal documentation needed for the government. Included in her staff were Case Managers, Counselors, Overnight Residential Managers, Cooks, Receptionists, Office Clerks, Janitors and Greeters.

She made sure that individuals living in the inner city neighborhoods filled all entry-level positions. Her mother quit working at the hospital, settling for an early retirement. The city offered Job Readiness courses and college preparation courses for participants in the program. "Save the Seed" program facilitated all the programs and group counseling sessions.

The Ford car dealership donated two 15-passenger vans. Their only stipulation was to make sure that a sticker with "Donated by Winner Ford" dealership was visible for others to see.

Two big "grand opening" events were planned for each group home on both sides of town. It was broadcasted on all the local radio stations, newspapers and posted throughout Delaware. Reporters came out to conduct interviews about the new program and "From my Hood to your Hood" Precioustymes Entertainment newsletter did a featured story on the fallen soldier, Mona Foster.

Yatta was extremely proud of his mother and how determined she was to stay clean and live out his sister's wishes. It was now time for him to take care of what he needed for Mona to rest in peace.

Rhonda was joyful, but her recent actions presented a dual message that she had to address before doing anything else. Since she had access to money at her fingertips, she didn't want that to tempt her chemical craving inside. This was the first time in her life she didn't have to trick, out slick and steal for money. Rhonda knew she had to seek help fast, very fast before something went down.

After taking a little nap, Yatta left home and gathered up Kevious, Dale, Bird, Ali and Maine from off 5th Street. Do Good stayed back to handle business. Every time he looked at Bird, he thought about Nee's slimy behind. Bird or Do Good didn't peep a word about taking the paternity test. Yatta was curious to know why. Maybe they thought he caught feelings for her, that was definitely not the case. Setting that aside, the Forklift crew had a job to do. They went to the hidden garages where they kept most of their weapons. They needed heavy artillery to battle against Camron's demon. Yatta rounded everybody in a group and explained to them exactly what was going down.

"Yo, check this out. This shit is real, the enemy is at our hands. If we play our cards right, we'll all come out of this alive. This is some do or die type shit. Anybody fearful or doubtful about the job, step down now. This demon we're about to confront is no joke and won't have a problem letting off seventeen shots from his black 9mm glock! This kid is known for putting people to rest. This is serious and very personal to me.

Most of you know from all the rumors that he killed my little sister: It's now time for him to pay. Now, this is how it's going down." He resumed the conversation after he gave them all the details about El'san. He had one of his female friends rent a Dodge Caravan with tinted windows from a crooked Pennsylvania car rental place just in case they needed a getaway car. He'd promised to let Nee in on the details, but wavered her out. This was not a situation for a female, let alone his baby's mother.

When the time was appropriate, he would fill her in. They were ready when the time came to go up top to the city. They were just waiting on El'san's call.

Chapter Five
That Was Then And This Is Now...

Camron had no idea that one of his archrivals, El'san from Kingsborough Projects, was home and in total control of the 'Borough once again. Life for the "fiends of the living dead" was shut down. Hustlers' pockets that were once bulging out with money knots now only possessed lint balls.

El'san cursed the day Cam was born. He heard about all the rumors through Riker's Island Prison when they were down together. He was determined to shut down the force behind him. If concealing Cam's brother's secret was not enough for them to step away from the 'Borough, he would expose them all. For a mid summer day, instead of the normal haze and humidity, the breeze lightly agitated the summer leaves.

El'san was sitting, rather laid back on the bench in front of the Kingsborough projects, chewing on a vanilla mint stick. His black sweatpants damn near dropped past his knees exposing his gray and blue-stripped boxers. He maintained his weight well, muscled up, biceps rippled. It had been one year since his release from Riker's and he was still able to preserve his body. The only part of his body that was unchecked was his thick Sunni-Muslim beard,

73

and even with that, his strong dark cheekbones blended well. Sitting on the bench was the norm for him, relaxing watching his surroundings. With his pit, Chyna Whyte secured with a triple thick metal chain around his neck, by his side. His life was the 'Borough, his family was one of the first families that moved into the apartment complex.

Every mother in the complex knew about little bad ass uncontrollable El'san. A terror since 3 years old, when he would throw rocks from his 7th floor bedroom window, cracking car windshields. His mother claimed he was beyond reach and his father didn't want nothing to do with him. So, just as young men without the presence of a father, to the streets he went to find that father figure. Instead, *"ghetto love"* is what he received. Instead of attending high school, El'san dropped out in his last semester of the 8th grade to become the *"King of New York"*, or *"King of the 'Borough"* whichever came first.

His mathematical skills were almost unbelievable for an 8th grade dropout. Many people in the complex would request his help during tax time. One of the old timers taught him years ago how to hustle taxes. He was grateful for that.

Some nights instead of robbing, he would prepare taxes for loot. Preparing taxes was a small hustle for him, and besides, no one else in the 'Borough knew ways to work around numbers to double client's refunds except him. This meant more money for him. If he secured a refund for $1000 dollars, he wanted at least $200, because in reality, they probably were only going to receive

$500 in refund money but after he got done, the refund doubled. He figured he'd be doing them a favor by getting them an extra $300 dollars. His main hustle was robbing drug dealers. He despised them like he despised employable women on welfare.

At any given opportunity, he would run up on one and take every cent in their possession. Because of him, the 'Borough was labeled "Robbinville". Niggas knew if they came through floss'n, they'd get got, or just by chance you were just strolling by, you'd get it too. The 'Borough loved new faces, they meant new money to them.

El'san had been shot at over twenty times, but only hit once in the palm of his right hand, his trigger hand. Sometimes that posed a problem for him due to the nerve damage it caused. His fingers would sometimes lock on him and cause delayed reactions when trying to let off shots. No one is his camp had the privilege of finding out that information. He had a crew of over forty. All of them lived in the 'Borough and nobody dared to step to the crew.

Despite his ill behavior with the drug dealers, El'san had a heart of gold. He was on a mission to keep the streets of Kingsborough clean from the filth of drugs. They were a very unique bunch. He sponsored many late night basketball leagues, organized many festivals with excessive amounts of free food, juices and sodas for everyone.

One summer, he rented a portable swimming pool the same width and length of the basketball court for the kids to swim in. Seeing that a public pool was never in question, he took it upon himself to contact a portable pool distributor who worked out a major deal for them to keep the pool for the summer months. The company even came out to change the filter and water of the pool weekly. It was all love. To satisfy the ball players, he purchased two traveling courts and placed them in front of the entrance walkway so that they too would be occupied. He was always looking out for his people. That's what he was known for, a Ghetto Robin Hood.

Watching the little kids playing basketball on the court, his attention shifted to one of the 'Borough's queens, "Sweetie," is what they called her. Sweetie was fairly new to the 'Borough and El'san hadn't had a chance to maximize off her yet. He was quite the ladies man in his hood, but Sweetie was different from the rest. She did her own thing and had her own style.

You hardly ever saw her go without. She would do whatever it took to get hers. The main reason he respected her was because she never brought other dudes up in the complex. He knew she didn't have a man. She came through slithering smoothly as a stray kitty cat, searching for prey. He observed her animated movements as she eased both legs into the cut. The cut was the hidden entrance, between buildings three and four.

"Look at this shit here." El'san thought to himself. Chyna Whyte lifted his chest, hopping on all four legs in attack mode.

Sweetie was almost 30 years old, still hanging out in the 'Borough. She didn't have any kids so for her age, she looked damn good. Her age did her injustice. She could, without question, pass for a young woman 21 years of age when necessary. Instead of the traditional Dominican wrap hairstyle, her hair was styled neatly in Bohemian Twists, which accented her appearance all the more. Her face, an unblemished bronze tone shone of natural beauty. The appeal she retained was subtle. Her idea of dressing fancy was wearing a long summer dress with wood carved jewelry dangling from her neck and ankles accentuated with platform canvas sandals. Her past wouldn't allow her to be Afro centric, so when given the opportunity, she never turned back. An only child, she was easily influenced by others.

Most of her teenage years were spent in the 67th Street Mosque. Introduced to Islam early in life, she was unable to enjoy what most young girls her age had, freedom and expression through clothing. Her mom was strict and her father was a dignitary in the Mosque. So whenever she'd try to break free, the possibilities were narrow. Her current situation made her even more depressed.

The expectations sought from her mother and father put her in an uncomfortable position. They selected a career in the medical field as a LPN, she choose a career as a Spoken Word Artist. Not living up to their expectations, she left home at an early age in the quest of becoming "*Sweetie, Queen of the Spoken Word*".

The 'Borough wasn't the best neighborhood, but the rent was cheaper than other apartment complexes in the area. Probably because of the recent rash of burglaries and the increase in volatile crimes.   Though struggling hard not to fall deep in the wickedness of the 'Borough, she was losing the fight.

Dressed in white Capri pants with a v-neck white tee shirt without a bra, freeing firm breasts and large supple nipples, Sweetie quickly unzipped her overnight bag searching for her Black Muslim garb. This was one day she was glad to wear it. There simply wasn't enough time to escape to her apartment, so the cut would do. The cut was an easy hidden entrance to throw someone off. If she tried to chance it, her cover would be blown. El'san knew something was suspicious and he wasn't going to let anything go down in his hood.

"What the hell are you up to Sweetie?" El'san yelled out. He knew something was going on.

"Non ya' damn business El'san!   Stop drawing attention to me and keep that beast of a dog tamed before he mistakes me for a meal." Sweetie said counteracting.   She was getting smart but knew all along that she loved the attention El'san gave her.

"Your sneaky ass up to something." He said, as he continued to watch her from the bench.

"Don't worry about Chyna Whyte, unless I tell him to get at you, he won't bother you."

With speed, she pulled the wrap around her face and began to smooth out any wrinkles. The garb covered her entire body just as she needed it to.   It was then she stepped cautiously, fearing Chyna Whyte, over to El'san.

"Why are you always in somebody's business El'san? You aren't my father. You might be too many of these females around here, but you aren't mine! So, whatever I'm up to is my own business!" She stared into El'san's charcoal black coal eyes. He stared back at her, giving her the same attention.

If being 30 years old and looking 21 years young meant acting childish, Sweetie was definitely fulfilling her purpose. Just then a young Hispanic male with a black hoody covering his head, crept slowly in his sedan as he rode through the 'Borough trying to blend in. El'san quickly noticed his actions and reached under his right pants leg to grab his peacemaker and started walking toward the vehicle.

"What are you doing El'san?" Sweetie asked, scared of what he might do.

"Just sit tight, I'll be back, al'ight." He responded, as he rose from the hard silver bench.

"Yo, homie! You best get outta here for you feel some heat. This here is El'san's 'Borough, in case you didn't know. The only person plotting on this turf is me. Ya' heard, son!" All the guys on the court stopped playing and the only other sound you heard was from the bouncing basketball. They were ready to take cover. When the Spanish guy saw El'san was serious, he put his car in 5th gear, pressing down frantically on the accelerator and squealing all four tires, trying to get away.

Sweetie sat on the bench, without remorse, looking directly at her victim. With the garb on, he wouldn't stand a chance identifying her. A few minutes ago, she was rumbling through his glove compartment when she lucked up and found $300 dollars in an envelope marked, *"Baby Mom's."* His *"Baby Mom's"* wouldn't see that money since it was left in the open for Sweetie.

Carefully slipping the bills inside her beige straw bag, she eased out the sedan while her new friend, she just met, was inside the corner store. Had he known a courtesy ride from downtown Manhattan would get him robbed, he would have left her looking puppy-eyed at the bus stop. He was trying to do her a favor by giving her a ride, and maybe getting her digits during the trip.

Sweetie was in her hood, so the back alleys were an easy escape. El'san walked over to Sweetie, mad that she played a part in the dude passing through.

"I told your ass before, don't you ever bring a damn buster around the way! Beat them niggas on their turf. How stupid can you be to bring them near your resting place anyway?" El'san questioned.

"That was one of the reasons I dug you first, cause you never did that shit. Yo, you slip'n. Times that damn hard? Now whatever you beat him for, I want half of it for bringing heat to the 'Borough." Standing with thick folded arms, he was serious as he motioned for half the money. She couldn't believe he was getting ready to tax her. She knew about all the people he'd taxed, but not her. She just couldn't believe it.

"Why you got to be like that El'san? All that money you rob people for, why you got to take from a petty hustler like me? I'm barely making ends meet." Hissed Sweetie. "I only got $100 dollars anyway."

"You're lying and I know it. If you're willing to tell me about a dove you probably got triple that. Now, come up off $150 in bills now. Yo, if you're in that much trouble, get a job then. Make some real money or get down with us in the 'Borough." Responded El'san, thinking this was definitely an opportunity to lure her in.

"Hold up, I ain't 'bout to be out here pulling guns out on niggas trying to rob them. My parents are already disappointed with me. Imagine what they would think if they heard that or if they knew I was playing with the Muslim religion. They may cast me to the river." She couldn't help but to smile.

"Come on Ma', I'm not talking about being a straight stick up kid. We're already holding that down. I'm talking about setting niggas up. You're *already* good at it, but you're making small change. What about making some real cash?" El'san asked. This was a sure way to draw her into his circle. He could make cash off of her and make moves to get into her panties at the same time.

"How so?" An inquisitive Sweetie sat as El'san began the smooth talk. This was a sure way to draw her in. Like an aggressive salesperson that reads the "No Soliciting" sign on businesses front doors, he knew Sweetie could easily be sold once he got inside her mind.

"Check this out, I'll give you every lead you need. The first job I have is this cat named Toby. He's from the Bronx but lives over in East New York. From my source, he's making a little dough and I want all or a large chunk." El'san said.

"So, how can I help get it and what's my cut." Sweetie asked readily, as if she were interviewing for a job.

"Easy Ma, I'm getting to that." El'san said assuredly.

"This dude is a sucka for a pretty face."

"Should I take that as a compliment? That's a first for you." She beamed.

"Yeah whatever, pay attention. One mistake can cost us money and flattery will get you nowhere. My cousin Shavonee lives across the street from this dude. I'm gonna hook you up with her number and she will put you down."

Searching his sweatpants pockets for a stray piece of paper, El'san pulled out an old grocery bill Receipt and began writing the telephone number down. He'd been shopping two days ago and forgot to throw the receipt away. Sweetie looked him up and down while he was writing the number down.

"Hold up! I know those are not the same sweatpants you had on two days ago." She asked, hating to see guys wearing the same clothes two days in a row.

El'san looked at her as to say, "And, your point?"

"What's it to you if they are?" El'san asked without a look of concern.

"I ain't got time to please these hookers by the way I dress. They know a nigga can get dipped if he wants to. You know dat too, you've seen me in my pretty-boy gear."

"I'm just saying though, you'd look a lot better in some clean clothes." She respected dudes that gave genuine concern about their appearance.

"Yeah, whatever ma. As long as my ass is clean and my mouth is fresh. I'm good I don't say shit when females call themselves getting all cleaned up by putting on new clothes and ain't even wash their ass before putting them on, or when they wear the same pair of jeans but change the shirt to make it look like they got on a new outfit. They wear the same pair of tight ass jeans without washing them cause they didn't get a stain on them. Now that's trife. What do they think, dudes can't smell 'em when the clothes peel off? Some of you hookers only take a bath once a day. Now, that's some nasty shit. Y'all know damn well you got to wash that thing at least three times a day or the shit ain't gonna smell right. Why don't you preach about that? See niggas, our shit don't stink like that. Granted, our balls can get a little stale but we wash our shit numerous times a day. You got my point? Now, do you want the information on the trick or what?"

Sweetie's lips were puckered curving to the left of her mouth. "Go ahead, you don't have to be so damn testy. All I was saying was, change ya damn clothes!"

El'san brushed her off.

"Toby drives a silver Jaguar, I think it's a 2000. He's a brown skin nigger with jacked up teeth. The two front teeth buck out like rabbits teeth and most of the side teeth double over. With teeth like his, he could probably cut through a barbed-wired fence. That's how sharp his teeth look. This fake ass nigga dresses like a wanna be thug, always wearing dress shoes with his wife beater T-shirts. He's a clown ass sucka for a drug dealer. Its dudes like him that don't belong working in the streets. He's making the streets look bad. You know what I'm saying. He know damn well he belong in Corporate America with those uppity dudes wearing tight ass ball huggers." He joked, chuckling afterwards.

"What do you expect me to do with a john jacked up like that? I mean, at least he could have been cute. It's easier to get in their pockets when they're attractive. Give me some type of incentive. Let me at least fantasize about the dude while I plot on his money. Oh, and I hope you don't expect me to sleep with him. I don't get down like that; he at least has to be a cutie. And um, that's fine Shavonee is gonna put me down but um, what about *my* money? You still haven't said what's in it for Sweetie."

El'san didn't like the comment that she made. "What was that last comment?" He quickly asked.

"What, when I said, what's in it for me?" She answered, without knowing his true intent.

"Hell no, that shit about, 'at least he has to be a cutie'. Are you telling me that if a dude was handsome, that you'd be willing to sleep with him? Where the da fuck is ya head at?"

Sweetie lifted her head in confidence. Play hitting him on his shoulder she said, "Nah, I was just playing you to find out where yo' head was at."

"Good, come back on that Sweetie." El'san responded, glad that she switched up. "Now what's this shit about, what's in it for Sweetie?" A distressed look appeared on El'san's face, if she even knew how he'd pistol whip a joker upside his head for second-guessing him, she'd never asked that question.

"All right, be easy baby girl, the nigga gross worth is about $500,000, but his net worth is more like $200,000. I'm figuring he's working off credit, so that means most likely he keeps $300,000 in a secured location to pay off debts. In his house, he presumably has at least $200,000. If you can get all of that, I'll give you half. If you get half of that, you'll get half. I know this nigga has at least the minimum.

One of his boys was on my pod in Riker's, talking all this 'rah-rah' bullshit about how Toby was blowing up in East New York. His stupid ass even told where he hides his drugs. I'm not interested in the drugs, only in the paper. It's always at least one dude giving up the tapes in the pen. Nigga, always running off at the mouth, and if it's like his boy was reporting he keeps loot up in his crib.

So bottom line, whatever you bring me, you are guaranteed to get half. If you haven't learned anything today, know that if you go to jail, never tell your personal business or your friend's business, cause it's niggas like me preying on weakling's just waiting for the opportunity to get broke off with what they've worked or hustled so hard to maintain. With the blink of an eye, the snap of a finger, it can be gone just like that." El'san's blood began to rush and he could feel the excitement swelling up in his crotch.

"Let's get this sucka for every penny he got!" An instant hard on came at the thought of him robbing another. He got off the bench, stretching out his stiff body from working out earlier, holding his nuts. Sweetie watched him. After stretching, he planted his feet wide apart and stared at Sweetie with a less than attractive look this time.

"One thing though Sweetie, don't play with my money. None of that underhandedness, you hear me." An excited El'san started walking toward the basketball court to loose some of his hypertension on the court.

"Yo, I got next!" He yelled out to dudes on the basketball court.

"I called next." A scrawny slender dude called out.

"Man, I don't give a damn. You gonna have to *wait*, I got the next game." El'san emphasized the word wait.

"I got the next game."

His focus was no longer on Sweetie but now on the court. "El'san?" Sweetie called out.

"What? Don't you have some business to take care of?" He answered, now ready to play ball and get her out of his face.

"Sure El'san, now give me the number so *I CAN* get down to my business! That nigga really drive a Jag, huh. Damn it's like that!"

He didn't like the fact that she marveled over Toby's material belongings.

"You only have a week for this job. If you can handle this, I'll put you on to another. Check back with me on Saturday, that gives you exactly seven days." El'san uttered.

"If you pull this off, I may put you down on a real nice pay off."

Sweetie grabbed the number from his hand and smiled as she made her way to her apartment.

El'san nodded his head cleverly thinking of his new *"get rich"* quick scheme. While Sweetie, on the flip side, daydreamed about how she would approach Toby's corny behind.

Scheming On a Nigga

Get into my thoughts understand my plot
I'm try'na take your nigga without a doubt
The night is warm, my flesh is hot
My pressure is rising, palms getting moist
How do I tell this nigga he has no choice?
Gotta come off of his dough, this ain't no show
Won't trick for it, lick for it or let you stick for it
Cause nigga, I consider your doe my doe!
So ease up and let it go before you feel the heat from El'san's forty-fo'!

Chapter Six
The Transition...

To have so little furnishing, it took two extra-long, extra-wide U-haul trucks to load all of the belongings from Camron's condo. He hated the fact of moving up out of Philly, but ever since Mona's funeral, he'd been getting weird telephone calls in the wee hours of the morning.

They'd gone unnoticeable for awhile, simply because he thought it was pesty telemarketers trying to sell a product or service, or possibly one of his many female friends, feeling abandoned from his inattentiveness. Since his last relationship failed, the attitude presented to women was that of dissatisfaction. For him, women came around for one reason and one reason only, to get screwed.

They tempted men for it, soliciting bare skins, breast, curvaceous buttocks unified with flirtatious habits. After he boned them, they were no longer needed. History, a done deal. The challenge was over; he'd be the victorious one. Another reason for moving, Yatta had been to the apartment on the strength of his sister and he wasn't taking any chances of him showing up unexpected.

He saw the indecent looks he received from him at the funeral and before another life was lost, *though killing really didn't bother him,* he'd go back to Brooklyn until things cooled down. Contrary to his uncanny actions, inside Cam longed for love, unconditional love. Love unseen or heard of, like extremely obsessive love, unpolished, ferocious, consuming, aggressive invigorating love from a woman. All the women he dealt with, leaving out Mona, conformed to his every need. None rose above the occasion or stood out in the masses. They were all the same, same clothing style (Gucci, Prada, Movada, Fendi, Fubu, Babyphat), same fake hair (long weaves, ponytails, micro braids), same hazel colored contacts, same tight ass hip hugging jeans or coochie cutting shorts, same low cut shirts exposing cleavage, same situations, fatherless daughters raising three and four kids without a clue to what motherhood is really about in low income areas. Acting as if they could afford buying expensive clothes instead of saving money to elevate them to the next level. Most not possessing a sense of originality, only following the current styles and trends. Concerned only with the outlandish lifestyle, the money, cars, jewels and attention.

It sickened his spirit and Cam could feel saliva dilating from the roof of his mouth. The trickle of spit solidified into a syrupy liquid known to most as a "hawker." With one hand rubbing intensively at the tip of his nose, the other hand rolled down the window to release the thickness spreading inside his mouth. The rustle of the back gliding door quickened his actions, for a second, he was pondering in his own thoughts, not someone else's.

"Let's go, man. It's a lot of shit in this truck." Kenny spoke in an irritated tone. "All the money we got, how come we didn't pay a moving company to take care of this?"

"You ever heard of the word trust?" Cam asked, seriously waiting for a response from his brother.

"What kind of stupid question is that?" Kenny responded, thinking where is this dude coming from now. Repeating the question again, but this time Cam positioned himself slightly to the right in the driver's seat almost touching the passenger's seat.

"Have you ever heard of the word trust? That's the question I asked," He stated firmly. "Webster's dictionary version of trust is a firm reliance in honesty, dependability, strength or the character of someone or something."

Instead of immediately responding, Kenny stood with a disorientated look rubbing his upper lip with his index finger. After placing the first box on the sidewalk he responded, "What the hell are you talking about? What are you trying to get across to me?"

"Nigga, I guess now you a scholar. The only degree you possess is from the School of Hard Knocks, don't ever get it twisted." Cam removed the keys from the ignition, lifted the latch and opened the truck door. Realizing he had an audience, he had to play it smooth. He brushed his hand gently against his Roca Wear denim jeans, trying to brush off invisible lent. It was all for show, there wasn't a particle of lent on his pants to get off. He lifted his arms to stretch out, yawning from the two-hour ride, letting his hands slowly fall right to the center of his crotch. He extended both palms wide to grab the bulge that seemed to be unmanageable. The onlookers turned away except for one young woman standing in the middle of the block sucking on a super blow pop. A young, moldable piece of flesh, she stood remaining focused on his rhythm. Catching her attention to detail, he asked her if she wanted something chocolate to blow on. Without saying a word, her right hand rose, eliminating all fingers but the middle one. His crackling laugh vibrated his bottom lip watching her actions.

"Are you going to continue with this trust bullshit or are you going to play games with Ma all day?" Kenny interrupted, hoping the vague conversation would end soon.

"She wants this thug muscle, don't she?" Cam spoke, loud enough for everyone on the block to hear.

"Baby girl, sucking blow pops don't impress me, but making an appearance in an adult movie just may."

She responded without thinking, "And baby boy, trick ass drug dealers don't impress me, but a hard working man does! So, get a job, Buster!" With that, she turned and walked over captivating the attention of all, to her side of the block.

A dainty, professionally dressed middle aged woman eased out her mouth, "There goes the neighborhood. Every time one of these young punks move into this brownstone the crime rate increases!"

"Move the fuck out then!" Cam yelled back. "Cause we ain't going nowhere *'block captain,'* we own this here. Both you bitches can eat a fat..." He caught himself as four little kids passed by on bikes giggling.

"These low life black women kill me. Here they are downing me when most of them halfway illiterate. Like honey over there, or the so-called executive working woman, working on the lowest level of employment holding an entry level job and they think they got it going on.

Look at them both. Honey got a slick back ponytail with what's supposed to be baby hair pasted with gel on the side of her face. To top that off, she has a little kiddie hairball, probably her daughter's or her neighbor's daughter's hair accessories, to hold it up. The fake hair coming out the back is nappy and the color doesn't match her natural hair. Now, how ghetto is that! She know damn well, if I slid over her crib later on she'd be trying to give it up or suck anything that she could for this wad of money in my pocket. She needs to stop front'n. It's written all over her face that she's an easy lay. I bet if we tried, we could hit in one night, just that simple. And Ms. Working Class citizen, she's wear'n those cheap ass hand me downs that look like they come straight out the picked over merchandise in a Forman Mills Department Store and cheap ass Payless run down shoes. She better stop listening to Star Jones on those commercials, she gets paid for saying that good shit. Now damn, Payless is the store where you pay less right? Then, why in the hell can't she afford to get a new pair when the heels run down? And, they dusty as hell, don't she know that everyday you should wipe your shoes from all the dust and debris that you walk on? Or, has she not been informed of that yet? Which is it?"

Cam was dogging both of them. Her face has two deep gashes on it, sitting center of attention possibly from a cut wound. Which tells me she's been into a fight or fights.

"So, how the hell, can either one of them pass judgment on me. We just moved here, and just because I have a materialistic appearance that expresses my love for designer clothing, jewels and immaculate sneaks, that doesn't mean I'm a drug dealer. Yes, just by chance I am, but not every man that dresses fly is a hustler. I wish people would get that stereotypical perception out of their minds. That stuff burns me up!"

Kenny was struggling, trying to get the boxes off the truck. Disregarding his brother's behavior, he summoned three dudes lounging in front of the building.

"Look like y'all need some work, I'll give you a couple of dollars if you help us unpack this truck." Without question, they came over for instruction.

"What are your names?" Kenny asked, laughing to himself at how eager they were to get some work.

"I'm Doon." Mustered the 5'6, light skin slender man who looked to be in his late 40's. The second man stepped to greet him. "My name is Skee, like in Skee-ball." He outstretched his hand to formally introduce himself to his temporary employer.

The third man replied, "Well, the best always comes last! I'm Twinkle, as in my steps are so swift, you'll never hear me coming. Ya' dig and not that funny stuff either, part'na."

Lost from impartial conversations, Camron started where he left off.

"Yeah, like I was saying, trust goes a long way bro." Not seeing Kenny, but three dusty looking men carrying the boxes, he hurried down to the second U-haul truck.

"What the hell y'all doing?" He questioned. Being the boldest of the three, Twinkle spoke up for his buddies.

"Look here man, we just doing our job. Your partner over there, pointing to Kenny, is paying us to move the boxes into his brownstone. We don't want no trouble only a couple of dollars for assisting in the move."

Camron stared at the man as if he was crazy.

"Ay Kenny, what the hell did you do, hire the black version of Manny, Moe and Jack?" Kenny couldn't control his laughter as he walked out the entrance down the fourteen steps in front of the building.

"Man, I ain't breaking my back trying to move all this shit. Let them do it, that's what I'm paying them for. Now, if you want to continue with your long drawn out conversation of trust, then go ahead, I'm all ears."

"Let's see, where was I." Cam stated trying to remember where he left off. Kenny interrupted him.

"You were at trust the last two times I checked!"

"Be easy, son. Have you ever longed for trust? Do you know anyone besides me, who is worthy of your trust? You know, ever since Mom passed and the whole situation with our family, I have never been able to trust anyone, not even you. Sometimes, I feel like I'm in this war alone. You act like a bitch sometimes and that shit burns me up. It's like you out to get me like everybody else. I'm afraid one day you might try to set me up, or something in that respect. Like you don't want me around. We're both victims of mistrust, believe that homie. With our backgrounds, we have no choice but to war against anybody coming against us. That's on the real, bro." Camron sat on the steps relieved to get his feelings out. Kenny looked cowardly at his younger brother, not wanting to respond.

"Well, say something nigga, let me know what I'm feeling is bullshit, or do you understand the words coming out my mouth? Break out in a sweat, raise up, act a fool, something. Convince me that I'm wrong!" Shouted Cam.

"Come on man, you're my blood, why are you entertaining evil thoughts about your older brother?"

"I never gave you one reason to think, let alone muster the thought of sibling rivalry. That's your own insecurity. If you'd never created chaos in our family, you wouldn't feel like you're being betrayed or that the trust was lost. You need to look inside yourself and ask yourself that question. Why is it that you don't trust anyone? It could be for one reason, you can't even trust yourself. Now, if you want a lesson on trust young blood, you better check your inner feelings first. Now while we're out here having a heart to heart family discussion, Doon, Skee and Twinkle may be pocketing our shit, so let's get inside and monitor what the hell is going on!" Cam agreed and walked inside the building to monitor the black version of the three stooges, but still didn't like the answer his brother gave him.

Kenny turned in the opposite direction and stood in position to face both trucks. He watched as the sassy mouth young lady with the lollipop monitored them. Instead of creating a scene, he walked across the street to meet her, and the way she was slurping on that blow pop, she was sure enough tempting him. Watching her take slow licks, he knew she had skill.

"Excuse me, Miss, can I have a moment of your time?" Kenny walked nonchalantly over to where she was standing.

"No, so take your tired ass back across the street." Her legs stood in a pigeon toed position, with her left hand on one hip and her right hand moving slowly in and out of her mouth with the blow pop.

"Slow down Ma, that was my brother blowing up your spot, not me. Don't disrespect me like that; I'm coming to you as a gentleman, make peace, meet the neighbors' type shit. That's all. What's your name?" Batting her eyes back and forth, she finally toned down her speech.

"I'll ask all the questions, ai'ight." She stated.

"First, who are you and who is that ignorant ass imposture of a man you are with?"

"Well, we're finally getting somewhere." He grinned.

"The imposture of a man is my little brother Cam. Baby doll, you'll have to excuse him, he can get pretty quarrelsome with women. He loves to start trouble, so the best way to deal with him is to ignore him. We're like night and day. Oh, by the way, I'm Kenny." He admired her dress.

"That's a nice white halter dress you have on, is that Donna Karan? Those quarter heels raising the calves on those pigeon toed legs go perfect with that dress."

By the expression on her face, brownie points for him were building up. She was glowing, showing all teeth as if she'd just hit the big lotto.

"How'd you know that? You're good with designer clothing." She smiled brightly cause she had his attention.

"Yes, this is Donna Karan, exclusively from Hecht's Department Store. The store located inside the Manhattan Times Square Shopping Mall. I purchased the shoes from there too. You like the outfit, huh?"

The tension in the air eased, allowing the sweet lustful spirit to take over. Her pigeon toed position switched to standing bow-legged, but by now, she was twirling her blow pop around in a circle with bright red lips.

"Yeah, sweetheart you are wearing that shit! I must tell you that blow pop does you an injustice though. Try sucking on a piece of candy if you want to suck something. Men will take sucking on a blow pop to another level and I can't stand for another man to dis' you like that." Kenny said, trying to shower her with flattery.

"It's a damn shame men have to be that way. I mean, for real, it's only a piece of candy shaped like a little ball." Thinking about what she just said, she recanted.

"Let me take that back before you take that the wrong way too. I've never done anything that gross in my life. All my friends have, but I think it's just nasty. Anyway, Kenny it is a pleasure to meet such a gentlemen as yourself. My name is Yvonne but everyone calls me Shavonee. Feel free to call me that if you want."

"How did you get the name Shavonee from Yvonne?" He asked, questioning the person who gave her the nickname Shavonee.

"Well, if you keep saying it long enough, it will start to sound the same. Yvonne, Shavon, get it? That's my name, *'Shavoneee'*."

"Well, Shavonee, it's a pleasure to be in your presence. Later, if you don't mind, maybe I can come over and chill since our house will be in an uproar. Would you like that?" Kenny asked, praying that she would adhere.

"I guess it will be alright. I don't have to work tonight, so you can come over. I live in the 2nd floor apartment." Shavonee didn't have job the first, her only job was plotting on men.

"I don't need to come strapped do I?" Questioned Kenny, not wanting any drama.

"Only if you want, it's not necessary though." Shavonee responded, hesitantly.

"I'll check you later then baby girl." He smiled, thinking later he would be the first to break her in orally and then exchange fuck faces. His nonchalant movement with his feet diminished as his pimp walk crept in.

Shouting loudly as he possibly could, he yelled out, "Yo Camron, come to the door." You could see Cam staring out the front window at this fool. His hands pointed to his chest as if to say, "Are you talking to me?" Kenny waved toward his direction.

"Come here, man."

Cam walked out, sipping on a brew so cold small pieces of ice trickled down his arm melting as soon as they touched his flesh.

"What do you want fool? I'm in here monitoring the base head 'goodfellas'."

"Why don't you try out for 'Coming to the Stage', since you think you got jokes." Kenny laughed at his corny ass.

"Man, Kim Coles ain't ready for a street nigga like me. I'd get up there on some straight bullshit like, your girl's coochie is so big, they had to recall the deaths of Biggie and Pun cause she was keeping them captive."

"Yeah, you're right. That's some straight bullshit. You best stay a local comedian." Kenny shook his head, not wanting to tell his brother his comedy line was garbage. Cam was steady laughing, spurting out beer as he exhaled.

"Seriously lil' bro, later on tonight I'll be across the street with honey that you dissed earlier. So don't look for me to return until tomorrow morning." Cam's laughter turned into a solemn look on his face.

"You mean the project chick sucking on a lollipop sitting at the bus stop? Nigga, you went over there begging to hit, didn't you? Let me school you big bro', project chicks like that you don't have to beg, they come easy. You could hit that probably in the stairwells, on the rooftop, in the alley, in a dark park, in the car, they just trying to get it in anyway they can. Take some of this good *'Purple Haze'* over there. I bet she'd start giggling at first, then hit her with a bottle of Remy, or something she ain't never heard of before, to make her feel special. Now, make sure to stop by the chicken coop and get a 15-piece bucket of chicken, add the extras, mashed potatoes, gravy, biscuits and strawberry shortcake if she has kids. She'll go through the process as every weed head, just let the process take its course.

After the first stage of giggles die down from smoking the haze and the drinks start filtering through her body, those spirits will assist you in the take over. That's why I love the L.Q. – liquor store. They help a brother speed up the process. Can you believe people go there to buy the liquid version of evil spirits? Ready to poison their thought process voluntarily. That's crazy dog! Once the spirits settle in, that lust demon is sure to surface. Your girl is going to start getting real freaky. You have her in the position you want her, under your control and horny ass hell. That's when you take advantage of her. You beat the coochie up, smack it, flip it, hit it from the back and then ram it right in her buttocks without warning and without using any lubricant either. She'll be screaming and squirming, don't let that bother you, just keep it coming. Make her pay for being an easy lay.

Treat her the way a slut should be treated, unwarranted like filth. Maybe the next time, she'll think about giving it up on the first night and won't be so damn easy."

You could feel the sincerity in Cam's voice as he spoke each word so passionately.

Kenny watched as the venom rose inside his brother. Instead of him, it was his counterpart, the darker side of him. It was like he transformed from a comedian to a dark evil demon out to steal the innocence from its victim without warning.

A side of Kenny wanted to quickly respond but he couldn't find the words to describe the feelings he internalized. That side of his brother was the grimy side of him that he hated so much. Cam's thought raised memories of Kenny's time in Riker's Island and the thoughts began to swarm his head.

Never physically spending an overnight stay in a penitentiary without his brother, Kenny was less than thrilled of spending the next 9½ years alone, behind bars. Since Cam's release, the first day was rough enough. Then to deal with other inmates down for more serious crimes made him swallow up in isolation. He was placed in maximum security with Big Thaddeus as his celly.

"Big T", is what they called him for short, was down for seven counts of armed robbery and five counts of aggravated sexual assault on a minor. He was a big black bald, 320-diesel joker fresh from Uncle Tom's farmland in Bucktussell, somewhere deep in the swamplands.

Kenny begged the Correctional Officers, requesting for an emergency modification in the tier. However, in order for an inmate to request such a change, he or she must be incarcerated in the facility for at least twelve months. This was only his ninth month, so his request went in and returned quickly from his Counselor, denied.

Living in the cell with Big T made life a living hell for Kenny. He wasn't known for squaring up or going toe to toe on the fighting tip. His pattern was tag teaming his victim with a crew or letting his brother hit him up a couple of times with his favorite Mac Ten. In this case, neither was available to help him. Everybody on his tier knew Big T was an outside "in the closet" homosexual. On the inside, the majority of the prisoners were well aware of that. It's a golden rule in prison not to leak information about the inside, all the things prisoners witnessed, they didn't witness. At least that's how they'd respond when questioned about any occurrence they'd witnessed. They didn't see a thing.

Big T had been in and out of prison all his life and each time released, he would move in with a woman from the projects spreading all the infectious diseases and germs. This last term he was tested for HIV and was later informed that he was infected with the disease. It was then, he decided to poison all the men and women he could.

Just before getting settled in the cell, the dinner bell rang. Taking advantage of the dinner meal, Kenny walked nonchalantly in his crisp white prison uniform out the cell. Just before his right foot hit the walkway, Big T pushed him forcefully to the ground. Other prisoners walked pass ignoring the commotion. Kenny grabbed hold of metal bedpost to lift himself up from the floor. That's when Big T kicked him maliciously in the groin. Soft moans escaped from Kenny lips as he knelt in horrifying pain. With quick course, Big T threw him, face first, on the twin bunk ripping down his white prison pants. Kenny wanted to fight but couldn't muster the energy to move, it was like his heart stopped beating. His vision clouded and his hearing was temporarily gone. Once his whites were down, Big T mounted him, exhaling his victory of conquering another victim. He pounded anxiously gripping Kenny's buttocks trying to bring him to climax. Blood was now soiling what used to be his white pants and white linens. Kenny's manhood was snatched without reason. Had it not been for another prisoner, El'san to be exact, yelling out to Prison Guards for help, not only his manhood but also his life would've been taken. Big T was known for sodomizing his victims and later strangling them to death. To thank El'san was the appropriate measure to take, but Kenny not seeing his savior wasn't able to match the voice with his face.

Camron glimpsed at Kenny as he saw the emotionalism that built on his face.

"Hey Bro', I know you're not shedding tears by me telling you to do shaw'ty grimy tonight, are you? What the hell happened to your spirit just that quickly?"

Lifting his head and leveling his shoulders out, he deliberately wiped away the salty tears that streamed down his face.

"Nothing man, I'm alright. I can't stomach the way you talk about hurting women like that. What's your problem? Ever since Mona, you've been acting asinine about other women. Bro, it's

over, you got your revenge, now let that shit go!"
He couldn't form the words to let his little brother
know he'd been raped. Cam was not about to
accept that at all.

Chapter Seven
The Set Up...

On My Grind

I'm on my grind, fine-tuning and hitting rewind
The mistakes I made last night, never mind
To slip up and trip up is seldom in this stick up game
It's a shame,
these niggas are lame,
but they have stakes for me to claim
Moving seductively the tricks chin drops
I lay him down to the side till his dick pops
Slip him a drink to relax him
Him not knowing later on I'm a tax him.
I'm on my grind nigga!

Walking through her apartment reciting street poetry in a long white linen dress accessorized with a white turban, Sweetie grabbed her cordless microphone as if a crowd was in her presence.

Scarface flooded the CD player with "My Homies" CD, Fuck Faces featuring Too Short, Tela and Devin.

"You must be used to all them finer things. Infatuated by what money brings. It seems to me you ho's will never change."

She rapped verse by verse, *"Man, I met this chick so fine, so bad she made me sick sometimes.*

107

Honey, must of missed being treated like something more niggas do than talking but beating, I did it, making Mack moves she came chasing. You must be used to all them finer things, them situations that the money brings" and danced around the large wooded rocking chair.

Scarface blazed the track. Her movement caused the chair to slightly sway back and forth. Whenever her mood desired a switch in her spirit, she let Scarface, Tupac, Biggie, DMX, Ice Cube, Jay Z, Beans, old or new CD's rotate in the chambers. She loved southern music so when she felt country, she let her down south cronies light up the room, Master P, Eight Ball & M.J.G., Youngbloodz, Lil Jon and the East Side Boyz, Ludacris, Trick Daddy, and most recently, the Ying Yang Twins. To put her in the mindset to hype herself, she would blast *"I'm slip'n, I'm fall'n and can't get up,"* on the Flesh of my Flesh, Blood of my Blood CD by DMX. That song motivated her like none other. DMX is a gritty rapper, so when the time was right to scheme, she would listen to his lyrics over and over again to give her non-caring attitude the victory. With her mind on the plot, she phoned Shavonee to set up her victim.

"Hello, may I speak to Shavonee." She said, politely speaking.

"Who dis is?" Shavonee questioned, while blowing huge bubbles from the wad of gum inside her mouth. Sweetie couldn't stand dealing with *"Ghetto Girls"*. This job would definitely have to be over in a short period of time.

She imagined Shavonee on the other end, hair twirling with her left hand, positioning her right hand against the phone. Her image probably matched her obnoxious ass vocals. Though she couldn't be rude, that would mess up her scheme of money if she blatantly disrespected her.

"This is Sweetie, dear. Your cousin El'san told me to give you a call about Toby. Do you recall speaking with him?"

"Oh, yeah that's right, what's up girl? It's Shavonee representing from the East, ya' heard me! I stay down on the get down, so when you ready to put it down, H o l l a!"

Sweetie squeezed her eyes tightly and sighed, shifting her tongue to the upper level of her teeth clinching the phone tighter against her forehead. Okay, play the game she thought, comprising her position.

"Yeah, yeah what's up baby girl, it's your world. You ready to get 'dis crumb snatcher or what?"

"Fo' sugadale, for sure, here's my address. Meet me here later tonight. Toby's an easy mark, you can hit him up in one day. Huh, ask me how I know. East New York baby, I gets mine in. I am not new to this, I'm true to this, Miss Thang. You ready to get on this grind or are you slow easy, hesitant?"

"Never that, mistake me for none you've seen, best make room for this Queen." Sweetie retorted, her free flow.

"Later, then baby girl. I'll get at you."

Shavonee hit the off button on her cordless phone and dropped it accidentally on the floor, causing the back cover to pop off and the batteries to roll underneath the Futon in her bedroom.

"Damn, messing around with this trick, my cordless phone done malfunctioned!" She said agitated.

Sweetie placed the telephone on the receiver and pouted.

"Why me? Why me? I can't escape dealing with these unsophisticated ghetto chicks. Can I meet some educated Sistas along the way? What's up with that?"

Elevate My Sistah Elevate

Step up my Sistah and please recognize
The plague that's filtering on your inside
Your heart is warm and easy to squeeze
Men and boys take advantage of you even in your dreams
Instead of uplifting, you keep lifting up your skirt
Until your heart bleeds and your feelings get hurt
A woman scorned is what you've become
Acting nigga-fied when the time comes
Letting emotions control instead of molding you
For what's to come
How can you teach
Let alone preach, to your sons and daughters
Your reactions speak negativity in their minds
And when they get older, you scold them for wasting time
Stop running girl,
The negativity continues to plague your mind
Help reach your seeds before they get left behind
Don't run, it's your destiny to plant positivity
And not negativity in these times...
"Elevate my Sistah, Elevate!"

The late afternoon commenced to the latter hours of the evening. Sweetie, dressed so elegantly in spectacular fall colors, burnt orange Khaki pants with A-line sage green and a burnt orange halter hanging enticingly over her shoulders outlining her hips superbly. Using the disposable razor, she touched up her arched eyebrows, afterwards applying a Mac Lip Gloss on her lips to give them the perfect shine.

"Mmmmaw." Came out of her mouth, kissing at herself through the mirror as the twists gently fell into place, she was ready for her victim. She grabbed her straw bag with limited accessories, turned off the lights, blew out the scented mango fragrance candles that filled the air and locked the apartment door.

Once in the hallway, she heard loud music coming from her neighbor's apartment. Blasting music was the norm for the complex so this was nothing new.

The building was kept mannerly and in sanitary conditions. Pop was the community Maintenance Supervisor for 27 years. This was his community as well as the residents in the building. A country man at heart and in spirit, he relocated to New York City after owning a home in the fields of Mississippi for 32 years. The farmland was a family inheritance for many years. However, not receiving formal education, Pop was unaware of his actions when he signed over the deed to the property to the Mississippi Town Hall. Signing the documents, affected his family years of sweat and hard work, by one signature coerced by the Town Legislator supposedly for his family to obtain more land.

Twenty-four hours after he signed, his family found themselves homeless and bound for New York City where his sister lived. Instead of humbling himself due to his actions, that situation made him easily agitated and undesirable at times to be around.

Finding a job in the city was easy for him because he was so handy. Although he'd suffer many beat downs on the strength of his impulsive bitter comments, he sputtered to anyone who called in with a maintenance complaint. Pop kept drama going, telling everyone's business at any opportunity. Being the maintenance man, he witnessed almost anything you could imagine, prostitution, drug deals, robbery, in the building, men and women cheating on their husbands, wives, girlfriends and boyfriends, young folks sexing in the laundry room, people getting high on the rooftop, property managers sneaking in and out of peoples apartment unauthorized. You name it, he witnessed it.

One day while coming from making repairs in a vacant unit, he witnessed El'san give a serious ass whooping to a petty hustler from the block. I mean he beat him down to a *"Bloody Pulp"* for selling drugs in his building. Pop didn't make a fuss about the beating, but he made the error of disrespecting El'san by calling him a low life thug and saying that he would suffer in hell for his wrongdoings. And, Pops' version of a thug was *"To Hell U Go"*! Apparently, he caught El'san at the wrong place at the wrong time, because from the anger built up inside of El'san that day, he couldn't help but to kick Pop down a flight of stairs, causing him to dislocate his left hip. That injury quieted Pop down for a little while, sixteen weeks to be precise. But, it also caused him to tell his story to people over and over again to those curious about the shortness and the limp in his left leg.

Walking past the loud blaring music, Sweetie looked at Pop as he moped and waxed the rear end hallway floors. In his blue maintenance uniform, he was bent over, sweat oozing from his forehead, fussing while continuing to mop the floor. He lifted his head, alerted by the footsteps coming through the hallway.

"Evening, Miss Sweetie. What your evening be like? You are looking mighty fine in them there seasonal colors. Mmmm, the smell of your perfume is so sweet." Pop lifted his upper lip, touching the tip of his nose. Reminding himself that he was on the clock, he tipped his blue and white maintenance uniform cap and spoke sincerely to Sweetie.

"No disrespect Miss Sweetie, I think a man ought to compliment a beautiful lady when she's in his presence. Would you mind sharing with me the fragrance that is so sweetly seeping out your natural pores?"

"Pop, if I didn't know any better, I'd think you were trying to pull a fast one on me. And, the fragrance I'm wearing is Cool Water for Women. But that's not the question of the hour. What are you doing here this late in the evening moping and waxing the floors?"

"Now Miss Sweetie, you've been living here long enough to know that if I didn't come sometimes in the evening to clean up this building, it would look like Vietnam War hit this place. With all the trash and those damn junkies, it doesn't make sense at all. I mean the government pays at least 70% of the rent for people living in this building. That's a respectable amount of rent the government pays, when you look at it that way. Residents are only responsible for 30% of their income and most of them are on State assistance, so they're paying zero or close to nothing in rent. Why they got to be nasty and live so damn trashy? They ought to inspect these buildings more than once a year. Cause, all these trifling residents do is clean up one time for their annual inspection. Half the time it looks like trash been dumped but scattered about. I see it with my own eyes everyday. I can't say it's all of the residents, but it surely is most of them. And, Miss Sweetie, if it applies then let it stick, if it doesn't, let it fly by. But, I am not holding my tongue for no one, not even that little demon El'san. Uh huh, no sir! The next time that boy disrespects me, it will be his last time."

Shaking his head intensely, he wiped the sweat dripping from his nose with a week old dirty drop cloth.

"No, it doesn't make sense at all." He couldn't resist the aroma. "That sure is nice smelling perfume, Miss Lady. Would you mind getting me a bottle for the misses? Our 33rd anniversary is coming soon and that sure would be a nice anniversary present."

Sweetie stepped over the mop and proceeded down the stairs.

"You mean to tell me you want your wife to smell like a young, sensuous woman like me? Or, and be honest with me Pop, are you trying to buy some Ms. Irene on the 1st floor? Come to think about it, that's probably the reason you're here late tonight. Ms. Irene was selling dinners earlier today. Did you get one?" Everybody knew the married maintenance man, Pop, was sweet on Ms. Irene. He used his job as a way to get away and be with his mistress.

"Yes 'Ma'm, I did. As a matter of fact, I bought two dinners from her, a chicken platter and a pork chop platter. You know Irene can sure burn up in that kitchen. I try to tell these young ladies in the building, the way to a man's soul is by cooking a delicious meal. Often times, they think fixing precooked encore frozen meals is a home cook meal."

"Don't get off the subject Pop! Are you hitting Ms. Irene off or what?"

Pop sullen puppy eyes drifted, turning to see if anyone else was in the hallway listening. All those late nights of cleaning usually turned into hours of adultery till the wee hours of the morning with Ms. Irene. He was an older man but when Viagra hit the market, his risks and his hormones built up like never before.

"Miss Sweetie, I don't imply about your personal life and I would respect it if you weren't in mine. This is my job and a part of my job is to resident relate. That's what me and Irene do, resident relate. Now, if you don't mind, here's a $20 dollar bill, please get me a bottle of that 'Deep Water'."

"No, it's 'Cool Water', and for the record, $20 is not enough. You need to pull off at least another $40 to compliment that $20. And, you just answered my question, you and Ms. Irene are boning, case closed! Now, pull the money out those nasty blue uniform pants, old man. You need to ask the Management Office for a couple new pairs, cause it looks like you had them for years and never washed them." He looked at his uniform pants like nothing was wrong with them.

"Pop, it's crazy how you in everybody else's business but when it comes to your mess, you try to keep that discrete. Remember, what you do in the dark comes to the light, and sooner than you think. Later!"

Sweetie made it to the entrance of the building without disturbance from any of the neighbors in her building. Her night was about to begin. She spotted El'san and Chyna Whyte sitting in the park on the basketball court bench.

Chyna Whyte was off the chain once again, chasing those inside the gate. People were terrified, climbing high on the 17" inch wired fence. El'san was in his glory, he loved fucking with the ballers like that.

In his peripheral view, he saw Sweetie come out the building and wondered what the hell took her so long. She had only a few minutes before she was to meet up with Shavonee, to swindle money from her first victim.

He was skeptical about giving her so much information on Toby's worth, but he figured she lived in the neighborhood, so what the hell. Either way, she couldn't escape him. Chyna Whyte would sniff her out if she tried to dodge. Finally placing the dog chain around Chyna Whyte's neck, El'san rose, with the help of his hyperactive Pit, to the concrete.

"Yo, Sweetie! Holla at ya boy for a minute."

Sweetie hated when he called her out like that. She didn't like neighborhood attention, she was more intimate, wanting one on one attention. Her response was low, almost a whisper.

"Here I come, El'san. Please stop calling me out like that."

"What did you say, I can't hear you girl?" He continued to yell.

Raising her voice two notches. "I said, here I come, damn! Give me a minute to get over there."

The streetlights bounced brightly off the basketball court, causing a glare in the direction of the building. It was pretty calm this evening. The fiends knew El'san and Chyna Whyte were out. So, instead of going to the front entrance, they met up with hustlers around the back. What they didn't realize was Chyna Whyte was trained to smell the scent of heroin, weed and coke even while bagged up in plastic. His nose was like a radar detector 500 feet away. When he smelled a deal going on, he was trained to bark a certain way. Two barks, then a growl, two barks, then a growl.

The hustlers loathed that damn snitching ass pit bull, and the owner for training him in such a way. El'san could have easily sold Chyna Whyte to the DEA for $50,000, but he figured he was doing his societal good deed by cleaning his neighborhood of drug abuse, by pushing the users away and through damn near eliminating hustlers from selling their product. Over 60% of Kingsboroughs population was consumed by users that had to make other means to cop drugs just to support their habit.

It was rough trying to deal with the "Jump Out Squad", but now they had to deal with their own personal DEA renegade in the 'Borough. El'san had the 'Borough on lock down. Nobody was using to their full potential or making mad money because of him shutting down the area.

The only time selling drugs or using was prevalent was when El'san was on his mission to rob another dealer from another area in New York.

"Well, are you just gonna stand there or are you going to say something to me El'san?"

Chyna Whyte barked once, then again, then growled. Ah, the shit was on.

Before Chyna Whyte finished his ritual, El'san let the dog chain loose and Chyna Whyte with spectacular motion, moved her shiny black back hind legs to catch the perpetrator.

"Get 'em Chyna Whyte, Get 'em!" El'san coached him on.

Sweetie stood in a trance as she witnessed Chyna Whyte rip the rugged pair of jeans on the dealer's backside.

El'san ran fast enough to catch the hustler and to retrieve his money and package.

"Please, please, someone get this dog off my ass!" The boy cried. "In a minute he'll be chewing on my balls. The perpetrator rested against the building in a "spread 'em" position.

"Nah, nigga, I told you not to come around my hood with this bullshit. You're killing the community flooding devils into the minds of our people. Do you realize how drugs are slowly assassinating families?" El'san was fuming, speaking directly in the young man's ear, and slightly touching his earlobe with his lips after every word. "Take a good look at this 'Borough son. Lil D is only ten years old. Do you realize this little man has to rob the corner store to provide snacks and to make a meal for him and his little sister because his mother is only concerned about sucking that glass dick! Do you see young ass fourteen year old Natalie, late night getting hit off by some perverted nigga to buy school clothes because her Mom is in jail for supporting her drug habit?

What about Ms. Irene, the sweet elderly woman who sells dinners just to make up for the rent money her son rips her off for to buy drugs?

Young blood, do you understand how pushing drugs on the corner is affecting your life? What, you think you'll retire and get a pension from selling drugs? It ain't happening like that, part'na. What's going to happen is the 'Jump Out Squad' gonna eventually pick your ass up on a trafficking charge. Your little faggot ass can't afford a lawyer, so you'll sit waiting for a trial date. When the trial date comes, the prosecutor will offer you a plea. If you fail to accept the plea, your case will be heard by a Judge or a Trial by Jury.

In your mind, you already know you're guilty, so when you decide against taking that plea, your ass is history. To the penitentiary you go, a young sweet and innocent virgin. Do you know what will happen to you once you get inside? That childhood innocence will give off a smell throughout the prison.

The rapists will smell you out waiting for the chance to steal the little bit of manhood you have. I've witnessed first hand hardcore dudes handling their business on the streets, but now they're on their knees or bent over getting fucked. Man, dats a horrific site to see, a man's strength, his courage and his manhood being taken away. In the pen, once you're labeled as a bitch, you're game for anything and anyone. Soon you'll be fucking, sucking and washing laundry for half the damn prison. Your butt hole will be so loose shit will just fall from your ass without you knowing. After a while, you won't be able to live with yourself anymore, so the drugs that you once hustled on the streets will soon become your best friend. It's a halo effect young blood, what goes around comes around! Understand the world's plan for the black man. They want us to inflict violence on one another. They want you to become a weed head, heroin addict, crack head or an all out junkie.

They want you to become accustomed to the revolving door of the penal institution. They want you to impregnate all the girls you can put your link dinker in and become a deadbeat father. This is all in the plan to decline the presence of the black man. Don't think drugs will escape you, if it's not you they find, it may be your little sister or your little brother. Do you know what it's like to see your mother tricking in the streets for a damn hit? Selling her ass, to White, Hispanic, Asian, and Haitian men, any man willing to give her $20 dollars for sex or $5 dollars for a blow job. Yeah that's right, $5 dollars to give some head to a dirty dicked mothafucka!

I hate little niggas like you that keep this shit going, the decline in parental involvement, the increase in high school dropouts, the increase in pressure to sell drugs, the decline in nurturing our brothas and sistahs, putting an end to the beginning of uncovering your dreams without the sense of right and wrong!"

The shit was serious to El'san.

Letting loose from his shirt collar, the young man fell to ground with Chyna Whyte still holding on to his rear end. The pressure from Chyna Whyte on his balls caused him to lose consciousness. El'san pulled out his forty-fo', ready to put an end to this pitiful young man's life. Checking the round, he only had three gold tip bullets.

"This might be your lucky day, punk ass. I have three rounds, I'll give you one chance to get up and get your sorry ass out of here."

He lay unaware of the choice he'd been given.

"So, you're not going to leave huh." El'san garbled.

A brave woman from the crowd couldn't stand the abuse and what she was about to witness.

"Let it go El'san, the boy looking like he half dead now! You've done enough. It's not our fault."

The woman's best friend grabbed her and covered her mouth with one hand, dragged her from behind and ducked into the large crowd.

El'san spit to the ground, allowing it to land right on his victim's jaw. White specs and bubbles sizzled on his face as he rested, sprawled out in front of the building as if he was taking a power nap. His mouth was wide open permitting the spit to slither inside the crevices of his lips onto his tongue. Viewers watched the ball-breaking scene, not uttering another word.

Skipping her face, Sweetie allowed droplets of tears to fall on her beautiful blouse. She'd seen enough and wasn't about to become an accomplice to a murder.

"El'san baby, come here! I think we have business to discuss." A distraction was the only way to get El'san's attention.

She opened her pocketbook, grabbed her compact mirror to double check her facial expression. It was cool.

El'san was in another world, his mind transformed, his body stiffened and Chyna Whyte stood at ease waiting for his master to modify the mood.

"Leave me the fuck alone, Sweetie! You know what you got to do. Just get it done." He responded.

"But baby, I need your advice before heading out on this mission." She had to say something to take his mind off of the situation.

Though they never shared sexual intimacy, the bond that Sweetie and El'san held was sacred. He had seen her at her worst and she'd seen him through the same. El'san was the first person who took a liking to Sweetie when she first moved to the 'Borough. He never consented to any other man in the 'Borough to develop a relationship with her. If she needed to talk to someone, he was the man she would come to, none other.

"Excuse me miss, do you need help carrying your things inside the building?" He could tell she wasn't from around the area and was just moving in.

"No, thank you, I can handle this myself."
Sweetie responded, not wanting him to think she was dependent on a man.

"Now, come on baby doll, there's no way
you can lift a love seat and a sofa from that pick
up truck. And, from the looks of it, the crack heads
that drove you over here aren't willing to help." He
watched as the crack heads rummaged around the
truck to, by chance, find a lost bag.

"By the way, my name is El'san, the leader
around the mothafuck'n 'Borough, and for the
record, I despise drug dealers and drug abusers,
So if you are one of the above, take your shit and
move around to Prospect Plaza cause I ain't having
it in my hood." He had to give it to her straight.
The pretty smile, the perfect brown skin, those
tempting eyes, was so innocent and pure. He had
to make sure she wasn't honing drug dealers in
his area.

"Well, so much for a pleasant greeting, Mr.
El'san, the mothafuck'n leader of the 'Borough!"
That was nice she thought, another ruthless,
renaissance trying to save the hood by his
lonesome.

Both of them shared a laughed as she
mimicked his words.

"There's no need to worry about me, I'm a
petty thief. I'm known for robbing small change
from the dealers." She spoke proudly. That's right
she thought, get it right, this is my hustle and I'm
not letting anybody come between that. You do
you and I'll do me.

"Is that right. That means you fuck for a
buck huh! Damn, is it that easy! From your
appearance and the way you present yourself, I
would have thought differently about you. Look at
you, dressed all neatly in your innocent white
Muslim garb. The length falls so eloquently down

*to your unspoiled white moccasins. Your hair
remains a mystery to me under that beautifully
wrapped white turban. I guess looks are deceiving
and I was dead wrong. That innocence is to shield
the griminess tucked on the inside of you. What
building do you live in? It's necessary that I keep
an eye on your slick ass. You're doing the Muslim
world an injustice, Queen. Here we go, another
African-American Queen using what she got, to get
what she wants. I have a lot of work to do, not
just to reach my Brothas but to reach my Sistahs
too!" He deliberated.*

*"I live in the second building on the 4ᵗʰ floor.
Why don't you stop by later tonight or help me with
my stuff like you first suggested, 'My brotha X'.
Maybe we can get to know each other on better
terms, cause I am not even like that. All of us have
two sides, I try my best to release the positive side
of me, but out here in these streets, it's a must I do
me.   The hustler's are helping to dissect the
neighborhoods anyway. Why not steal from them?
They steal from the mouths of babies, corrupt the
minds of mothers and fathers, buy stolen goods for
70% less than the original price from people, who
most likely stole it from someone else in the hood.
You know! You do dirt you get dirt, El'san. So,
what's your story?"*

*I bet he has a story to tell, she said to
herself. Don't no man knock hustlers just for the
heck of it. What, is his mom a crack head? Is his
father a heroin addict?   What's his beef with
hustlers? I mean they trying to eat like the rest of
us.*

Finally, getting within arms reach, Sweetie
gently stroked El'san's right arm. Because of his

nerves, his hand locked on the forty-four holding a tight grip.

"Let the forty-fo' go El'san!" Sweetie demanded, trying to make sense of the situation. "He's not worth going back to prison. We need to talk anyway."

Taking heed to her delicate touch, he patted Chyna Whyte on the rear motioning for him to move. Now able to control his nerves, he let go of the trigger and placed the gun inside of his gun strap under his right pant leg. In an instant, it was like he came back from his blackout.

"Yeah, go head Sweetie, what's up?"

"I wrote this poem and would like your honest opinion of it. Okay? Listen closely, it's dedicated to you. Here it goes:"

Lift My Mood

Sometimes, I just need someone to lift my mood
Give me some of that extra attention
That I'm not used to
Not be judgmental about the issues
I'm going through
Sometimes, I just need someone to lift my mood
I mean it's not an everyday occurrence
That I need this Boo, Open up your arms
To squeeze those ill feelings to the top
Let's pray together that the spirit is loose
When you feel that "Pop"
Sometimes, I just need someone to lift my mood
When the stresses of street hustling
Dampers my livelihood
I mean when I've made a bad decision and

Try to reverse it but it comes back void
Sometimes, I just need someone to lift my mood
When I witness my young sistahs get caught
Up in young motherhood
When I see my young brothas selling drugs
Struggling in neighborhoods
Sometimes, I just need someone to lift my mood
After holding a conversation with a teenage friend
That has fell victim to addiction over and over again
The stresses, the worry, the poverty, the Enslavement
of our minds, the purple haze, the craze
It's killing our time
I can't stand it, I didn't plan this,
To enter my mental thoughts
Please stop me, before they drop me
To the psych ward
Sometimes, I just need someone to lift my mood
El'san, would that someone happen to be you?

The words glided from Sweetie's lips and the shine from her Mac Lip Gloss glistened as she finished up her last verse. El'san was mesmerized, this was the first time someone genuinely expressed love by way of poetry. Sweetie stood there waiting for an informal response when, without warning, El'san grabbed her hair pulling forcefully, yet seductively, by her Bohemian Twists. Then letting loose Chyna Whyte, he lifted her off her feet into a carrying position. Sweetie didn't know how to respond. She submitted to the force of his eyes telling her to surrender her love. Speaking in an adorable low sound, Sweetie finally initiated conversation.

"El'san, what are you doing?" Looking at him deeply, yet carefully, over his facial features, she noticed he had shaved off his Sunni Muslim beard. She stared without a blink looking past his anger. From where she lay, his silhouette favored more and more like that sexy ass chocolate actor, Mehki Pfeiffer. His skin was untarnished, even after shaving.

He placed his right index finger over her mouth, summoning her to keep quiet, as he walked straightforwardly to his building. Chyna Whyte watched his master as if he knew what was going on, walking proudly beside them like they were a King and Queen. Even with the mounds of people standing around the building still waiting for the young man to gain consciousness, El'san proceeded as if nothing ever happened. Sweetie's weight was easy to maintain, hell he lifted at least 320 pounds in weight everyday. A mere 165 pounds of a voluptuous soft woman was an easy task. He mounted the twelve steps then opened the brick red metal door with his left hand, slipping through sideways to avoid Sweetie hitting her head. Once inside the building, Pops had made way to begin to mop and wax the floors of this building. He lifted his head, positioning his glasses from the sweat, causing them to fall from his nose and couldn't believe what he saw. He mumbled under his breath about how the thugged out disrespectful creeps always ended up with the good girls corrupting their gullible minds.

"Chyna Whyte, grab the keys from my pocket." El'san spoke as if his dog was a human being. Listening to his owner, he rose on two hind legs, pulled the key chain from his master's navy blue sweat pants and seized them.

"Good boy. Good boy. I'll give you a treat when we get on the inside." He said, to reward his dog for his good deed.

El'san opened the apartment door and the sweet aroma of Home Interiors' specialized Apple Cider Spice candles filled the room. Once Sweetie took in a deep inhalation of the sweet aroma, she exhaled long and gradually. The apartment had a pleasant and welcoming environment to it. There were pictures of the late Martin Luther King, Jr., Malcolm X, W.E.B. Dubois, St. Clair Drake, Dr. Daniel Hale Williams, Satchel Paige, John Hope Franklin, Langston Hughes, Benjamin Banneker, Frederick Douglass, Reverend Daniel Payne, Elijah Muhammad, Walter Rodney, Thomas J. Martin, Toussaint-Louverture, Marcus Garvey, King Ramses, Bobby Hutton, Booker T. Washington, Granville Woods, Nat Turner, Duke Ellington and many more.

All of which represented the true meaning of being black and struggling in "White America." They embodied the strength in organizations, leading through ministry, patenting industrial inventions, authoring and publishing books, educating in segregated school systems, composing music, founding Revolutionaries, leading in Christian discipleship, Muslim discipleship, becoming an Anthropologist, claiming All-time baseball records, just a few great black men most not seen or heard about in our schools and communities or even during February's once a year "Black History" month.

And, here they were framed so stunningly in a so-called thug's apartment.

The Afro-centric appearance blended well with his sandstone sectional furniture with recliners resting on both ends. The round center glass table was outlined by carefully carved wood incisions of African dancers. The scribes became visible once you moved in closer to the table. Underneath the table, a soft sandstone and black furry rug captivated the attention. He had a nice surround sound of music mostly a collection of Bob Marley or mellow sounds from the Temptations, Bobby Womack, Teddy Pendergrass, Bloodstone, Curtis Mayfield, Marvin Gaye, Stevie Wonder and the O'Jays. Though he listened to rap music fluently, the only music played in his apartment was from the Black classic music magicians. By this time, he placed Sweetie to her feet and permitted her to walk around his apartment to admire the many portraits and relieve some of the tension from the earlier invigorating scene. How sweet it was.

In one corner of the room, alone a computer desk with a top of the line Dell with about ten Turbo Tax programs and at least forty other software programs for his leisure.

His mother fell in love and married a man she met at work. When he asked for her hand in marriage, he also asked her to relocate with him down to Florida. She was more than thrilled to go, but sad at the same time, because she knew her eldest son wasn't willing to relocate. He was grown, so he made his own decision to stay. So, she packed up her and her youngest son's belongings, married and moved to Florida.

Since the apartment was once for his mother, brother and himself, there were three bedrooms. Now, there was only person occupying the residency, one bedroom remained untouched, while Chyna Whyte occupied the spare bedroom.

The master bedroom, of course, belonged to El'san. He had a great big king size black Victorian bed with huge thick head posts that barely missed touching the ceiling. The headboard covered almost the entire width of the wall. The two dressers and small chest matched the color of the bed frame. For this to be a subsidized apartment, the bedroom furniture almost didn't belong.

His closets were neat. His clothes were placed neatly on hangers and instead of sweatpants just hanging in there for his everyday apparel, it was mostly Italian tailored suits, khaki pants, a selection of jean outfits, casual shirts, designer shirts, and of course, dress shirts for his suits. His shoe collection was better than a woman's. There were no less than a hundred pair of designer shoes and sneakers lined up on the top racks and placed down in the bottom shoe racks.

El'san summoned for Chyna Whyte to go inside his bedroom. He went inside the bathroom, turned the knob to the hot water, lifted up the lever for the water to spray out the shower nozzle and undressed. Sweetie was still in admiration of the African leaders. She grabbed a photo album that was sitting alone on the coffee table and rested, rather reclined her body on the recliner. Her mind started to race.

"What the hell am I doing? I was supposed to be meeting the ghetto chick Shavonee an hour ago. El'san must be tripping picking me up in front of everybody, like he's my man or something. I must admit, it damn sure felt good to be in a man's arms once again. His muscles were tight and I could smell the Versace Blue Jeans steaming from his body. What is he up to? I know he didn't just get in the shower and leave me out here alone. He must trust me a little bit to leave me inside his apartment, especially since this is the first time he's invited me in. The apartment is nothing like I imagined for a drug dealer stick up kid. He's more spiritual and Afro-centric than I would ever imagine. I'm kind of feeling that to. What am I doing? I should just turn around and leave, complete my mission like planned. There's money to be made and time is being wasted sitting up in here. Come on Sweetie, stick to the plan. No need for falling in love, particularly with El'san, the mothafuck'n leader from the 'Borough. Snap out of it, we cool that's it, not lovers, companions, none of that shit."

She was afraid to leave as she paced back and forth through the apartment. The shower had since stopped and her heart raced, skipping three or four beats. Her palms began to sweat and her breathing increased. She could see her breasts rising after every breath. Her chest protruded faster and faster until, her oxygen just about stopped.

El'san stepped out of the bathroom with water still dripping down his well-mounted bare chest. The steam from the shower slowly escaped from the door opening. He stood firmly with the towel wrapped tightly around his waist with his penis lifting the towel from its erectness. He watched, looking intently as Sweetie paused in a daze not knowing what to say or do. He smiled in her direction knowing for the first time, he had control of her. He thought to himself.

"Is this all it took, a shower and a few droplets of water on my body. Imagine if I put the extra shine baby oil on my skin! I'd been had her panties down exchanging juices."

Instead of walking towards her in the living room, he walked at a snail's pace into the master bedroom. Sweetie dropped the photo album forgetting it was in her possession, trotting behind him into the bedroom. She shut the door and began to make advances at him. El'san let the towel, little by little, drop on the carpet. In an unhurried tempo, he turned to show off his body parts. Sweetie was astounded.

"God damn, milk sure does the body good! Look at that masterpiece. All this time you've been holding back A L L T H A T!!" She didn't mind letting the lust demon control her emotions.

"Sweetie." El'san called out.

Pure and innocently she answered. "Yes, El'san."

"Yo, what the hell do you think you're doing?" I came in here to get dressed, ALONE! I didn't request your presence, or rather, I don't need your assistance to get dressed. His mind destabilizing, thinking back on the scene he was escorted from.

"What?" El'san, I know you're joking right?

"No." He said. Sweetie did not comprehend.

"Why would you lead me on like that? I mean come on, the sweeping off the feet, that has to account for something."

"Queen, let this be a lesson learned. Granted, I have a connection, along with an attraction for you. Our spirits compliment one another. Don't get that misunderstood. When I first met you, you warmed my soul but baby girl, don't play yourself. This is just another way of tearing down our community."

A disturbed Sweetie bowed in disgrace. "How is this tearing down our community El'san?"

"Sweetie, you are thorough in many ways, but also weak in many. You are an African-American Queen and live that to the fullness that God intended you to. We are partners, not just in the hood but partners in crime. How can we effectively create a plan to rob jokers when, by the sight of some big dick you get aroused and all horny? That lets me know you'll fall for the 'okey doke', *the get over.* Make a man interested in you for who you are. I'm not gonna front, that poem damn near sent me over to the realm we've never experienced. But, as I carried you and watched those beautiful full eyes, crying out for a man's love, I knew I couldn't take advantage of you. You are someone special and I would never take that away from you.

Listen baby-boo, as an Afro-centric woman, I mean, let's even take that away, as a woman, it's your duty to make a man work to gain your respect, your trust, your love and especially you're most precious gift. This is your first time in my apartment and you would so freely and readily give it up?   Maybe that statement you made about 'a nigga gotta be handsome for you to sleep with him' was true.   If I was really on some 'rah-rah' big head shit, I would have went for mine, not caring how I abused your body. Imagine if we let our lust demon control our moves.   What next?   The thieving demon may advance and we may start stealing from each other.   I mean if we took it to that level, we could never do business together.   I never mix business with pleasure.   When we get on some other type of level see me then.

You see, I don't have females flocking from all over tearing down my door with no drama. They are all in check, ain't no drama over here.   I don't have any kids, so that baby mama drama shit is dead.   I'm strengthening it.   That's on the real!   And, I am not ashamed to say that I've been passing up plenty of pussy that came my way. I'm waiting patiently for my Queen to enter into my life.   When she does, all this shit is over, the robbing, the violence, the late night creeps, the set ups, all this shit.   It's a war training to fight against the war on crime.   The government doesn't want this shit to end."

El'san really took it to another level spoiling Sweeties mood.   He wanted her but he wanted her as his main girl.   He was trying to tighten her game up.

"Who do you think authorizes the movement of cocaine and heroin in the United States?   Cocaine is grown in Columbia and heroin cultivated through India.   How then, does it get to America?   Somebody, an elected official, must know about it because the drugs are here.   It's prevalent all over the states. Drugs flood the cities and mostly the urban neighborhoods. Yeah, I know most boys, and I'll call them boys, because only boys that haven't developed into manhood feed drugs into our communities. Come on Sweetie, you're too sharp for me to have a conversation like this with. Don't let the game play you, you play the game. All right, baby girl?"

Chapter Eight
Stumbling Blocks

"Yo, enough of that we're still moving in bullshit! It's time we get back in the hustle of things. There's been enough time to situate some furniture, get your bed in order and arrange your clothes for easy access." Cam was persistent and expected Kenny to move at his command.

"Listen here, I told you I'm not one of your flunkies. Stop demanding me like I'm a bitch!"

His nose started flaring open as he inhaled heavily, while he patted on the table and beat loudly, he said, "I'm a man! And, don't you ever forget that." Since the prison incident, he had to continuously remind himself that he indeed was still a man. "I told you earlier, I was going to see Shavonee, the chick we met earlier who lives across the street."

Puzzling up his face, Camron responded, "Shavonee, who the hell is a Shavonee? What kind of ghetto nickname is that? I know she's at least 21 years old. That 'Shavonee' shit should now be Shavon for short, right? Sounds like she's still on some little kiddie shit, *'Call me Shavoneee'*. And, you be dealing with these type of chicks, but you call me a hater. Man pleez, I don't understand you. You seem to always pick up chicken heads and ghetto rats.

Let's put the facts on the table, you're a good looking brotha, you keep cash in your pocket, you drive a nice car, you live in a nice house and you have me as a brother. Something still doesn't add up, what seems to be the problem? Is your self esteem low, your confidence shot? What's up big brotha? If you insist on seeing her, don't let her ghetto ass play you. Bro! Wait, let me check your vitals. Do you have a fever, lumps in your throat or a sudden rash outbreak? I think you have that I-D 10 T illness?"

"What the hell are you talking about?" Kenny asked looking at his brother.

"The I-D 10 T illness. You know what that is fool. You're an IDIOT! Get it, slow learner. That's why I never trusted you with the money. Your analytical capabilities are worse than a ten year old."

Kenny was sick and tired of his brother's philosophies. Even when things didn't go Cam's way, he always found another way to make matters worse. Like the taunting insults almost everyday. He was tired of the same routine. Ever since they were kids this had gone on. Granted, he wasn't a leader or a fighter like his little brother, but when it came to morals and values, Kenny was the victor all the time. Frustrated by his brother's comments, Kenny left the house. Before closing the door shut, he glanced at the mirror to see his reflection. His smooth brown skin, dark brown Betty Davis eyes, curvy full lips with a razor sharp shape up and fade, were enough to convince him that he was still the man, regardless of how his brother felt. The red and gray Rocawear T-shirt was without wrinkles. Looking down at his faded blue jean shorts and his new white on white S. Carters, he was ready for the evening.

While outside, he watched as the normality of New York commenced, hoping Shavonee slipped into something revealing and easily accessible to set the evening off. Opening the door to the apartment building he could smell the sweet scent of herbs mixed with an Italian style cigar.

"Let me follow the smell." Kenny thought. A blunt would unquestionably come in handy after taking two shots of Henney at his house to set the mood. He pushed the bell to her apartment and waited for her response.

"Yeah, who dat is? Sweetie is that finally you? Child, I've been waiting all night for your ass to arrive. The suspect is probably gone by now."

Her mouth ran a mile a minute before Kenny could respond. Everytime he opened his mouth to speak, another word would come out of hers until he finally cut in.

"Shavonee please slow it down! This ain't no Sweetie and what suspect are you talking about?" Startled by the sound of his voice, she responded.

"Oh, shit, who 'dis is then?"

"It's Kenny from across the street."

"I'm sorry Boo-Boo, I thought you was this chick named Sweetie I've been waiting for. She was supposed to be here hours ago and the slick hussy never called to tell me she'd be late. Anyway, what's up?"

"Well, I'd like to continue our conversation, but at least can we hold it in your apartment and not in the doorway?" Kenny questioned, ready to go inside her crib.

"Oh, sure Boo-Boo, I'll buzz you in. Come on up." The door buzzed, making clicking sounds as Kenny pulled the door towards him. Almost too excited to get up the stairs, he missed a step causing his feet to fumble and his hands landing flat out on one of the steps.

"Shit." He thought as he wiped his hands clean from the cigar shavings.

The stairwell was unclean from old pieces of paper, wrappings and cigar fillings. It was obvious people didn't have a concern when it came to sanitation in her building. Reaching his destination, he saw that Shavonee left the door open for him. How sweet of her to do that he thought. The incense smell *"Lick me all over"* swarmed the two-bedroom apartment. The aroma was pleasant and sweet. Walking with her feet almost in a U-shape, one would believe that Shavonee was pigeon toed and bowlegged. However, this was not the case she was front'n for real.

"There you are Boo-Boo, come on in. You smoke trees?" That was her first question. She tried passing the blunt in his direction.

"I have some real good herbs that will set you in a tizzy, for sheezy! Ya feel me! Well, I guess not yet, maybe you'll feel me in a few hours." She said, as playful laughter eased from her mouth. She was already medicated after smoking two blunts by her lonesome and was feeling real nice.

Kenny searched around the almost bare apartment, which consisted of one love seat, a small thirteen-inch television and a faded black and white fur bear rug that had dirty brown claws gripping the floor. The one lamp on the right side was missing a lampshade and the coffee table was missing the inside glass.

"Yes, please let me hit that!" To get through the night his mind, beyond a doubt, needed to be altered. He started to invite her over to the crib but he didn't want Cam to embarrass him or her anymore than he already had.

"Come on into my bedroom Boo-Boo, that's where I keep my stash." She said without hesitation. Hoping the bedroom was more appealing than the living room he followed behind her like a disappointed child. Shavonee plopped down onto the queen sized poster bed, patting the bed signaling him to sit down.

"Right here Boo-Boo, come sit next to me." She was sure he was ready and willing.

In spite of what Kenny thought, the bedroom was presentable. Smoothing out her comforter, she asked Kenny if he liked her bedroom décor.

"Yeah, it's nice. It's surely a step above the living room set up." He didn't want to hurt her feelings, but he was telling the truth.

"Don't trip Boo-Boo, Rent Central will be here sometime this week to deliver some furniture for the living room. I rented my bedroom furniture from them about fourteen months ago.

The payments aren't that bad, in fact, it's almost paid off."

She didn't understand that was part of the problem, using the rip off center as a furniture resource. Not wanting to spoil the mood, Kenny responded as if he didn't feel a certain way about what she just said. Fact being, he never figured out why people rented from rip off centers. Didn't they realize that they'd end up paying twice, almost three times as much when they finally paid for the merchandise? It was highway robbery and another way to rob urban communities of the few dollars people had. That's who generally paid for the living room sets, bedroom sets, dining room sets, computers, lamps and sometimes even artificial flowers, poor black folks! He thought of where most of the stores were located, mainly in surrounding urban cities.

Just to continue conversation, he conversed on a positive note.

"Well, if you're sure of the quality and pricing of the merchandise from the rip off center, I mean the Rent Central, then do you baby girl! If that's all your budget can afford, then this conversation is dead."

Shavonee walked around the room, still pulling on the blunt, finally grasping what Kenny was trying to get her to comprehend.

"What you talking 'bout Boo-Boo, Rent Central was the cheapest, they don't conduct credit checks and their selection of goods is real cute. Don't trip, I know your Momma done bought some furniture from Rent Central sometime in her life. All black people have, so

143

don't try to front on Shavonee." The body language and sassy tongue proclaimed what she was trying to say until she proceeded on.

"Besides, this is a Section 8 apartment. Now, why would I doctor it up like I own it! Anyway, I was thinking, maybe you can help me out with the payments."

"Easy, E a s y! This is my first visit over and you're already hitting me up for some dough. Damn, you sure don't waste time do you?"

"Sure don't Boo-Boo." She unzipped her dress, which gracefully fell to the floor. Underneath she had on a red lace push up bra to help out her 34B cup and a size 6 red lace thong that had a snug fit on her butt. She walked over to the CD player and pressed play. Jaheim encircled the room in sounds with track seven *"Ghetto Love"* off the *"Ghetto Love"* CD.

"Don't be afraid to look Boo-Boo, this is all me." She spun around dropping it like she was hot, smacked her butt so it could wiggle for him. She grabbed hold to the bedpost and twirled as if she were at a strip club.

Kenny inhaled a substantial hit of haze, his eyes lids lowered as he watched Shavonee move in his direction. This is going to be easier than I thought and I didn't even bring a 3 piece special meal with me, he thought. He scooted back on the fluffy pillows watching as Shavonee's body moved erotically. The percussion and bass flowing out of *"Ghetto Love"* seemed loud and clear. The red lace thong barely moved when she bent shaking her buttocks from left to right. With his eyes barely open, he tried to concentrate on staying focused. He couldn't help but to massage his manhood watching her sexual innuendos.

Her body was tight, and even though her breast, were a little small, they were perky. The flat stomach led directly to her curvaceous hips and her sweltering romp shaker. Just refreshed and smelling good from a shower, Kenny began to undress. Though he wasn't very muscular, the little muscle surrounding his flesh received plenty of attention from the ladies and men.

Shavonee adjusted one leg on the edge of the bed allowing one hand to grip the end of the bedpost again. Only this time, with creative movement, she lifted one leg high exposing what was in between her legs.

"Whoa." Escaped Kenny's mouth, watching her extract the center of her lusciousness.

"Girl, you are phat in more places than one! I can't wait to taste that."

With one finger placed on her lips, Shavonee slid the other very lightly inside of her mouth wetting it. She moved her finger in and out very slowly.

Kenny was in la la land.

"Well, from the looks of it, you can't wait to taste me either." He mumbled.

Shavonee was so willing to give of herself freely, she wasn't even trying to learn about the inner person of who Kenny really was. She had no idea this man had a past of participating in homosexual acts. In fact, she was ready to go raw with him. Her sacrifice to give her love just to get a few dollars, was it worth it? Time and time again, she succumbed to a lustful man's request to violate her sexually. She didn't even realize that the little money that she was hustling from them was never worth it.

Camron jumped into his new creamy honey mustard colored 745 BMW with a smoked tint, he was boss play'n fo' real. "A quarter to eight," that's what most people called his ride. He kept changing radio stations until it landed on, Hot 97. The Funk Master Flex show was on and he knew the DJ mix would be on fire, instead of the same old sounds that other wack radio stations played. Sean Paul started the mix off with the smash reggae hit *"Like Glue."* Blending into that, was a new track from Controversy's CD. Cam gritted his teeth just listening to the echo of his voice and picturing him on stage at a concert rapping this very song. He couldn't help but reflect on how Controversy played him with his old girl, Mona. Let the truth be told, he was the reason why this whole mess started. It was such as mess, a famous author decided to use their story in the Urban Tale *"Blinded."*

Cam talked out loud, sharing a conversation with himself. His blood pressure began to rise as he reminisced.

"This bitch ass sucka tried to play me! That trick most definitely got it coming to him. He's gonna see Cam and when he do, I'm gonna make sure it's known. A nigga gonna know the golden rule, don't ever, I mean ever, cross Cam! Shit happens when a mothafucka cross me."

He smashed down on the inside dash, damn near creating a permanent dent in the board. His fists were balled up tight. The people riding beside him watch his callous actions in a car all alone and wondered what was wrong with this deranged man. They tried not to stare too hard. They didn't want any road rage. Cutting one of the onlookers off, he made a sharp corner turn with his right hand in circular motion. His watch gleamed as the light reflected against it. Opening his cellular phone, he dialed Yatta's number trying to figure out why he hadn't heard from him this week. Not getting an answer on the receiving end, he left him a voicemail message.

"Yo son, this is that '*P I M P G A N G S T E R,*' Cam nigga, straight gangsta! I haven't heard from you, yo! What's the deal? Get at me in a short. One!"

He started to feel strange vibes from Yatta since the incident with Mona. When it came to business though, all the personal feelings and shit had to ride. He swerved in and out of traffic, checking the blocks, now occupied with some new faces. As he rode through the streets of the 'Borough he noticed that something was seriously odd.

"Damn, it's like a ghost town out this motha. All the money made over here, this shit doesn't even seem right. Jump out squad must have rode through here a minute ago." He drove about five more miles and then pulled his car into a parking space.

Securing his vehicle, he walked into the apartment building where Slowdown's woman, Aiesha lived. He rang the bell three times before Aiesha came to the door. Cam looked at her, scrutinizing her bare appearance. The sheer black dress shirt exposed her black bra and her hi-cut thong panties. To match her undergarments, she had black thigh high boots on with a sharp clear heel. Her appearance didn't bother her one bit as he searched her body up and down with his eyes. She greeted him as if nothing was wrong with her outfit.

"Hey Cam, Slowdown is in the bedroom getting dressed. You know I had to hit him off a little something, something before he hit the streets with your whorey ass. Now, it won't be any reason for him to be looking for some trim. I blazed him just right. Now, let that be the reason he bring his ass home tonight."

Aeisha was a sexy chocolate female with short silky black hair. Her body was explosive and when she tottered in movement with those thigh high black clear heel boots, her steps became the image men dreamed of. Cam didn't want her to finish telling her nasty escapades about her and freak nasty Slowdown, so he cut her words short.

"Aiesha, do you always dress like a hooker? I mean every time I come over here you're dressed like a tramp. Trust me, I know that's your profession but do you have to let everyone in on it? What makes you think that he won't run up in another chick? He probably only got off one nut with you anyhow. Don't you know, the average nigga got at least four nuts up in him. In about an hour, he'll be ready to get up in some more pussy and after that, give him another two hours, he'll be ready to bust off in another. I never understood why a woman would think that just because she hit her man off, he wouldn't be interested in running up in some other broad. A nigga gonna fuck regardless, especially if he come across a hooker like you." He pushed her aside and then stood with one hand on his chin.

Turning her back to him, she casually walked into the kitchen ignoring his comment. Rather than reacting rudely, she showed hospitality.

"Would you like something to drink, Cam?"

"Yeah, what do you have in the refrigerator, malt liquor or a picture of Kool Aid? I know this is a typical black house. Which one do you have?" He said, grinning.

Aiesha knew how Cam was, so she continued to ignore his arrogance.

"Actually, there's a ginger ale and a bottle of Sparkly in here, which would you like?" She stood with the refrigerator open waiting for his response.

"I'll take a glass of ginger ale with four cubes of ice. You do have ice, don't you? And, I hope the ginger ale is not the store brand, I only drink Seagram's ginger ale."

She pulled out the ice tray running cold water over the ice for easy release. Before placing the ice cubes inside the glass, she kindly spit down inside the bottom of it. Afterwards, she placed four cubes inside the glass to cover the spit. Then, she poured the ginger ale in it to fizzle the soda with the spit. She grabbed a napkin placing it underneath the glass and handed it to him waitress style.

"Here you go Cam, a nice cold glass of Seagram's Ginger Ale. Drink up and enjoy! Now, let me see what's taking Slowdown so damn long." When she turned away she raised her eyebrows as Cam took a gulp of the soda.

"Serves him right." Aiesha said to herself.

"Slowdown baby, Cam is in the living room waiting for you!" She hollered out.

Slowdown was sitting on the edge of the bed pulling up his jeans and putting on his sneakers at the same time. He snatched his fitted New York Knicks hat and stood up walking towards the bedroom door with his shoestrings hanging. Surprised by Aiesha's attire, he questioned her judgment of exposing her body like that.

"Girl, you didn't go to the door like that did you?"

She looked at him with a smirk on her face.

"Damn, you showing all my goods like that?" He smacked her on her right cheek watching it jiggle, as he waited patiently for a response.

"Yes I did, come on now, it's only Cam. You act like this is his first time seeing me like this."

Slowdown stared at her for about a minute or so before he responded. Aiesha remembered the time Cam videotaped her and Slowdown for one of the many adult films selling around the city. It wasn't her fault Slowdown got caught up in the moment and decided that she should be his woman. It was only a job for her. She was trying to get paid that's all. So, it really didn't matter if it was Slowdown, Earl or Cam that hit her off in the flick.

"Ma, slow up on that!" His disbelief of her words showed on his face. He spoke firmly and slowly when he responded to her. With his back slightly turned, he walked into the living room to greet one of his main men.

"What's up Baby Boy?" He gave Cam some dap and plunged down on the soft sofa.

"I hope you washed your ass good. Buddussy is a bad smell to carry around." Cam said, as he burst out into laughter.

"Shut up, man. I washed my ass." Slowdown insisted.

"I can't tell. When you plopped your stinky ass on the sofa a big puff of stank ass blew up in my face." Cam continued to laugh.

Slowdown grinned with a wide spread smile. "Enough of the jokes, funny man. What's the deal son? You seen Richey and Earl? I called earlier trying to check them but neither one of them hollered back, you know."

Cam didn't waste any more time on jokes. He let Slowdown in on his thoughts.

"I sent those niggas to dirty Jersey to handle some business. 'Dem niggas al'ight. Yo, what's up with the 'Borough? It was like a ghost town when I rode by."

Slowdown gave a puzzled look. "Son, you haven't heard that the nigga El'san got the 'Borough on lock down?"

Cam sat up in his seat.

"What the hell do you mean this nigga got it on lock? Niggas must be out their mothafuck'n mind if they think we ain't getting a piece of that. You mean to tell me this dude is making money and we're not getting a piece of that gold mine? All those junkies over there, man we are sure enough missing out! What's the deal with that?"

Slowdown nodded his head in agreement.

"I hear you son, but the dude ain't on that type of shit. Yo, don't get it confused, El'san isn't making money slinging.   He's straight up '*Rah Rah*', robbing cats."   Cam's movement became still as he listened attentively to Slowdown.

"Check this out, not only did he shut down the money makers in the 'Borough, but he makes it his duty to rob them of their money. This cat is on some Black Power clean up the neighborhood type shit.   Fiends are vexed they have to cop damn near five miles from their house."

The worried expression on Cam's face showed his skepticism.

"Yo, who the fuck does 'dis nigga think he is?" Cam felt crossed.

"Word son, how long has this shit been going on?" He said, trying to figure out how much money he was losing.

"It's been going on for a minute. Ever since he got out of Rikers Island on his second bit. You know the nigga. He hung out with Birdie and about fifteen other dudes on the pod. All of them became inseparable in the pen and was on some rah-rah shit up there. Those niggas all maxed out about the same time. You know Birdie ain't never been a hustler. He was always the credit card scammer. El'san took over as the ringleader when they got home. All of them stay in the 'Borough. Check this out, El'san got some fly females on his dick. Instead of him playin' them out, nigga got 'em all on the setup. Every last one of'em is shacked up with bitches over there. They runnin' shit and gettin' paid." He paused for a moment.

"And, gettin' paid without slingin'. You can't be mad at them, cause they doin' their thing. It's really not something we should worry

152

about cause this joker has been in and out of jail since he turned eighteen. Give him another minute, he'll be back in. Once he goes back, the other dudes gonna fall wayside. They can't piss without him holding their dicks. That's why nobody is really making noise about it. Its El'san dat niggas is worried about. With some luck, he'll be back in Rikers in no time."

Cam wasn't trying to hear that.

"What do you mean nobody's making noise? Nigga, I'm about to make some ruckus in the 'Borough! Imagine that, a so-called black power rebel and a bunch of fake ass S1W's, shutting down a 'Borough of five hundred plus apartments. Now ain't dat some shit? Nah son, ain't nobody creating stumbling blocks for killa Cam. I'm going over there to straighten this shit out, regardless to that other bullshit."

Slowdown retorted. "Before you do, make sure you go over there ready to take out his trained pit bull. Yo, the dog is vicious. Nigga trained him to sniff out like vice squad dogs. He'll take a nice chunk from your ass."

"Word, son?"

"Word!" Slowdown responded, giving him the word he heard from the streets on Chyna Whyte.

Aiesha listened carefully from the bedroom as they continued to communicate.

Chapter Nine
I Gotta Get Mine!

Back in her apartment, Sweetie could not believe what just transpired between her and El'san. She started to feel queasiness in her stomach, just thinking about how she made a complete fool of herself walking into his bedroom without his consent. After all, they shared the same vision and she thought more of El'san than the average robber. He was doing it for a good cause. He was more than inquisitive about Black awareness. He thirsted to share and inform others of his knowledge. He had a solid belief in uplifting communities even in the midst of his pain and his dislike for drug dealers. She knew whatever his reasons for denying her request to entertain him intimately, it was for the best. Instead of sulking about it, she lit three candles, a white candle for peace, a pink candle for love and a black candle to rid darkness from her life.

On the pink love candle, she wrote El'san loves Sweetie on it just as the lady at the worship shop informed her to. It was hard not to allow her personal feelings to interfere with the business relationship that they shared. She knew it was time to catch her next victim Toby under the same trance El'san had her in. She'd already let one day pass, even failing to contact Ms. Ghetto Fabulous herself, Shavonee. It was best that she go over to her crib instead of calling her on the telephone, cause she knew the conversation would lead nowhere.

Unconsciously, picking up the telephone, she dialed El'san's house number. El'san didn't have a caller ID, so he didn't have a clue that it was her on the receiving end.

In a raspy deep tone he answered. "Yeah, this is El'san."

He was laid back on his couch stroking Chyna Whyte's back. He was relaxing listening to Stevie Wonder's classic, *"A Ribbon In The Sky"*. He'd just taken his t-shirt off because of the sweat that soaked it. It was routine for him to do a thousand push-ups a day. This was a daily regimen for him in the pen.

Startled by his manly vocals, Sweetie's heart jumped realizing she called El'san's apartment.

"Um, what's up with you?" She spoke very softly unwavering in the thought of his blatant rejection of sleeping with her.

"I'm relaxing with Chyna Whyte and who is this, my Beautiful Black Queen?"

"Your Beautiful Black Queen?" Hesitantly speaking, Sweetie went on.

"Obviously you have the wrong person because you've never called me, nonetheless, considered me your own personal *Beautiful Black Queen!*"

El'san sighed before responding. His eyes looked toward the ceiling. Out of all the women he dealt with, he thought Sweetie would be the one to appreciate his genuine compliments.

"No, what is sure enough obvious is that you would mess up a wet dream. It's also clear, that you haven't experienced a real man who compliments his woman. Or, you haven't been in a real relationship if you're on the defense about me calling you a Beautiful Black Queen."

Sweetie was still argumentative. "Don't get it wrong, your exact words were My Beautiful Black Queen."

El'san was somewhat in wonderment as he listened to her jibber jabber. He couldn't understand why she just couldn't accept a man calling her a Beautiful Black Queen. Obviously, getting a tad bit frustrated, he spoke very clearly and convincing.

"Alright, check this out, if you don't want to be my Beautiful Black Queen, you can be my Sweetie."

"Yeah, now she will get it." He thought to himself.

Sweetie sucked her lips and those hidden insecurities began to seep out in her reaction.

"I knew you didn't know who this was. How many females call your spot, huh? Why now would you be calling me your Sweetie?"

El'san spoke powerfully into the telephone.

"Hold up baby girl." He thought about that and quickly switched up his words.

"Maybe I shouldn't call you baby girl because you'll probably have something to say about that. Now, I refuse to waste valuable time going back and forth over some pet names. I've known who this was since you first opened your mouth to speak."

157

I can't understand what her problem is today. Was it because I didn't hit her off last night? 'Cause women tend to think if a man turns her down, it's because another woman is involved. Sometimes, that's just not the case.

"I called you my *Beautiful Black Queen* because that's what I consider you as. Come on now Sweetie, we are a team. Don't let the situation that happened in my apartment get to you. You know damn well. I don't have females calling me or coming to my crib like that. I'm working on self right now. Why else would I decline a proposition from a sexy ass stunning woman, such as you? For sure, I wanted to make passionate love to you for unlimited hours, but like I said before, I want more than that. Now, it's up to you to fit the pieces to our puzzle. What happened to the fire you had? Don't go and get syrupy on me. I realize that you have strong feelings for me, but don't let those insecurities override those secure feelings that you have. I told you before, El'san is here for you, and only you. So, keep that thing tight for me. In due time, I'm a break you off just right."

Sweetie was blushing from ear to ear thinking about how childish she was at the start of their conversation. She was consumed with guilt and felt she owed him an apology.

"I'm sorry baby, I'm just so use to dealing with clowns, I mean men that play so many games, that I misjudged you. Will you forgive me?" She pleaded.

"Sweetie there's no need to apologize because I don't feel that you violated me. What you should do though, is apologize to yourself for allowing yourself to act out of character. Stop thinking that all men are like the clowns you used to deal with. I'm a real mothafucka, ya heard. I'm not even going to give you a speech on that cuz, it's not my place. Your father should have taught you better."

Sweetie listened without responding, realizing that she never gave her father a chance to teach her about men.

El'san waited for a slick reply but received none. Since she never answered, he continued to speak.

"You called for a reason, what's up?"

By this time, El'san was up off the couch feeding Chyna Whyte a slab of raw beef. His jaws opened wide exposing the sharp edges of his sharp white teeth. In seconds, they were consumed with red stains from the bloody meat. Blood dripped from the sides of his mouth.

"Damn, Chyna Whyte! You putting all that blood on the kitchen floor. Whose going to clean this shit up?" El'san questioned.

"Sweetie? Are you still on here?"

The phone was still silent.

She responded in utterance. "Yes, I'm here."

It never ceased to amaze her how El'san could use reverse psychology to play with her mind. His comments always made her think.

"Well, did you call to talk to me or just sit on the phone and listen to me breath?" El'san asked, with little patience.

She was wasting too much time just sitting on the phone.

"Actually, I dialed your number by mistake. My mind was set on getting with Shavonee today so we can take care of Toby and make some money. So, let me get off the phone with you so I can handle my business. I'll stop by later and help you clean your place, alright."

"Al'ight, do you baby girl and make sure you stop by to see me in the cut when the job is done."

"Alright, I'll talk to you then." Sweetie hung up the telephone, went over to the lit candles, blew them out, grabbed her keys and headed out on her mission.

After walking several blocks, she began to question her judgment.

"Why in the world didn't I ask El'san to use his car?" Sweetie's pulse increased with every footstep. Walking alone now for about thirty minutes or so trying to get to East New York, in a hurry. Fortunately, she dressed lightly in a long linen dress, just delicately touching the bare of her skin. Her shoes, thank God, were from the Easy Spirit Collection so they were very comfortable and the hip length natural straw bag draped evenly over her thighs. To shy away from the sun, she wore an oversized natural straw hat to cover her twists.

Today she was especially angry with herself, for one, taking so long to complete this job and two, not using the resources that were available to her. To ease her mind she let her creative juices flow.

I Played Myself

Without thought, without question
I compromised my very being
So willing without consciously allowing my
Intellectual side to get the best of me,
I played myself
When temptation and peer pressure stood so tall
Boasted and proud, the inner weakened spirit, drifted
away like summer clouds
It was at that very moment temptation and peer
pressure settled inside of me
I played myself
Maybe it's true I'm a weakling providing small
Cracks and spaces to overcome my very being
The stronger I get, the weaker I become, for small
Things that I tend to overlook like
honesty, loyalty and trust
I bend those characteristics of me when I'm in a
crouch
I may even comprise for a little lust,
I Played Myself
This is a battle that many have a tendency to face,
Ripping apart the insides of their spirit man
Who is fighting so diligently to stand!
What happens when the lust, lies and grimey
behaviors consume the best us,
Please someone help me to learn not to any longer
Play myself!

She smiled as if she'd won a Spoken Word
contest. "Sometimes I wonder why I don't just

enter a Spoken Word contest. I'm sure eventually I'll make more money legally for my creative flow. I'm blocking my own blessing, I know." This thought always registered in her mind just before doing dirt.

The streets of New York hadn't changed. Rats and mice ran from drain to drain, chasing one another without gesturing when humans tried to cross the street. The "whoop, whoop" sounds of the police sirens sounded frequently, summoning double-parked cars to move or be forced to get a ticket. Many times if the perpetrator moved, police officers would give a verbal warning not wanting to create anymore paper work than necessary.

The hustlers and project chicks were always posted in front view of the high-rise section 8 building, watching movement from all angles. They spotted new faces like eagles spotted dead prey on highways and byways. And, like crack heads spotted crumbs of rock, mostly everyone was on point.

Sweetie felt a little odd. She had the feeling that someone was watching her. It made her feel very uneasy. Her brown eyes peered to the left and using her peripheral vision, she glanced at a gentleman riding at her walking pace. Before stopping, she checked her surroundings for a quick escape. There were three escape outlets just in case, this was one of her many victims. A corner store crowded by the general population, a brownstone with an open door from people moving out and an old Cadillac running without an owner inside. Those were her three quick getaway outlets. One was bound to set her free.

So, if something were to jump off, it was on. Without any further hesitation, Sweetie turned to face her target.

Rather than being a skeleton in her closet, it was absolutely a new opportunity. They stared at each other for about twenty seconds before either made a move, just as a lioness searched out her prey. Sweetie decided she would make the first move.

"Yes, can I help you?" She asked.

The gentleman shifted the toothpick cornered in his teeth around his kissable lips.

"May I ask why you staring at me like that? I hope there's not a possibility of you being a stalker." She insisted.

He continued to look her directly in her face without commenting. Sweetie started getting agitated with him. He drove slower and decided to stop the car beside another vehicle parked on the street.

Sweetie continued walking, but kept her attention on him.

The gentlemen opened the driver's side door and eased out the vehicle. He had long athletic legs and a caramel complexion. Dressed in a pair of black chukkas, black jeans and a George "The Iceman" Gervin, San Antonio Spurs throwback jersey. The extra size San Antonio Spurs fitted hat, with the white do-rag underneath of it, gave him a sure enough thug persona. Sweetie could tell he was on point but didn't care. She was on a mission for her man and nothing was going to sidetrack her this time. A couple of females leaning on a fence tried to holla at him.

"Fuck her, you need to be checking on this here." A dark skinned female yelled out, while turning around to smack her ass.

"Nah, what he need to do is stop checking on a no name bitch and get with 'the real' like me!" Her friend responded.

Sweetie and the gentlemen ignored both their comments and continued to stare each other down until they got in reach of one another.

"What the fuck do you want from me? Do I know you or something?" Sweetie asked, with an uncaring expression on her face. Even though the dude was sharp, he still didn't come close to her El'san. She had no idea how to handle the words that were about to part from his lips.

"Yo bitch, you must be out of your goddamn mind confronting me like that! Let's get one thing straight, never in my pimp history have I stalked any chick. In fact, it's just the opposite, the bitches stalk this good looking nigga right here." He popped his collar and brushed off his shoulder. Looking at her he asked, "You wanna brush off fo' me?"

Sweetie's eyebrows rose up. The disrespectful dude kept on talking.

"And, after a few hours of talking with me, you'll be riding my dick just like the other bitches. I'll end up adding your name to the stalker list with all the rest of those hoe's."

An "Oh, no he didn't" look swept across Sweetie's flushed face and that casual pose quickly altered to a defense tactic. Her nostrils opened wide and she took a deep breath. She was about to let this cocky son of a bitch have it.

"Cocky, no you're more like an arrogant individual. What makes you think I'll want a nigga like you?" She pointed her finger in his direction, almost invading his personal space.

"Perhaps, you're probably used to dealing with those low class ghetto girls or chicks with low self-esteem, like these." She pointed over to the females who were trying to holla at him just a second ago.

"I am neither, but rather a clever, highly seasoned Black Queen." The words transitioned smoothly, as she thought of El'san.

"One, who surely wouldn't give you the time of day. Just because you drive a nice car, flash a little jewels and have somewhat, and pay attention very closely, I said '*somewhat*' of a handsome appearance. That does not mean every female wants you!"

She turned her head in dismay.

"*Oh, I get it, you're the big man around the hood.*" Her thoughts turned into voiceful words.

He leaned his body against a pedestrian's car and gazed at her with an expressionless look. Her mouth was still moving.

"No, no, don't give me that surprised look like you can't believe the words coming out my mouth. We all see who you're trying to be. It's just so obvious, the image that you try to portray. That's the problem with you lowlife hustlers, drug dealers, grinders, whatever the hell you choose to call yourselves. You let the money dictate who you are. Make you think you're invincible or some shit like that! How cocky is that, thinking all females want you because of material gain? Well, Mr. Hustler, Drug Dealer, Grinder, let me put you down on this, not every female is willing to compromise their being to be with a slum of a man like you. You're a punk, scared to live life without the hustle of selling drugs. You fail to benefit the black community. Why don't you crawl under a rock and let somebody ride over you to speed up your death. Because, you are slowly killing yourself by your own actions. Your path by now is set before you and your dumb ass can't even see that. So which are you ready for, jail or the coroner?"

She was on a roll and nobody could stop her. Those in passing stopped to listen to what she had to say. The crowd grew larger and she spoke louder and louder.

"Just for your information, there are people out here just waiting for a chance to rob a loser like you."

Realizing that she'd gone to far, subconsciously leaking information, she silenced herself. Her words caused the gentleman to rise completely up from the laid back position. His finger pointed to his chin taking in every word she said. You could have brought him for a nickel.

"Bitch, apparently you haven't a clue who I am, because if you did, none of those words would have ever passed through your vocal cords." He gritted his teeth.

"I should pay one of these bitches out here to beat the shit out of you."

"I'll do it!" Hollered out a dark skin goddess with three gold teeth in her mouth.

Another chick with her hair pulled back into a high ponytail with skintight jeans on, stepped closer to him.

"She can get it.   I'll do it just on the strength for you, cutie."

Sweetie looked at both of them, sizing them up.

Instead of authorizing the beat down, he decided to kill her with words.

"Listen up, you half Politician, half Christian, half Muslim, half community activist, this time I'll let you pass.   I'm going to respect your take on a man of my stature but I'll tell you what I can do for you."

He reached down and instantly Sweetie moved far from his reach.   Watching her squirm, he made his words loud and clear.

"Oh, Miss Bad Ass, don't get scared now! Not with all that mouth you have." Called out one of the females in the crowd.

To show her how much he cared for her thoughts, he threw out of the driver's side window ten balled up hundred dollar bills.   People standing around fought to get the money thrown out the window.

"Take this money for your thoughts, cause evidently you were trying to win an Oscar or a Grammy for your acting performance.   Is one thousand dollars enough?   Or would you like to work for more?"

"Throw out some more!"   A female in the crowd yelled.

Not too ashamed to pick up what she could of the money, Sweetie grabbed five balled up bills, punching one woman in the face who was trying to snatch them from her.   She quickly placed the money inside of her swathe handbag.

"See? That's exactly what I thought. You bitches are all the same. All you want is money and you willing to do anything for it. And you wonder why hustlers, drug dealers, what else did you say? Oh yeah, lowlife grinders are so cocky. Maybe it's because we know what moves you. If it isn't the product that can get your ass high, it's damn sure this green." He flashed three rubberband wads of money. Now the roles were reversed, but this time, you could have brought her for a penny.

"For the record, don't you ever try to play a nigga like Cam, like that ever again! You never know when the next time we'll cross paths and the next time may not be as pleasant."

He turned his back to her and walked over to his creamy honey mustard colored 745 BMW turned on the ignition and sped off down the block.

Cam, Cam, the name rang over and over in Sweetie's mind. She'd heard so much about a guy named Cam from the Brownsville area. Could that be him though? All the horror stories she heard about him, she was afraid of what was to come. Did she overstep her boundaries? Later when she finished her job, El'san would have to let her know. Her adrenaline was racing in her veins and her steps moved rapidly in motion. How ironic was it that only two days ago she wrote this poem.

Someone Is After Me

Your black cold eyes follow me
Denying my very existence
Is it my body that your heart intends to violate?
My precious thoughts or are you jealous
of my high self-esteem?
Would it please you if I lowered my standards and
expectations?
My morals or my capabilities
What is it that you want of me?
To try and boost your own self-esteem
Because you are too weak to build a strong
foundation to carry out your inner dreams!
Do you call yourself the man when you continue to
down play each and every individual that comes your
way?
Or could it be the small boy tucked deep inside of that
masculine body lashing out just hoping
and praying someone will cast him out?
I see through the harden shell, it is no longer you but
the spirit of the one who comes directly from hell!
Maybe after all, it's not you who's after me
but the evil chameleon fronting to be...
Someone Is After Me!

Finally reaching the destination of
Shavonee's apartment, Sweetie transformed into
ghetto girl mode, knowing that if she didn't,
Shavonee would take her there anyway. She had
to deprogram the female rebel that dwelled on the
inside.

The door was open to Shavonee's
apartment building, so she kindly let herself in.

She climbed the stairs to the third floor and beat relentlessly at the door. Shavonee, stunned from the loud knock, ran into the bedroom and removed her stash of Purple Haze. She lifted up her bedroom window and dumped out the remains and paraphernalia that the Purple Haze was in out the window for it to blow away. Positioning one eye, she cautiously looked through the wooden door peephole, only to see Sweetie on the other side.

Sweetie moved closer, looking back at Shavonee through the peephole.

"Open the door Shavonee, I know you see me out here!"

Shavonee couldn't believe her paranoia. "I'll be goddamn, this trick done made me dump my shit!"

The door swung open and Sweetie stumbled in with the force of air that pulled her forward.

Shavonee looked her up and down.

"Uh, uh, what the hell is wrong with you knocking on my apartment door like you the Po-Po or something? Girl, you done made me dump out all my damn haze! Trick you owe me for that shit!"

Sweetie had a yeah-right look on her face. She wasn't about to reimburse her for that garbage that she polluted her mind with.

"Ain't nobody tell your suspicious behind to panic from a simple knock at the door. Start living right and you wouldn't have this problem." Sweetie didn't give two shits about Shavonee and her schizophrenic self.

Shavonee shut the door and immediately put on the double deadbolt lock. She spoke as if someone else was in the room besides her and Sweetie.

"Check Miss Thang out, here she comes a day late philosophizing to me and I'm the one not living right. Well, well! For your information trick, I mean Sweetie, making money doesn't stop because of your lazy ass."

Her lips curled as she spoke.

"You probably had your nose so far up El'san's ass you couldn't think straight."

"Look, the hell with all of that Shavonee, let's get down to business. I'm not even trying to hear that. Have you seen Toby today?"

"Yeah, as a matter of factually."

Sweetie shook her head in disgust.

"Shavonee the saying is 'a matter of fact' not, 'as a matter of factually'."

Shavonee stood there with one hand on her left hip and started waving and snapping her fingers at the same time.

"Girl, you knew what I was trying to say so don't trip! You know I'm the Queen of E B O N A Y!"

"The queen of what?" Sweetie asked, unsure of what she was trying to say.

"You heard me, Queen of E B O N A Y!" Shavonee said, without a breather.

Sweetie laughed very loudly and Shavonee looked at her like, what was so damn funny.

"Oh, bless your heart ghetto girl, it's Ebonics! Now what are the chances of a project chick taking Ebonics to the next level. Ebonics Part II, I guess. Just ask my girl, Shavonee she'll put you down on the course!" Both of them started to laugh at the joke.

171

Without prolonging the job, Shavonee gave Sweetie the details that she needed.

"Toby is home now, so this is the perfect time to catch him."

Sweetie looked around the apartment that seemed to be in desperate need of a good cleaning. Clothes were piled up in one corner as if Shavonee hadn't washed in weeks.

"What's his address?" Sweetie said inquiringly, after stepping over three piles of clothing.

Shavonee hadn't paid any attention to the clothes, this was the norm for her laundry. She watched Sweetie inspecting every damn thing but didn't care.

"Shavonee, may I ask you a question?" Sweetie insisted in a quiet manner.

"You already did." Shavonee answered.

"Damn, does that run in the family? El'san always says that to me when I ask him that."

"Whatever! This conversation is not about my cousin. It's about the mark, so pay attention."

Shavonee knew from the chicks in the 'Borough, how lately Sweetie's general conversation was about El'san. Even if they were on another subject, somehow El'san's name would come up. She didn't want to rain on her parade, but El'san was not the man she thought he was. Shavonee knew him for what he really was.

"He's the third brownstone to the left and his apartment is on the first floor."

"Follow me." instructed Shavonee.

They walked into the kitchen that had a perfect view of the brownstone building occupied by Toby.

"See that silver Jaguar XJ-S right there? That's his."

Sweetie moved closer to get a better view. She stood side by side with Shavonee, invading her personal space. She had no idea how much Shavonee really disliked her. The closer she moved towards her, the closer her nose came to a stench of foul odor.

"Hey Shavonee, no disrespect, but is that your breath or your ass, I'm smelling? I hope to God it's not your ass, cause if it is, that's a damn shame."

Shavonee cupped her hands over her mouth to conduct a self-breath test. Her hands stayed covering her mouth as she spoke.

"Oh, no you didn't go there with me Sweetie, sweet cakes. It may be my breath, but it's damn sure not what's between my legs. I wash several times a day, with real vaginal cleanser. Not with the traditional douche either. I get the *'real'* cleansing products."

Sweetie continued to tease her about her tart breath.

"I'm sorry, I didn't hear you clearly, your words were a little muffled. Speak up a little bit. But um, please don't speak too loudly, your breath smells stank, like a skunk and shit on a stick combined! You need to leave that damn Purple Haze alone cause it's starting to come through your pores child!"

Still running off at the lips, Sweetie purposely looked out the kitchen window to avoid

Shavonee embarrassed ass, which was headed into the bathroom to brush her teeth. Along the way to the bathroom, Shavonee spotted that Sweetie's straw handbag fell off the couch onto the floor, exposing what looked to be balled up dollar bills.

"Oh, this trick wants to play huh!" Shavonee eased over to see if Sweetie was paying her any attention. When she saw that she wasn't, she opened the handbag and stole every balled up dollar bill that was in there. Shavonee had a smile on her face.

"That should be enough to cover my loss for that blazing Purple Haze that I threw out the window earlier. The other money, I can use for my consultation fees. Ain't nothing for free."

Shavonee placed the bag back into place, as it previously lay and went to brush her teeth. She hurried up and stashed the bills underneath the bathroom sink inside her tampon box, just in case Sweetie noticed her money was missing.

Not a clue as to what Shavonee had done, Sweetie scanned over the small kitchen surroundings and watched as baby roaches made their way from the crevices of the electric stove.

"Ewe, that is so nasty!" She said under her breath.

"The momma roach must have her nest hidden somewhere in the stove."

"*Sha-von-ee!*" Sweetie yelled out loudly.

"You might need to get an exterminator in this roach infested kitchen to spray. You have baby roaches coming out of your stove. I hope that you haven't been cooking on it lately, cause, it can use a professional touch of roach defusing."

The toothbrush agitated Shavonee's teeth and toothpaste oozed from the sides of her mouth. She sucked up the excess toothpaste before it dropped down on the bathroom sink.

"Yeah, whatever!" She responded, not giving two shits about Sweetie.

Sweetie brushed off Shavonee's nonchalant attitude.

"I'm getting ready to bounce out. I'll get at you when I'm back in the 'Borough."

"And while you're in there, just make sure you get the tongue real good. That's where all the bacteria lives anyway, on the tongue. It's no sense in brushing your teeth if you don't get the tongue, cause your breath will still be stinking and the bacteria, which causes gingivitis, will still remain alive. So scrub everything in your mouth with that toothbrush until it makes you damn near throw up. That's when all that gook will come out that's been living in your mouth for hours. Well, in your case, for months probably. That's how bad your breath smells."

Spitting out the last bit of toothpaste and gargling with extra strength Listerine, her mouth was now fresh. She patted her mouth with the hand towel hanging on the towel rack. As spiteful as Shavonee was, she had to get Sweetie back for her insulting comments.

"Don't worry about me and my damn mouth! What you need to worry about is how you're going to get that money for El'san. For he beat 'dat ass, if you come up short. Know that, for '*S u g a d a l e*'?"

Soon as she heard the name El'san, Sweetie stopped in motion and waited for her to finish.

Shavonee paused, knowing that now she had her attention.

"Girl, you are tripping, El'san would never put his hands on me."

"Oh yeah, okay whatever. Ask one of his old flames, most of them live in the 'Borough. You see them everyday in passing. Plus, I heard he's still hitting a few of them off from time to time."

Seeing the look in Sweetie's eyes, she rubbed it in even more.

"Don't get all bent out of shape with me. It's not me that's intentionally hurting your poor little feelings, it's your man you need to confront. He's the nigga that's playing you, my dear."

She rolled her chunky eyes and cocked her head to the side, as she finished her last word.

Sweetie was appalled.

"I know you tripping now because I'm the closest thing he has to a woman! Don't no chick have El'san's heart the way I do. You're just jealous of that cause you thought your girl was the one. Oh, I guess you thought I didn't know that, huh!"

"Well, I'll be damn, cousin done ran the 'okey doke' on Miss Sweet Thang! Girl, my cousin had handfuls of bitches before and during you, and will after he's finished using you. One thing I don't understand, why is there always one who falls head over heels for him?"

"Cuz's game might be tight like that!"

"Yeah, since you already know, ask my girl Tiff. That was the last woman who thought El'san loved her. And, he had her ass swinging poles making money for him. At first, they were inseparable but then, 'bah dow', the door blow hit

176

her and off to the club she went trying to please him. Now, need I go on, cause I can tell you plenty more stories about the rest of them ho's El'san bagged in the 'Borough. Yeah, he always starts off treating his woman real lovely and giving them the utmost respect. That's a part of his pimp game. I got to give it to cousin, he's a straight up hustler. He knows how to get a woman to get that money for him. No wonder he chose you, you're to damn naïve to recognize the game."

"What the hell are you talking about Shavonee?" Sweetie didn't really want to listen anymore than she had to, but curiosity played with her intelligence.

"I bet he's fronting like you the only one. Like he's holding you real special to his heart. Did he dick you down one good time yet? Cause cousin is known for backbreaking sex sessions. He got that bomb ass shizzo, so the hookers tell me."

Falling right into the trap, Sweetie answered.

"Honey, how is he playing me when he hasn't even hit this yet? Besides, we are waiting for that special moment."

Saying it very sarcastically, "What the fuck, girl you dumber than I thought, El'san is getting more trim than a damn john is from a prostitute. Lisa just called me the other day, talking about, she just sucked his meat."

"Lisa?" Sweetie wondered if she was talking about the Lisa who lived two doors down from her.

"Come on, now. Don't act like you don't know your neighbor, Lisa. Yeah, uh huh, he's hitting that too! If I were you, I'd be ashamed to show my face in the 'Borough, let alone tell everybody that you and El'san are a couple. Those bitches be laughing all in your face and doing your man when you're gone. In fact, one's probably getting it on with him right now. Oh, and you think he's holding out just for you. Girl, you better check yourself."

Sweetie listened with suspicion.

"I don't believe you. You can say whatever you'd like, but this I don't believe!"

Shavonee knew she had to break it down to her.

"Listen Sweetie, men are playing the very same game women been playing all along. Now since when you know a handsome young man like El'san, which has been down in the pen for some years, horny ass hell, deny some coochie? Girl, never! Pay attention to his game, that's all I have to say."

Shavonee waved her hand goodbye.

"C-Ya! Goodbye, I'll holla at you later."

Sweetie wanted to say, "Fuck you Shavonee, ya' project chick." Instead, she left without showing her burning emotions that boiled on the inside.

"Oh, wait one minute, don't forget your little pocketbook." Shavonee handed Sweetie the handbag less the balled up hundred dollar bills.

The heat outside couldn't compare to the temperature that boiled on the inside of Sweetie. Was El'san really using her? She thought they were more of a Jada and Will Smith, an inseparable combination. She knew the chicks were on him, but never did she imagine that he had this many women sexing him.

She walked across the street trying to quickly clear her mind. She didn't need any costly mistakes on this job. She contemplated not doing it, just going back to the 'Borough to confront El'san. However, she needed the money bad. She checked the area thoroughly; the honey mustard colored 745 BMW parked across the street appeared to be the same one that ignorant ass dude named Cam was driving. Maybe it was just a coincidence. She walked pass, hoping her intuition was wrong. She glided up the brownstone steps with much caution. Not wavering to ring the doorbell of Toby's residence, she stepped up like she knew him for years. A husky voice rang out from the intercom system.

"Yeah, who is it?"

Sweetie changed up her voice to a softer and a professional tone.

"Yes hi, my name is Karen. One of the neighbors informed me that, this is your silver Jaguar XJ-S parked right in front of the building. Is that correct?"

A little resistant to answer, he responded.

"Who wants to know again?"

"My name is Karen. I'm a collector of vehicles and I would like to discuss with you an opportunity to check yours out for a possible purchase. Have you ever thought about selling it?"

Still not giving in, Toby kept up with the questions. The chances of a car collector in East New York were damn near impossible. However,

179

a week ago when he was outside of the train station waiting on his run, a couple did share their interest in his Jag. They exchanged information but he lost theirs. They informed him they were only in town on business and said they would contact him in a few days. He thought it may have been them and was happy they followed up. They were giving him an offer he couldn't refuse.

"And, what did you say your name was again?"

Not getting impatient, Sweetie played along with the game.

"It's Karen. Karen Jamison, I'm in from Virginia visiting one of my relatives in Manhattan."

He was a little unsure if that was the woman's name. The fact that she was visiting relatives in Manhattan, went right over his head.

"Are you from this neighborhood Karen?"

"No, I told you I'm from Virginia, Richmond Virginia to be exact. I'm just passing through on business." Sounding convincing enough, he let her in.

"Alright, I'll buzz you in." When he opened the door, he was instantly stricken by Sweetie's natural beauty. He said to himself, "Hell no, this is not the woman I talked to but this woman, whoever she is, is a dime."

"Oh Karen, it is my pleasure to meet such a beautiful young lady." Sweetie almost gagged when he grabbed her hand and pulled it up to his face to kiss it. The sharp edges of his teeth grazed her thin skin. His teeth were jacked up, and even that was giving him a compliment. The shape of his mouth extended forward about a half inch because of the way his teeth protruded forth. If he paid a visit to the orthodontist, maybe he wouldn't look so bad.

Sweetie eyed the unit before entering. It was very neat and clean for a man's apartment, even with the basic black leather furniture décor. It wasn't colorful at all, just black basics. A black couch, black loveseat, black coffee tables, black dining room table, a black runner rug, two black and white pictures hanging on the wall and two black lamps with black lampshades.

"What's with this damn black?" Sweetie asked herself. Seemed like fifty percent of black families had a living or dining room set of black furniture.

"Please have a seat on the *L o v e* –seat." He stressed the word love.

"Can I get you something to drink?" Being very polite and accepting, she responded.

"Yes, I'll take a glass of soda if you would."

"No, actually I was talking about a glass of Henney or some of this Thug Passion I have on chill."

"That's alright, I'll just have a chilled glass of soda." Sweetie responded.

Practically running to her request for something to drink, Toby inquired about her passion of collecting vehicles.

"So, what kind of vehicles do you have in your collection?"

Not expecting him to ask that kind of question, she thought quickly and rebounded.

"Uh, I have three Jaguar XJ-S's. One is a collector's dream. It's a 1964, original body style, chrome stripping on the trim. That baby is clean."

Selling her story to him, she almost convinced herself that she had one.

"The other two are newer models, both identical, with the exception of the color. One is red and the other is black."

Toby still couldn't be too careful, so before handing her the drink, he slipped a 1oz bottle of the date rape drug, Roofies in her soda. It was a small amount, but if he kept her, in about an hour or so, he was sure to be in her panties after the Roofies drug set in. She was sure to be zooted and horny out of her mind. He sat down very close to her on the *L O V E* –seat and handed her the glass of pineapple soda diluted with the drug. He was destined to get some of that.

"Tell me Karen, what drew your interest to my vehicle if you already have three of them?"

Getting deeper and deeper in the conversation she continued.

"I admire the rims you have on it. It makes the vehicle stand out above the rest, especially with that silverish creamy paint job. Mine are not that flashy. By the way, where did you go to get that kind of paint job?"

She took a sip of the pineapple soda, waiting for a response like she was really interested in hearing more about the location. Her antennas didn't go up and she forgot about one of the golden rules when you're on a victimizing mission, always accept a drink, but never ever drink from the cup a potential victim gives you.

"There's a place down in Brick City." He explained.

"I'm sorry, where is Brick City?" She played as though she never heard about or been to dirty Jersey.

"That's right, you are a Southern Bell. I forgot you're from Richmond, Virginia. The state for lovers right?" Snuggling closer to her.

"Yes, and Virginia natives really live up to that name to!" She giggled in a childish manner.

Thinking he was about to cash in on a winning lottery ticket, he made a serious offer.

"Maybe we should cut the talk about my vehicle and find out just how much you live up to that name." He eased his arm around her shoulders and started to nibble on her ear with his goat mouth. Sweetie jumped off from the sofa spilling droplets of soda on the wood floor.

"Back to business." Sweetie demanded.

"How much are you willing to sell your vehicle for? I mean I'm not trying to cut your money short or anything like that, but I am on a strict budget. I can only pay so much. I know you'll be depending on my money to replace this vehicle, so I'll take that into consideration when making the offer." Toby had to prove to her finances wasn't a problem.

"Come in here, Karen. Let me explain a few things to you." He grabbed her hand, walking in the direction of his bedroom.

"Wait a minute, you're not going to try something crazy are you?" The effects of the date rape drug hadn't taken full effect yet.

"No Karen, I would never do that!" I'm trying to show you something that's all."

B I N G O! His stupid ass, he took her straight to the stash. She walked with her glass in her hand and this time she took a few gulps until the glass was empty.

"You know, I haven't drank a pineapple soda in years. This sure was tasty." Sweetie had to admit to him. She was steady thinking,

"This dumb ass easy mark. Is he really that damn dumb to show me his stash? What's it been, only twenty minutes, since I first met him?"

"See all that money in this basket?" He had several wads of bills wrapped up tightly with about three to four rubber bands around them.

"I can sell that vehicle and still have enough to buy all three of your vehicles. So how's that, do I have enough money to buy you, I mean please you?"

Feeding right into his ego, she expressed her interest in him. "Oh, that's very impressive Toby, but you need a lot more money to buy me, I mean please me." She shook her head and frowned slightly, causing her forehead skin to ripple in layers. Before the situation got heated up again she made a suggestion.

"Now, when can we go check out the vehicle?"

Since she knew where the stash was, she could play along a little longer. They walked out of the bedroom and Toby picked up his house keys. Escorting her outside, the sound of two men arguing could be heard from the short distance.

"Nigga, I told you it's time for business. You let that tramp, Shavonee hold you up from making a $100,000 dollars last night! I was handling business with Slowdown and you were supposed to get up with me to drop off the package to that Jamaica Rasta in Queens. Since you were a 'no show,' he's taken his business to those dudes over in Flatbush. That was our money, yo!"

Cam was very relentless, not caring who was listening in on the conversation.

"Just for that, you're not getting paid for this month! You costing the business."

Kenny didn't care. He had money put aside for rainy days. Missing out a month's pay wouldn't even put a dent in his pocket. He stood there paying attention to his brother's alter ego going on and on. After being embarrassed for fifteen minutes or so, he sat on the steps nonchalantly with his back turned, facing Shavonee's house. He blocked Cam out and reminisced about the pleasantly pleasing time he shared with her yesterday.

When Sweetie realized it was Cam, she took two steps back.

"Toby if you don't mind, I have to use the potty before we go outside to check out the car." She didn't want her cover blown.

He was too busy worrying about the battle between his new neighbors. He handed her the keys without doubting her ulterior motives.

Sweetie fiddled with the keys trying to find the right one to open the door. This was her chance to take what she needed and get the hell out of dodge. Just so he couldn't back up and get inside the apartment, she put both locks on. The deadbolt lock and the knob set lock.

She went right into the bedroom, opened the basket and put all the wads of money in her handbag. It was easy because his money was stacked so nice and neat. The money didn't even disfigure her straw bag.

After getting the money, she wrote on an old electric bill, "Call me later Toby, 1 800 U GOT PLAYED, Smooches, Karen!" She put it inside of the basket for him to see when he got back home.

When she got outside, Cam and the other dudes accompanying him were gone. With a sigh of relief, she had to now figure out how to get rid of Toby's tired ass. He was wiping down his Jaguar XJ-S like it was a Bentley.

"Toby!" Sweetie called out. Her head started to feel light and a tingling sensation came over her body, just a little bit. She thought it was strange but passed it off as the adrenaline rush from beating her mark.

The sound of her voice made him melt.

"Yes, Karen." He responded with a goat smile.

"Ewe." She thought.

"What year is your XJ-S?"

Saying it with pride he responded, "It's a 2003."

"Yeah, I figured as much. Can we take it for a ride?"

"Oh no doubt, I would love to ride along side of a beautiful woman like you. Trust me, I don't mind at all!" He began licking his lips with his long lizard tongue on his extended goat mouth.

"Disgusting." Sweetie said under her breath, after watching his movement. Toby

opened the driver's side door for her and waited patiently while she situated herself and her pocketbook, then shut the door.

Shavonee watched out the kitchen window at them, shaking her head in skepticism, not sure if Sweetie was capable of getting the job done.

"Bitch." Shavonee muttered under her breath.

Toby walked conceitedly over to the passenger's side door, like a proud father seeing his baby for the first time outside the womb.

Sweetie didn't delay putting the car in gear. Her body was feeling crazy and she longed for something wet to drink.

"My throat is really dry all of a sudden?" Sweetie exclaimed.

The tire made a loud stretching blast pulling out of the parking spot. They drove down one block when Toby started to get a little too comfortable with the ride.

"Is that right? You need me to wet it up with some moisture?" He leaned over to give her a kiss, opening up his goat mouth and rotating his lizard tongue. Sweetie almost hit an on coming car as she jumped, trying to avoid his mouth.

"Please do not try and kiss me again." She said in a very distressed tone. He placed his hand on Sweetie's knee and then let it ease up her thigh.

She wanted to yell, "Please take your hand off my leg." But the soft sensation of his hand on her thigh made her feel good. Fighting back the feeling, she asked him to remove his hand.

"Please take your hand off of me." By this time, his hand had reached her crotch.

"Come on pumpkin, ain't no harm in touching a little leg. Don't go acting all stuck up now when you're the one announcing that you are from Virginia, 'The home of lovers'." Sweetie was annoyed by his company and replied in such a manner.

"That doesn't mean we're going to be lovers. Get it right!" She wanted to get the hell out of dodge. Her eyes were burning and starting to blur. She fought hard against the sexual feeling that she desired so badly.

It seemed that Toby didn't get the drift, because he unceasingly kept the conversation going. What he didn't know was that Sweetie had tuned him out. Finally arriving in reach of the 'Borough, Sweetie changed their plans.

"Hey Toby, how much did you say you wanted to sell this car for again?" Toby shrugged his shoulders.

"Why buy it? And you can drive it anytime you want. Just be my special lady friend. By the way, how are you feeling on the inside?"

Playing right into his ridiculous request, she said, "I don't think that's a bad idea after all. But first let me pull over and call my cousin in Manhattan to let them know I'll be late coming home tonight. This will also give me a chance to get something to drink. Oh, I'm feeling fine, what made you ask me that?" Toby started rubbing his hands together.

"I just thought you might be feeling a little sweet on me right about now, that's all."

Sweetie was a little bothered by his remarks, but went along with her plan.

"Wait, you can use my cell phone. I have free unlimited long distance service." He said, trying to be of assistance.

"Oh no, that's all right, I don't want them all up in my business. This between you and I."

"That's cool. Please don't be long in the store. I'm ready to go back to the apartment." Toby ran his lizard tongue overtop of his goat mouth.

"Ay Karen, you know what I'm known for?"

"What's that?" Sweetie responded.

"I'm the downtown King. See this tongue right here." He let his tongue loose out of his mouth and let it drop down past his chin.

"Not only can I lick you down, but I can stick you down with it to! I know you'll love that!"

As frisky as she was feeling, the thought of receiving some oral sex, wasn't a bad idea.

"I'll only be a few minutes. I'm ready to go there too." She grinned at his evident stupidity. Her hips swayed in the dress, causing Toby's mind to go stark mad.

Sweetie walked into the corner store, straight back to the exit entrance like she'd done many times before. Once outside, there wasn't time for being sluggish. Her body wasn't really trying to cooperate with her mind. This was especially important after beating someone for money. She had to get gone with blinded vision and all.

The Cuban man at the counter knew what time it was when Sweetie passed off a sign that she'd just beat another. Later on, she would send

189

a runner back to the store to hit the owner off for allowing her an easy exit. This was the normal routine. When the victim realized that Sweetie was inside the store too long, he would come inside searching around for her. Without a doubt he would question the Cuban store owner, who played like he didn't understand English that well.

Sweetie ran as fast as should could, feeling like she was high off of drugs. She ran through alleyways, dipping and dodging in between cars after each exit, until she made her way back to the 'Borough. Toby was still sitting calmly in the vehicle waiting for her to return. Almost out of breath with a face full of sweat, Sweetie glimpsed over near the basketball court where she sighted El'san. He was on the court shooting hoops with a gang of niggas, trying to instill knowledge in a few of the younger boys out on the sidelines of the court.

Sweetie didn't know if she wanted to wild the hell out on him or go over there and plant a sloppy french kiss on his lips. The way she was feeling, he could get some right there. Knowing damn well she wanted to stop, it took all the strength to keep moving to the apartment, as opposed to stopping and talking to him. El'san noticed her but waited patiently for her to come to him. When she didn't, he continued talking to the fellas.

Pop, the maintenance man, was in the hallway patching up a few holes from vandalism. His grim face developed into a smile when Sweetie came marching in.

"Hi there, Miss Sweetie M'am. You fit'na go clean up, cause you look a little like the farm got the best of you. You been out milking them cows again?" This was his way of letting her know he knew what she was about.

"By chance, did you get them there uh, bottles of perfume for the misses?" Pop asked, sniffing his nose in the air to get a whiff of her scent.

Happy to see Pop, Sweetie answered with glee. She really didn't feel like holding a long conversation with him. She knew her response and physical balance would seem strange to Pop. He paid close attention to everything.

"Hey Pop, what's going on? To respond to your questions, yes, I am tired as a slaughter man after a hard days work, and yes I did get 'them there' bottles of perfume. They are inside of my apartment. How long are you going to be in this building?"

"Well, by the looks of these holes, I'll be patching in the building all day and maybe most of the night."

Sweetie puckered her lips as to say, yeah right. "You sure Miss Irene doesn't have something to do with you staying in the building most of the night."

"Now, Miss Sweetie, you're meddling in grown folk business!"

"All right, I'll respect that. Let me freshen up and I'll be out to see you later. I know where to find you, if it's not too late."

"And where's that, Miss Sweetie?"

"Stop playing Pop, you know you'll be over Miss Irene's. Come to think about it, is she cooking dinner today?" Pop lit up like a holiday Christmas tree.

"Yes M'am, she sure is. She's got southern fried chicken, crispy battered catfish, big thick beef ribs, chicken and dumplings and jumbo fried shrimp on today's menu."

The main course meals made Sweetie's mouth water.

"What are the sides?" With his country accent, he responded automatically.

"Are you alright Miss Sweetie? Cause it seems like you can't keep your balance and your speech is slurred." She didn't feel her body swaying from side to side.

"Yes, I'm fine, Pop. Now, what's on the menu?"

"Well only if you say you're alright, I'll believe you. But, you sure don't look alright." Sweetie closed her eyes and waited for his response to the question. Her head was spinning round and round.

"Homestyle mash potatoes, fried potatoes with onions, candied yams, fresh collard greens, potatoe salad, macaroni and cheese, french style string beans, and for dessert, a homemade triple layered chocolate cake. Mmmm, I love it when she makes those melt in your mouth triple layered chocolate cakes! Do you want me to put in an order for you?"

"Would you please Pop? That's so sweet of you, but rather than one, could you make it two dinners."

She was going to prepare an intimate evening for her and El'san.

"One, chicken and dumplings platter with collard greens and potatoe salad and make the other, fried catfish, fried potatoes with onions and green beans. I'll also take two slices of that triple layered chocolate cake. It's always delicious. Boy, I tell you, Miss Irene sure puts her foot in that!" She licked her lips slowly across every crevice. Pop was a little doubtful about the order.

"That other meal wouldn't be for that heathen El'san, would it? Cause you know, I ain't going to do nothing for that little bastard!" Grabbing his hat, he repositioned it on his head.

"I'm sorry, excuse my french Miss Sweetie, but the boy makes my stomach rumble. The nasty little buzzard." To get what she wanted, she knew she had to lie.

"No Pop, both the dinners are for me. Now, let me get you the money. That's $14.00 dollars right?" She stumbled against the wall.

"Yes, it is M'am. Miss Sweetie, are you sure you are alright?" She reached into her pocketbook searching for the crumbled up bills Cam threw at her early today. She didn't hear a word Pop was saying. She was in her own world. With the extra money, her intentions were to bless Miss Irene with purchasing two dinners and allow her to keep the change. She moved everything from side to side in her bag looking for the money.

"Now that's strange." She thought to herself.

"The money was in here earlier. Did I drop them out at Toby's?" She quickly let that thought go astray.

"It's no way, I could've done that. And, my bag was closed when I was running." Maybe it was her blurred vision she thought. Maybe it was her slow response. She didn't know. All she knew was the money was gone. "What the hell happened to my money?" She didn't want to pull one of the wads out in front of Pop, so she told him to hold on for a minute.

"Hold on Pop, let me go inside the apartment to get the money. I'll be right out." She locked the door behind her and stumbled onto the couch. She dumped the contents of her bag out on the living room table.

"No balled up bills in this damn bag." She was feeling some type of way. Her head snapped back and she quickly pulled it back up. Thinking back through the course of her day, the light bulb went on in her head. She remembered Shavonee specifically telling her not to forget her, *"little pocketbook"*, as she put it. She even remembered leaving it in the living room while she was in the kitchen.

"I'm telling you, if that ghetto ass girl had the audacity to steal my money, I'm going to steal her!"

"I'm not playing. When it comes down to my money, bitches better beware!" She absolutely had to call her to feel Shavonee's vibes. If she acted the slightest bit funny, she was gonna get got!

Sweetie was fighting the feeling of being high off Rookies, being horny as hell, blurred vision, being displeased and dealing with all that unnecessary bullshit Shavonee took her through earlier about El'san.

"What the hell is going on with me?" She asked herself, while dialing Shavonee's telephone number.

"Yeah, who 'dis is?" Shavonee answered, anxiously thinking it was another mark. Even with a slurred speech, it was evident in Sweetie's tone that she was pissed.

"Who 'dis is? It's Sweet-iee?" Shavonee wasn't taken aback.

"Oh, what's up Miss Trick? How did it go? I bet you didn't get a damn dime from Toby's trick ass and he's an easy ass mark. You're a sucka!"

Sweetie, still high out her mind had a strong come back for Shavonee. "You know what, it's awful strange that you, just by chance, today have all this negative talk and negative comments about me, my life and my game. I realize that a real trick like you, can get jealous over a *real* woman, running *real* game on these niggas. You wouldn't happen to be a little bit envious of me would you, because it seems that way to me?"

Shavonee sucked her lips. "Why would I be indigenous over you?"

"What?" Sweetie asked confused. "Let me repeat myself loud and clear, why would I need to be *I N D I G E N O U S* over you?"

Sweetie was irritated with Shavonee's illiterate ass self. "I didn't say that dumb ass, I said envious!"

Shavonee was very unshakable and not catching on to what Sweetie was trying to say to her.

"And, that's what I said too, dumb ass!"

"Let me try to put it to you in your terms since you can't comprehend proper English, "Why

195

are you hating on me? I bet you understand that with your Ebonics speaking ass!"

Shavonee's voice ran across the entire building. "What I got to hate on you for, bitch?" What I got to hate on you for?" She repeated her words.

"You better ask yourself why those chicks are hating on you in the 'Borough, cause chicks not feeling you at all and to tell you the truth, neither am I trick. Be glad that my cousin is in on this deal with Toby cause if he wasn't, I'd send his ass straight to your front door! Oh yeah, your little pocketbook should feel a little lighter shouldn't it? Ha! Ha! Peace trick!"

Sweetie managed to get her words out just before Shavonee hung up. She had to take it back to the hood on her ass.

"You grimy little bitch! I'm a beat that ass when I see you."

After that conversation, she opened her refrigerator, pulled out a cold soda and gulped it down like an ice cold Mike's Lemonade.

Her footsteps were heavy walking over to her CD player and scrolled through her CD collection to pick out a CD that fit her mood. Her fingers went up and down the rows searching for the perfect tunes. Tupac Shakur seemed to stand out above the rest on this day. *"All Eyes On Me"* CD, 'Wonder why they call you bitch' track.

Sweetie zoned out, throwing her hat on her bed and pulled her dress over her head. She bopped her head straight to the bathroom, opening the shower curtain to turn on the knob for hot water. Letting it run for a few seconds, she balanced out the temperature with cold water.

"There that's just right." Her image reflected in the double mirrors. The four-prong silver chrome bathroom light fixture reminded her of an intimate poetry night event. Going to poetry night had gotten just as bad as her visiting her mother and father, which was almost never. Her passion and love for Poetry and Spoken Word would never permit her to get comfortable with the life she was living.

This is what lifted her spirit, made her smile and gave her an abundance of happiness. Why did she let her dreams go to the wayside? Why did she continue to betray and play with her religion? Why had she developed feelings for El'san? Why the hell did everybody know that he was a whore besides her? Why hadn't she visited her mother and father at the Mosque?

The dancing slowed down to non-movement. She stood in a trance for a moment, then covered her face and cried from all the hurt and anger built up and living inside of her. The steam from the shower, at once, filled the bathroom.

All high up and forgetting that she still had her panties and bra on, she stepped right into the shower. She cried remorsefully after realizing the mistake she made.

"How can I be good at anything when I can't even remember to take my underclothes off to take a shower? What is wrong with me?"

The Dove soap started to soften up from the constant stream of hot water hitting it. The thick cotton washcloth massaged her body with the lather from the soap. She touched herself very personally. It was past due time for her to receive some loving. Taking a thorough wash, cleansing all the nook and crannies, she stepped out the shower, only to take into account that she didn't bring a towel in the bathroom with her.

"Damn." She sighed. El'san couldn't have said it better, "I would mess up a wet dream." Her vision started to clear, but she was still horny as hell.

"I know that trick Toby slipped something in my drink. I know he did." She said, convincing herself.

"I've never felt like this before a day in my life." Sweetie dressed in a white linen pantsuit with a white turban over her head. She applied dabs of pressed powder foundation to control the oily places on her face, then applied a small amount of clear Bobby Brown lip-gloss instead of the Mac Lip Gloss on her lips. Her white and silver leafy earrings complimented her look. She decided to wear her slides with a little more heel than she was used to. Using her candlestick, she lit the new lemon lime scented Yankee candles that were delivered to her. She'd pulled out a hundred dollars and walked outside of her apartment to pay Pop for the meals. Pop was on the outside pretending to be working, but actually paying very close attention to an argument that Sweetie's neighbors were having.

"Here Pop, tell Miss Irene she can keep the change. And, you need to stop snooping into people's business! That's how you always end up in the middle of things." Pop looked down at the bill and started smiling.

"Oh, Irene is going to love this tip." He said. "Miss Sweetie, I'm just making sure the man don't beat the brakes out of his lady. It's my duty to pay attention as head maintenance man of this complex." His chest started to stick out. "I take my job very seriously and if err, that means going above and beyond, Pop will do it!"

"Well, alrighty Mr. Superintendent of Maintenance! Miss Irene surely does deserve large tips. I just hope her son doesn't get a hold of any of it. She needs to stop pacifying his behavior and have the state come admit him to a rehabilitation center. That heroin is eating him up. He looks sick, if you ask me. I hope he's not close to the food. I don't need any of his germs. He's the one you need to be calling a nasty buzzard."

Pop was offended by Sweetie's cruel comment.

"Now Miss Sweetie, Irene would never allow that boy in her house on the days she cooks dinners. She would never make a dime. All those junkie friends of his would be full for days." He laughed after his words.

"Looka here, I'm fit'na take this money over to her now. Do you want to pick up the dinners or do you want them delivered?"

"I'll pick the dinners up. I have some business to take care of." She pulled the door open to grab her keys from the entertainment stand. Pop watched her walk down the hallway looking like a beautiful black angel.

When she reached outside, El'san was seated on the bench. While Sweetie was in the house, he'd went home to change from his basketball gear to casual clothes. He had a nice pair of khaki pants and butter cream Timberland boots. His belt was a leather khaki colored custom made by "Precious Designz". They both shared eye contact with each other until Sweetie arrived within the distance of his personal space.

"What's up Sweetness? Did you handle that?" He asked, hoping her response would be yes.

"Is it like me not to handle my business?" Sweetie answered condescendingly. Her stomach was doing somersaults and her coochie was twitching in the worse way. She was eager to question him about what Shavonee said and eager to get him into the bedroom, as well. She could see through his khaki pants his large manhood print.

"No doubt, you take care of business. Why don't we leave the park and go to my crib to discuss this? Besides, I don't like the way other jokers in this park are watching you."

When he stood up, he whistled over to get the attention to all those on the basketball court. "Yo, see this Queen right here, this is me, she's off limits understood!"

One of his boys, whispered to the next dude. "Damn near all the ho's he got in the 'Borough are off limits." They gave each other some dap and then snapped their fingers.

The guys brushed him off. Everybody already knew that El'san and Sweetie had a love hate relationship thing going on. They were just admiring her beauty.

"Why did you tell them that?" Her body stumbled to the side. "You know I'm not your woman. In fact, I had my eye on that dude right there." El'san paid close attention to the gentlemen she pointed out.

"Who, Devon? That's my man and I know he wouldn't even disrespect me like that. So stop playing mind games, Ma. Not nare one of these dudes living in the 'Borough better not ever push up on you, and that's word to motha. Now let's go, and what the hell is wrong with you? You walking like you had a fifth of Remy by your lonesome." He placed his arm around her neck and then embraced her from behind.

This was the first time in public he'd ever shown her any physical contact. She was smiling on the inside and happy as hell. She just knew they were going to get it on.

By the time they got to the apartment, Sweetie remembered that she had to pick up the dinners from Ms. Irene's house.

"Hold up for a minute El'san, I ordered us two dinners from Ms. Irene's house."

"Are you sure you're going to make it? You need me to come with you."

She quickly responded, "No, that's alright. I got this. You go ahead to the apartment."

"If you say so, I hope you ordered me the catfish." He responded, loving the way Ms. Irene battered up the crisp catfish that crackled and lightly filled your mouth when you bit into it.

"Yeah, I did. I know that's your favorite platter. Anyway, I'll be right back." She walked down to Ms. Irene's apartment. Pop was sitting on the couch watching television.

"Are you on a break Pop?" questioned Sweetie.

"Yes, M'am. I'm keeping Irene company, for a little while. I know how lonely it can be living alone."

"How would you know that Pop when you live with your wife at home?" Sweetie said, pulling his card. Miss Irene came from the kitchen.

"How ya doing Miss Sweetie?" Miss Irene walked out with her red apron, red house shoes and flowered housecoat hanging underneath the apron. She was a big boned, fair skinned woman with naturally curly hair. Her husband died years ago from cancer and Pop was the only man she took to after that.

"You sure do look like a fashion model in that outfit. Every time I see you, you get prettier and prettier. No wonder that boy sniffing all around you. That cat of yours keeps on purring and he keeps on answering to your call."

"Y'all shut your mouth!" Miss Irene giggled after her comments. Sweetie burst out in laughter. "I can see why Pop admires you so much, you are one of a kind Miss Irene."

"You really think so?" Miss Irene responded.

"Well, I tell you what, 'I know so'." She smiled in return.

"The dinners are ready for you. I threw in a bottle of whip cream just in case you need some with the triple fudge chocolate cake. Let me give you a lesson young girl, you know you can play all kind of games with that. Isn't that right Pop?" Pop kept his head down.

"Miss Irene you better behave. You got Pop over there blushing." Sweetie answered.

"Don't I know it? Man don't even want to go home to his wife. That's all right though, I'm plenty of woman for him. By the way, thank you so dearly for that liberal tip."

"Shoot, you deserve more than that, all those dinners you let go for free. I know you enjoy cooking and all those groceries are expensive. You better learn to make the money off your hustle and don't let the hustle break you." Miss Irene listened closely as Sweetie spoke. "I'll see you two love birds later." Sweetie stated.

Pop hung his head again, knowing that he always denied any sexual involvement with Miss Irene. However, Miss Irene made it clear that they were bumping and grinding. Pop was definitely cheating on his sweet southern bell that was at home.

Sweetie carried the bag very carefully so the juices from the dinner wouldn't spill over. Directing too much attention to the dinners, she didn't notice the dark skin female until she brushed up against her in the hallway.

"Excuse you!" Sweetie stated, throwing her shoulder against the other female.

"No, excuse you! You were in my way." The bitter young woman responded, throwing her shoulder back in return.

"You don't even know me like that so you better step." Sweetie was uncertain if this was one of the females Shavonee was talking about. It could have been because she was coming from the direction of El'san's apartment.

"Who are you anyway? Do you have a problem with me?" Sweetie asked, waiting for her to say something stupid.

"Go ask your man, he'll tell you!" With that, the female walked off. The platters almost dropped out of her hands because she was moving so fast to get to El'san's apartment. He'd left the door open for her. She was ready to go full blast on him. Instead, when she walked in, he greeted her with a dozen white roses wrapped in gold ribbon.

"These white roses are for you, my Beautiful Black Queen. They symbolize the purity of our love. What we share no one can come in between." He stressed the words, "*no one.*"

She was stuck on whether or not she should confront him about the chick that she just encountered or about the comments Shavonee made even with his sentimental gestures.

"You can place the food on the counter. I'll set up the table for us to eat." El'san instructed as he prepared the table.

He lit the center candle and placed a porcelain vase on the table with water in it to house the dozen white roses. The surround sound stereo system played Street Wize I soundtrack with the instrumental jazz Hip Hop tunes at a minimum.

"You can go into the bathroom and freshen up before we eat Sweetie" That way I'll be finished when you come out."

"Alright." Sweetie responded, puzzled by his sudden intimate interest. She was so elated. El'san removed his shirt revealing his white wife beater and perfect rounded muscles. Soon as Sweetie came out of the bathroom, she discovered his shirt located across the couch.

"See, he's playing games." Sweetie thought to herself. El'san was already seated and waiting for Sweetie to take her seat vertically across from him.

"Let us bless our meal before we eat." El'san requested.

They both parted hands turning their palms toward their face and together recited: "Bis Mill Allah Ah Rah Man Ah Rah Heem" and El'san started to eat. Sweetie's head was still down like she dozed off during the prayer.

"Sweetie!" El'san called out. He tapped her shoulder. Slobber came from the side of her mouth.

"Yeah?" She answered, like he was bothering her.

"What is going on with you?" El'san questioned. She was really starting to feel the full effects of the Roofies drug.

"I think the dude Toby laced my drink with something." She dozed off again. El'san was baffled.

"I know you didn't drink anything out of his house. You know better than that!" Sweetie lifted her head up.

"I'm sorry baby. You know I know the rules of robbing. I slipped up and made a big mistake. I feel high and horny out of this world."

The table was set up like they were in an exclusive restaurant. The aura was blissfully exquisite. El'san and Sweetie fixed their eyes on one another. Her eyes were blood shot red as she gazed at him. The thoughts in her head were going rampant. It was like she was going in and out of this drugged out zone. She tried to concentrate on eating dinner, but needed to release some of the feelings bubbling on the inside of her.

"El'san, can I ask you a question?"

"You already did." El'san responded.

"Come on seriously." Sweetie replied.

"Go ahead Sweetie, you have my attention. You're always prolonging things." El'san had little patience when it came to people questioning him.

"Well, I was over Shavonee's getting the information about the job, when out the clear blue she starts talking about..." El'san interrupted her.

"Hold up, I know you are not getting ready to blast on me from remarks that my ghetto ass cousin made."

"Yes, I am because it all boils down to this. Number one, the trick ended up stealing five hundred dollars from me. Number two, I called on her on it and she totally flipped the script on me. Number three, she told me you still hitting off major chicks living in the 'Borough. Number four." her head dropped down and she dozed off again.

El'san tapped her again. She started talking like the conversation was never interrupted.

"Number four, when I left to go get the dinners, a dark skin trick bumps into me and when I questioned her, she told me to come see you! Now you tell me, what the fuck is up!"

El'san rubbed his temples as he witnessed the frustration in Sweetie's tone. He didn't want to ruin the evening, but he didn't want her to become suspicious either. It was apparent she was high. He didn't want her to flip out, so he kept it calm.

"Whoa! Stop right there. Let me first say this, don't you ever talk to me in that tone and use foul language when you are talking to me, understand!

You are a queen and queens don't represent themselves like that. Especially, not a queen partnered with El'san.

Now, you want truth, I'll give you truth. My cousin Shavonee has a big mouth. Yes, she's very good friends with a lot of these hookers over here. Tiff is her girl, and like all the rest of the hookers, I used to hit her off every now and then. She was never my woman just a fuck buddy. The dark skin girl, I'm sure was her.

When you left to get the dinners, she stopped by my crib. I stopped abusing her sexually two weeks ago. I was tired of just screwing to be screwing. I'm trying to fall in love and make love to my woman. None of these tricks could ever fit into that category. They are to easy and always have been, for that matter. Chicks that aren't a challenge turn me off.

I can't stand a woman that doesn't have her own agenda. Women who are ambitious, ones that know what they want out of life turn me on. Women who don't let men dictate who they are. Not an over confident woman that thinks she doesn't need a man, but a woman that knows how to balance out her career and her family. I see those qualities in you. Yeah initially, I was thinking of just hitting that from time to time, but that changed when I realized your full potential."

Sweetie's head snapped back and a loud sound from her snoring captured El'san's attention.

"You're not even paying attention to me. Here I am pouring my heart out to you."

El'san sat looking at Sweetie all highed up. She jittered in her seat, and then turned her head in the opposite direction.

"No, don't turn away now. You asked for the truth and the truth is what you are going to get." He continued where he left off.

"The more we conversed, the more I started to develop intimate feelings for you. From the first day we met, I was drawn to your beauty. However, it's the inside of you that makes me inhale and exhale. Yeah, you may be on some foul shit right now, robbing jokers, but you're doing it to elevate us. You down for a nigga like me. I trust and respect that gangsta in you. I love that shit!"

Sweetie started to smile. She didn't particularly like the ordeal with Tiff, but at least he was honest.

"Okay, we cool with that?" He asked. She shook her head yes, not knowing for sure what he was talking about.

He walked over to her, grabbed her head back and stuck his warm tongue down inside her mouth. She reciprocated by giving him more tongue than he could handle. He lifted her up from the seat and she wrapped her arms around him. All the while, they were still passionately french kissing.

He pulled her face away from his with his hand on her cheeks. "I love you, girl! Do you hear me?" He asked, omitting all the bad occurrences that happened between them. Her eyes were closed and she dozed off again.

"Come on, wake up Sweetie. This is an important night for you and I."

Once she heard that, she popped up out of her seat, went into the bathroom and patted cool water across her face. She was going to fight this high no matter what it took. From the way El'san was talking, they were about to get it on!

"Oh, you said Shavonee took five hundred dollars from you. How do you know that?" He asked her when she came out of the bathroom.

Feeling just a little refreshed, she responded still looking high as hell.

"Because earlier today, I forgot to tell you, I bumped into this rude nigga named Cam. I believe that's what he called himself."

El'san frowned up his face. "What was this cat driving?"

"He was driving a gold, almost a honey colored 745 BMW." El'san shook his head.

"I know exactly who you are talking about. We did time in Riker's together. As a matter of fact, he has a brother named Kenny that was bidding with us. He's the same nigga I'm plotting on for this dude from Delaware."

Sweetie didn't understand what he was talking about cause he hadn't let her in on this job.

"Anyway, he was trying to holla at a sistah, but I gave him the spiel about selling drugs. I don't think he appreciated that too much, because that's when he got really nasty and threw out five crumbled up $100 dollar bills at me.

"Did you pick them up?" El'san questioned.

"Of course I did, silly!" Sweetie responded.

"Well to make a long story short, when I was over Shavonee's house, she stole the money from my bag without me knowing it. I didn't find out till later when I got home that the money was missing. That's when I called her on the telephone and she flipped out on me. Talking about, she basically took mine right in front of my face! Oh, and before I forget, the dude Cam lives across the street from her. But, we need to be careful because remember so does the mark Toby."

"Word." El'san muttered.

"We will deal with Shavonee, don't worry about that. You want to beat her down, tell me what you want to happen. A little one on one or do you want to jump her ass!"

"I want to beat her ass dolo – *solo!*" Sweetie hurriedly responded.

Coming up with a better plan, she explained to El'san. "For real though, I think we can kill two birds with one stone. I heard her make mention that she's hitting off this new dude in the area."

"That couldn't be Cam, she's not his type." El'san responded.

"How do you know that?" Sweetie answered.

"I told you I did time with the dude. He was always boasting on the dimes he toted. Shavonee don't fit the category he sang praises about." Sweetie continued, "Okay, but it's not Cam that she's messing with, it's the dude Kenny."

"Who?" El'san questioned.

"The dude Kenny. The one you said was his brother."

El'san took a fork full of catfish and became silent. He remembered so clearly how Kenny was violated in Riker's, now his cousin was putting herself at risk. Lifting his head slightly, he stared at Sweetie with a discerning look on his face.

"What's the matter?" Sweetie asked, floating higher than birds traveling down south in the winter.

"Nothing, baby. Come here and sit on Daddy's lap." Her feet didn't hit the floor fast enough. The dining room chair fell back, hitting the floor.

"Slow down baby, I'm not going anywhere." El'san said.

"You don't have to ask me twice. I don't see any need in wasting any more time than we have to." Sweetie said in return.

She sat down slowly on his lap, centering her ass right on his private parts.

"Damn, that feels so good." She said to herself.

El'san searched her body with his hands. He roamed to all the places Sweetie wanted him to go. He raised her white linen shirt and disconnected her bra.

"Turn around." He softly said to her. She straddled him from the front with her breasts hanging underneath the loose bra.

He lifted her shirt and opened his mouth to suck on one of her huge black nipples. He sucked and licked each nipple very slowly. Sweetie's eyes darted to the back of her head. She was high as hell but feeling marvelous. While sucking on one nipple, he fondled the other with his gentle hand. Sparks were shooting through Sweetie's body. El'san's manhood was poking at her with a wide smile. Letting go of the nipple that occupied his mouth, he looked up at her in amazement.

"Why did you stop?" Sweetie asked.

He put his index finger over her mouth. With very swift motion, he hauled up her body, pulling the drawstring white linen pants down. He placed her tenderly back on the chair. He parted her thighs and situated his body in between her legs.

Now, down on his knees, he licked her inner thighs, giving her forceful wet kisses. He pulled her black thong to the side and her fatty girl stared at him. With his mouth, he ate in between her legs like she was Miss Irene's dinner meal. Sweetie moaned and groaned, not wanting him to stop. This was the first time a man treated her genitals like he was.

"Oh, El'san this feels sooooo good." She whimpered.

He didn't respond by talking, but rather, stroked harder with his tongue until he felt her bottom quiver with joy.

"I'm cuming baby. I'm cuming." She screamed out, no longer fighting the pleasure.

El'san got off his knees and wiped the juices from his lips. He snatched up Sweetie's hand and led her back to the bedroom. Chyna White cried and scratched at the bedroom door to be let out. They bypassed the room he was in. Sweetie was in la la land. She was ready to share juices with her man for the first time. He pushed her body down on the bed and for once, Sweetie decided to take the lead.

"Uh, uh, this is not how it's going down. I want you to lie on the bed." She proclaimed.

El'san undressed and laid his butt ass bald naked self on the bed. Sweetie was mesmerized at what was hanging in between his legs. She pulled her shirt over her head and removed her hanging bra. She slid her black thong and her shoes off. El'san admired her body. Her body was perfect. She didn't have any kids, so there wasn't a sign of a hanging gut or stretch marks on her belly.

Her body slowly motioned like a sly stray cat, onto the bed to straddle El'san. Her breast rested on his chest and his hands groped her buttocks. She opened her legs real wide, ready for her tunnel to be filled my El'san's manliness. When he entered her, she rose up off of it a little.

She whispered to him, "Take your time, it's been a long time."

He eased himself in, little by little. Sweetie hinted with sexual noises that his strokes were pleasurably, but painful. Her genitals were juicy wet but it still didn't help any because of El'san's thickness. He pulled her bottom down on him easy, but harder with every stroke. Sweetie could feel herself coming again. Her back arched, riding his manhood like she was a porn star. They were both sweating and ready to cum simultaneously.

"Oh, oh." Sweetie and El'san moaned together. "I'm cuming again baby." Sweetie said with a slight murmur.

"I'm coming too." El'san said, as his body jolted back and forth.   They both climaxed together and held each other close.

For the rest of the night, they laid cuddled as one.   Sweetie's head was spinning, but as least she went to bed with a smile on her face.

Chapter Ten
It Hurts So Bad...

With the rise of dawn shining through the window shades, El'san gently lifted himself from the fetal position with Sweetie. He didn't want to wake her as she was sleeping very peacefully. Chyna Whyte must have sensed he was up, because his wet nose was snug at the bottom of the dog's bedroom door. You could hear him panting and breathing heavy to be set free. El'san opened the door slowly, he didn't want Chyna Whyte to get hit in the face. When the door cracked just a little, Chyna Whyte's body was squeezing between the little space, trying to break free.

"Slow down boy." El'san said, watching him trying hard to get through. "Ready for your morning walk?" He asked his best friend. Chyna Whyte was excited beyond a dog's belief. Just like an inmate set free from jail on a bright sunny day, he was in pure bliss.

Sweetie woke up with an excruciating headache, as she rolled over searching her surroundings. This was undeniably not her apartment. With the covers secured tightly under her legs, she didn't want to move. She was in El'san's apartment, in his bed, in the buff. From the vague remembrance of last night's happenings, the only thing she was sure of was that she was drugged by goat mouth Toby. Even though her actions seemed functional, the last thing she remembered was talking with Pop. Everything after that was a vague impression. She was hoping, since she was naked, her and El'san had gotten it on. But, was she poised to question him without him taking it offensively?

The warmth of the covers was enough to keep her content. Her mind was telling her to get up and out of the bed, but her body was screaming, lay down!

"Where the hell was El'san?" She asked herself. Little did she know, he was taking Chyna Whyte for a walk.

The morning was bright and the sounds of the public buses sounded as usual. The early risers were getting situated on the bus before they reached their destination. The 'Borough was rather peaceful this morning.

Knowing that it was against the law to let a dog roam free without a chain, El'san ignored it anyway. Chyna Whyte ran free all up and down the street. You could see the fear on the passerby's faces when they saw this fifty-pound dog come trotting their way. El'san knew better than that. He tried to caution them by telling them if they remained still, Chyna Whyte wouldn't bother them. Now ain't that a bitty? What else could they do, run? If they ran, chances are they'd be caught and suffer the wrath of this beast of a dog.

On this particular day, El'san decided to run a short distance, meaning around the block. After seeing so many people jump on cars or stay frozen in movement like a dead possum, he put the dog chain around the dog's neck. You could tell Chyna Whyte was a little discouraged because he resisted, throwing his head around from left to right.

"Calm the fuck down, Chyna Whyte!" El'san stated in command. He adhered to his master's request, but without delay, rose up fierce and started barking hysterically.

"What's the matter boy?" Chyna Whyte's front legs jumped and jumped, trying to get at his target.

El'san turned around to find out why Chyna Whyte was causing so much commotion. Much to his shock, Cam stood there holding tight to his black 9mm.

"Nigga, whuz's up? Long time no see. I believe Riker's was the last time we bumped heads." Cam had a sly grin on his face, knowing he had the upper hand with the 9mm pointed to the mid section of Chyna Whyte.

El'san tried to calm him down. He was boiling at himself that he didn't carry, at least, his small 22-caliber gun on his person. Normally, he wouldn't need it this early in the morning. He wasn't sure what Cam was doing over in the 'Borough, but he was sure about to find out.

"Yeah, what up Cam? What you doing in **this** part of the projects?" El'san said, aiming out his index finger and swaying it around the 'Borough. Chyna Whyte sat on his hind ready to jump at the gesture of his master's request.

Flashbacks of Riker's Island crowded both of their minds. Cam reflected on how so many people congregated to El'san's side like he was a king. Irrefutably, he had power on the inside.

His commissary stayed overfilled, he never went without. Even when he gave items out on credit, he didn't tax them like another would.

Cam didn't want to believe that El'san was the man to watch. Especially, if you were selling drugs. It was quite apparent that he didn't know El'san that well. El'san sized Cam up. Cam picked up a few masses of muscle since their last encounter, but he still was no match for El'san. He wondered if all the rumors were true about him murdering his own flesh and blood siblings, but Cam like Cain, had done just that. Not to mention, his ex-girlfriend from Delaware, Mona.

Murdering his girlfriend didn't seem far from reach but come on now, his own brothers and sister. How did his brother Kenny let that ride? If the rumor about that was true, then the murders were done in vain because the real culprit, his stepfather Jab, was still alive and well after murdering Cam's birth mother. He wondered if Cam knew about the horrific experience that Kenny went through after Cam's release. If he didn't know, now was the time to inform him.

"El'san, that's your name right?" Cam questioned, knowing the answer already.

El'san looked at him like, "Come on Cam, stop trying to play with my intelligence."

"I have two small problems with you, that if remain undressed, can turn into two real serious issues for me." Cam calmly stated.

El'san instantly knew what one of the problems was, definitely money. Shutting down the drug connection in the 'Borough was killing the Kingsborough projects and the pockets of the drug lords. He didn't take one eye off of Cam who spared not one moment with his gun still pointed at Chyna Whyte.

"Where the hell was everyone at this morning?" El'san thought. Usually a few of his boys, Tone, Butter, Leon or Andre would be creeping in this time of the morning on the low. This morning, wasn't a damn soul in sight.

"Yeah well, I don't know what I can do about your little problem." El'san answered, without flinching.

"I think you know exactly what to do about my problems. For starters, let's begin by cutting loose the restraints on drug selling in *T H I S* project. It would be so much easier on the both of us if you do that. Call off your group of S1W's. There's money to be made, and if you were really smart, you'd tap into the water fountain of money that pours nonstop in your hood."

El'san shook his head, no.

"I can't do that man. This is where I rest my head. My conscious will not allow me to pollute our mankind with the white man's drug. This is what they expect of us. They want us to kill each other with that poison you are infesting our communities with. If I give in, it makes me no more of a man than you are. Ask yourself, what have you done for the black community, besides continue to tear families down?"

El'san's grip on Chyna Whyte was physically powerful. He knew in any moment his dog would lock jaws on one of Cam's essential body parts.

"Nigga, who died and made you *'that nigga?*" Cam asked, with a screw face look. His

219

hurried expression to respond let El'san know he didn't care about what he was saying, he wanted to be heard.

"Cats like you are funny to me. You ain't no better than I am. Just because you rob a hustler for his 'ready made' money, that shit don't make no difference.

In fact, I think it's the coward way of saying, "I really want to hustle, but I don't have balls enough to get out and hustle for mines! So instead, you'll rob them of their hard earned hustling money. You talk about what the white man is doing, you're doing the same thing. They rob us of the money we truly deserve and you rob us for the money we work so hard to make. They leave us with scraps to take care of our families, and dudes like you, leave us with scraps to take care of our families. You're a thief just like they are, out to rob and destroy. The only difference is you rob within the community and rob us in our territory. Yet, you condemn my hustle? Fuck you, nigga! You ain't jack shit! You're taking the coward way out, if you 'ax me. If you really want to get down for yours, you should read up on some true black renegades and stop front'n like you on some *R E A L* renegade shit."

El'san felt the intensity solidify around the muscles in his neck as Cam spoke the word coward. It echoed over and over in his mind. He didn't hear a word after that. Though both of them were strong and egotistical, neither disrespected another until today.

"Coward?" El'san repeated to Cam.

"Yes nigga, loud and clear. In fact, if my recollection serves me correctly, I called you a motha fuck'n coward." All that El'san had on the inside of him concealing the events that took place on Riker's with Kenny was dying to be released. A heavy load would soon be lifted from El'san holding this secret.

"Pussy, coward must be you and your brother's last name. The only power you hold, is in your hands! Without a gun in your hands, you ain't shit. And, your brother, that's a fucking joke. This nigga is so much of a coward that another man snatched his manhood less than a week after you were released from prison." Cam's face twisted in concern.

"Didn't he tell you about that?" El'san asked.

Uncertain where El'san was going with this, Cam abruptly shot him down.

"What the fuck are you talking about? My brother ain't no damn punk and he ain't never been punked! We had it locked down in there. Didn't nobody step to us." El'san responded, very confidently.

"Yeah, ask around nigga. As soon as you left, so did the fake ass security blanket that those niggas claimed to have around you. I was the one who saved your brother the first time he was violently raped. Ask him who assisted him when he was down for the count. I'm surprised it didn't get back to you. Maybe, because he kept it on the hush. He was humiliated. He's probably one of those 'down low' brothers out on the streets, running up in all kinds of women knowing that he's a punk for another man. It's jokers like him that are the reason why our HIV cases increase every year."

"Yo nigga, what the fuck?" Cam didn't have a defense. He couldn't fathom why El'san would say these things. If it were true, his brother was a bi-sexual.

If he were raped, would he still be considered as a punk? Not if it were a one-time occurrence. Now if he continued to engage in homosexual acts, then he'd be considered a punk by choice and not by force. It's different when someone violates you rather than giving it up freely.

El'san had a way of changing the conversation to suit him. Cam played right in his pocket. This was the only time fear showed on Cam's face so evidently. The pain was written all over his face. What El'san said wasn't unbelievable. He knew his brother was soft and showed some female traits, but he didn't know this was the reason. Kenny had to be holding this in for a very long time. How was he able to keep it on the down low this long?

El'san posed a half smile, followed with an, 'I got under your skin' expression to Cam. Instead of showing his immediate feelings, Cam was on a verge of a blackout. This happened every so often when someone took him over his tolerance mark.

"Shut the fuck up!" Cam yelled out. "Don't say another word!" El'san didn't give him the option of controlling this situation.

"Man please, you've been shut the fuck up!" He laughed. El'san reached for Chyna Whyte to get on his feet.

Cam must have thought he was summoning Chyna Whyte to attack. He released his trigger finger and all you could hear was the sound of an echo from the 9mm gun. 'Back'em, back'em, back'em,' was the sound of the gun. Three shots hit Chyna Whyte. His body jerked like crazy. Before Cam exited the scene he told El'san what his last problem was.

"Yeah, my last problem was that damn dog of yours. Now, he won't be a problem. Ha! Ha!" After saying that, he ran to his vehicle and sped away. He knew he was in another man's hood. In seconds, the 'Borough would be filled by El'san's crew.

A stream of blood trickled from his open wound. El'san was speechless, stroking Chyna Whyte with one hand and the other trying to apply pressure so that the bleeding would stop. Finally, he picked up Chyna Whyte who was moaning very faintly.

"If I can just get him to the vet, he'll make it." El'san considered. He whistled and whistled, giving an all call to those in the 'Borough. Minutes passed and the crew filtered to the yard, all in disbelief. Chyna Whyte was a member of the squad. El'san was surrounded by his people while they watched him mourn the death of his best friend. Chyna Whyte didn't stand a chance. He took his last breath looking intently into El'san's eyes.

Trying to wake up from a terrible dream, Sweetie lifted her head only to see El'san was still not present. The sunlight blinded her when she tried to look out the window. She heard a lot of commotion outside and wondered what was going on. She grabbed El'san's robe and went into the bathroom to brush her teeth. Good thing El'san

223

kept extra toothbrushes because this morning, her breath was humming. She looked into the mirror, wiping the cold out of her eyes. The door was open to Chyna Whyte's room and that's when she realized that El'san was taking him out for his morning walk. Her body was weak and she needed a vitamin to boost her stamina.

Just when she was about to snoop into El'san's medicine cabinet, the phone rang. She stood there for a minute very impatiently waiting for the next ring.

"Hello," she answered. The dial tone went dead. She started to dial star 69, but forgot that El'san refused to pay for that service.

"Damn", she expressed. Before she could take two steps away from the phone, it rang again.

'Briing, Briing!'

In the blink of an eye, she speedily picked up the phone.

"Hello!" No one responded.

"I said hello. Who do you wish to speak with?" Silence still overpowered the other end. "Click-up", the phone went dead.

"Screw this, I don't have time to play these little games! Let me put my clothes on and go home to get dressed." Sweetie was ready to go home and freshen up her body. Her legs ached like they'd been worked out.

"Whew, I must have got some last night. My legs are killing me." She walked back into the bedroom when a forceful knock hit the front door.

Sweetie moved to the door with nothing but El'san's robe on. She figured El'san must have left his keys behind and needed to get in. She didn't even ask who it was on the other side. When she opened the door, Tiff stood there ready to start some shit.

"What are you doing in my man's crib?" Tiff asked. If it was games Tiff wanted to play, then Sweetie was ready for her.

"If this is your man's house, then what am I doing in here like this?" Sweetie opened El'san's robe to flash her bare essence.

"Chile please, no wonder he still wants this." Tiff was really jealous that Sweetie had the perfect body. She, on the other hand, had two kids and a pouch they left her with. She couldn't wear those cute little stripper outfits that she previously wore cause the stretch marks would show.

"What do you want? El'san is not here and I'm getting ready to shower and get dressed. So, you need to check with 'your man' later."

Another neighbor named Rena, who live four doors away, came running down the hall. "Chyna Whyte just got shot! Chyna Whyte just got shot! They say El'san is going off."

"What?" Both Sweetie and Tiff said in unification. Tiff ran behind Rena, even though she couldn't stand her either. El'san was known for hitting her off too.

Sweetie ran back into the house and threw on the clothes she wore last night. It sickened her to put on the same pair of panties from yesterday, so she just went without any. She rummaged around for El'san's house keys and proceeded to lock the door.

Pop was in the hallway sucking in all the details from the other nosey neighbors. It hurt him to see Miss Sweetie coming out of El'san's apartment that early in the morning. He'd seen so many women rotating in and out of his apartment like a revolving door.

"Miss Sweetie, before you go out there, let me share a few words with you." Pops requested.

"Not now Pop, I need to find out what happened?" Sweetie said in hurried motion.

"Please Miss Sweetie, it will just be a second." He pleaded. She respected Pop, so she adhered to his request.

"Make it quick Pop, I have to make sure El'san is alright!" Pop looked at her in those dark homely country eyes and said, "They say some murderer from the Brownsville area named, Tam, Sam or Cam, something like that there or another, came over here and shot that bad ass boy's dog. The dog dead and gone now. I reckon many folks 'round here gonna be happy as a fox let loose on a herd of baby sheep. All I'm saying is be careful Miss Lady. You are too beautiful and too smart to get caught up in that boy's drama. He ain't been nothing but drama since I've been working in this complex."

Impatiently waiting for Pop to finish, she responded. "Thank you Pop. Now is that all?"

"Yes Ma'm, I've done my duty to warn you." He replied, thinking he did his good deed for the day.

She approached the corridor, and for a second, she was afraid to see what lay beyond the building door. El'san was being consoled by at least ten females, none of them family, each fighting for a place to rest their hands on any part of his body. Sweetie's heart dropped. Were her feelings a game to him? All of the talk about commitment, was it bullshit? Did he sincerely have feelings for her? These are all the questions she wanted to ask, but knew this was not the time. She saw the image of Chyna Whyte sprawled on the ground in a puddle of blood. Everyone was standing around like they were at a spectacular event. Sweetie decided to break the ice by approaching El'san and ignoring the other females flanking around him.

His head was down and from his body posture, his feelings were hurt and hurt real bad. The conversation he had with Yatta earlier vaguely crossed his mind. He was supposed to be helping them take Cam down. Their plan had been ruined, Cam got to him first. He would just have to tell Yatta now the vendetta is personal. It could not go down as planned. Cam made it personal, very personal when he shot and killed Chyna Whyte in front of his master. At this moment, he didn't want anyone else to play a part in his revenge. He figured Yatta's family suffered enough. It would be an injustice if something were to happen to Yatta also. El'san himself would carry out the dirty work. Besides, he didn't have time to wait. An immediate, but careful, plan of action had to take place during the next seven days.

"El'san!" Sweetie called out, wanting to hear his voice.

Hearing Sweetie's voice, El'san slowly came out of his trance. He didn't even realize that he drew a swarm of females blocking the attention from others. Most of them he hadn't dealt with in months. Why now were they concerned about his well being? It was surprising how women can hate a man so much, but when he's in jail or laid up in the hospital, everybody is still in love with him and God forbid he passes away, all of them would be acting a damn fool at the funeral. Sweetie was different from the rest, in his book. He lifted his head and arms, and pushed against the females that held them away. His arms spread wide for her, and instead of her consoling him, he consoled her. The women were right away infuriated by his actions.

A white cover had been placed over Chyna Whyte until the SPCA arrived. El'san would lie to rest his best friend the way that any other human being was, in a cemetery. Sweetie held onto El'san for dear life. As an alternative for coming back to El'san's apartment, Sweetie suggested they go to hers.

Inside, El'san laid across Sweetie's bed hoping this was a bad dream that he would wake up from. In less than fifteen minutes, El'san was asleep. Sweetie took this time to shower and dress. She knew the shit was about to hit the fan when El'san awoke. Sweetie hurt for El'san, and about El'san, but didn't know how she was going to approach it.

Shavonee invited Kenny over for a home-style cooked breakfast. Even though at first, she really didn't care for him, she thought enough of him to prepare a meal or two every now and again. He was keeping her pockets full, that's the least she could do for him. Lately, she'd been feeling a little flustered and weary. Her body just wasn't acting right. I mean she could throw down on some french toast, fried potatoes with onions and a side of scrambled cheese eggs. However, for some reason her stomach would not tolerate it.

Kenny was glad that he had the crib to himself. Cam had been really busy lately and hadn't spent much time in the house. Shavonee had become Kenny's crutch. He talked to her like she was his wife. All the worries of the world were placed in her lap, with the exception of his hidden past. For a long time, he was confused about his sexuality. Shavonee made him feel like a man again. He was a man. Just because a sick individual raped him, it didn't make him less of one. It wasn't his fault, he wasn't to blame. However, he carried that weight around with him everyday causing him feelings of low self-esteem and suicidal thoughts. He was beyond himself most days. He submitted to the belief that he was gay. That's why he got high to ease the pain on the inside. He'd even participated in other sexual acts outside of the prison walls. His state of confusion led him in that direction.

Working through his issues were tough on him, especially when the only support person he had was his non-caring unsympathetic brother Cam. If his mother were alive, he would have been able to talk to her. The first thing she would have done was, rub pure holy oil on his forehead and pray for days that the demon come up out of him.

He was tired of living in a shell. Nonetheless, Shavonee was just like Cam, out for herself. All of those late night conversations she had with him, she was mostly high as hell and never remembered. She'd go into the bathroom and laugh her ass off from the most intimate secrets he would tell her. She treated him no different than any other man, her only focus was digging into his pockets. She gave all her men the love, affection and all the sex'n they desired. She stroked every man's ego. In turn, she'd get her bills paid, freezer full of food, expensive clothing and money in her pockets. She was good at it too, nothing short of being a prostitute, except for one thing, she was her own pimp.

Kenny washed his face and freshened his mouth with mouthwash. He'd just stepped out the shower and put on a pair of blue jeans, a new pair of butter soft Tim's and an Ecko polo shirt. He looked outside of the front window to see if Shavonee was watching him. Normally, she was all up in the kitchen window waving out of control, waiting to capture his attention. She'd sit in the window all day if she had to just for him to acknowledge her presence. Today, she wasn't standing there. That didn't concern him much because she had recently given him a door key to her crib.

When he walked in, Shavonee was bent over in the bathroom toilet.

"Hey baby." She managed to say. "I don't feel so good." She said with a sour taste in her mouth.

"What's the matter?" He asked her, unsure of what to say. "Do you want me to take you to the hospital?"

"Fool, don't you know I don't have health coverage and I'm not on Medicaid either. You'll have to take me to the clinic down past Fulton Street. They know me personally over there."

"Ai'ight then, that's where I'll take you. But if you want to go to the hospital, I'll foot the bill." He assured her he was on her side.

In between the gags of throw up, she stated, "The clinic is fine, I can go there."

While she was in the bathroom throwing up her insides, he felt there was no need of letting good food go to waste. He warmed up his plate in the microwave and sat down on the breakfast table nook he purchased for her. At the same time as she moaned in agonizing pain, he swallowed every bit of food on his plate. After she finished in the bathroom, she slipped her clothes on and off to the clinic they went.

Shavonee and Kenny waited patiently for the nurse to call her name. The waiting room was filled with ailing people. Both of them tried hard not to focus on anyone but himself or herself. Kenny sat with his arm around Shavonee.

For once, she felt like a man really cared for her. She was sitting there thinking to herself, *"I betta not be pregnant. I betta not be!"* She wasn't thinking about having a baby for no man. Especially not having a baby out of lust. She wanted a man to love her unconditionally for who she was, not for who he wanted her to be. That was always the problem with most men she dealt with, they were always trying to change her ways. Didn't they realize God was the only man capable of that? She would act as if for the first few months, maybe even the first six months, but after that, she could no longer play the role. The real character in her was destined to be exposed in her daily actions. When they got wind of that, they were out of there.

"Sha- Shavon- yeah." The nurse called back.

"No, it's Shavonee. The E with a long sound over it." Shavonee said, with an attitude.

"I'm sorry dear, it just names today are ridiculous. Parents need to stop harming these kids with all these crazy names. I've come across some names like Alize, Zambeasy, Zaquina, Yuasinia, Azu'rea, Otha, Aquawantay, it's preposterous. These kids can't half way pronounce their names, let alone spell them correctly. Then the parents get mad when they continue to spell their names wrong." The people in the waiting area chuckled at the nurse's remarks.

"C'mon back Shavonee." she said pronouncing her name correctly this time.

"Is your husband coming back with you?" She asked.

In quick defense Shavonee responded, "He's not my husband!"

"I'm sorry, I assumed he was." She returned, apologizing for her mistake.

Frustrated by the woman's comments on the name and now the mishap of believing Kenny was her husband, Shavonee was pissed.

"You assume-mid-ed wrong! Now can you take me back to the room so I can get checked out! My stomach is hurt'n real bad." Shavonee cried out.

"All that attitude is unnecessary." She placed Shavonee's lengthy chart down on the table for the Nurse Practitioner when she came into the room. She took Shavonee's temperature and blood pressure during the pre-screening

232

process.   Shavonee had been there on several
occasions, mostly for her annual Pap smear and
encounters with a venereal disease.   Seemed like
she had at least every disease once in her young
life.   She asked herself when she was going to get
the picture and start to use condoms?

The Nurse Practitioner came into the room,
very pleasantly picking up her chart to find out
what was ailing her.   From looking at the chart,
she immediately requested for Shavonee to pee in
a cup for a urine sample and prepare for blood to
be withdrawn.   There was a bad 48-hour virus
going around and she wanted to make sure she
covered all angles before giving her a simple
pregnancy test.

"Shavonee, we're going to run some tests
and the results may take 3 – 5 days to come back.
In the meantime, I'm going to prescribe you an
antibiotic to clear up any infection you may have.
Call me if your condition worsens and we'll call
you when the results from your tests are back.   Is
that okay with you?" She asked.   Shavonee was
cool with that for the time being.   However, she
would follow up to get her results.

Three days passed and her condition had
not changed.   She'd taken the antibiotics
prescribed by the clinic and her symptoms
remained the same.   She called the clinic to follow
up on her results.   She hadn't heard from them,
so no news, meant good news.   Kenny stayed by
her side the last three days taking care of her.
The attention he showered her with showed her
his worth, other than money.   While waiting for
the receptionist to answer the phone, her line

beeped in. She started not to answer it but did anyway.

"Hello, can I speak to a Shavonee?" It sounded like the Nurse Practitioner from the clinic.

"This who it be. Who dis is?' She asked right ghetto-fied.

"It's Angie, the Nurse Practitioner from the clinic." She answered, without sounding to enthusiastic about it.

"Oh okay, what's up? You know my stomach is still balling out of control."

Unable to dissect what Shavonee was trying to tell her, she asked Shavonee if she could come back down to the clinic today.

"For sugadale, I'll be right down there" Shavonee responded to her.

"Kenny, let's go. They need to see me back in the clinic. Maybe we can finally find out why my stomach is doing those sumner salts."

Kenny responded to her, "Do you mean somersaults, like your stomach is being turned upside down?"

"You know exactly what I mean, stop playing yourself." She told him.

Here they were back in the same waiting area, but this time, surround by a new batch of ailing people. Shavonee went up to the front desk and registered her name to see the head nurse on duty. The woman at the receptionist desk gave Shavonee a weird look.

"*What the hell is her problem?*" Shavonee thought to herself. After an hour passed, the same nurse who called her back a few days ago graced her presence.

"Good afternoon Shavonee, c'mon back. It may take a few moments for the Nurse Practitioner to see you. Do you have the time to wait?" She asked.

"I'm here aren't I? If I didn't have the time, I would've never came here for help, ah, duh!" Shavonee uttered.

The nurse retaliated this time, "For a woman that's not feeling so well, your mouth is definitely not the problem from the way you keep running it." She left the room, leaving Shavonee alone. The Nurse Practitioner came into the room and swiveled around in the chair.

"Hello Shavonee. How are we today?" Her presence was graceful every time they met. That's perhaps the reason why Shavonee didn't mind coming back to see her. Cramps formed in Shavonee's stomach and she bent over in pain that humbled her.

"Doc, I'm feeling the same way I did a few days ago. Ain't nothing changed." The test results were in.

Kenny sat in the waiting room reading the latest Essence magazine. The model on the front cover was especially beautiful. He gloated on her beauty to another man in the waiting room.

"You'd love to wake up to this honey on the magazine wouldn't you?" He asked the man. The man nodded in agreement.

"She is beautiful. I bet her man's pockets stay on empty trying to please her." Kenny stated.

"Kenny King." Stated a nurse, interrupting Kenny's brief conversation with the man.

"That's me." Kenny answered.

"Please come with me." She demanded.

He walked behind her watching her walk casually in her baggy pink and blue flower print uniform pants. She pointed inside the room where Shavonee and another woman sat. Shavonee's hands covered her blood shot eyes. He took a seat beside her and comforted her by placing his arm around her neck.

"What's wrong?" He whispered to her.

"I'm pregnant! That's what's wrong." She blurted out. Kenny's body became warm on the inside. He was finally going to be a father.

"Well, that's not anything to cry for." He reassured her. "It's a blessing from God." He smiled. This was the first time in his adult life that a female claimed to be pregnant by him.

"OH, YEAH NIGGA, OH YEAH!" Shavonee yelled. Kenny couldn't understand whey she was so distraught.

"It's not that damn bad Shavonee!" Kenny insisted. The two nurses sat inside the room watching their actions, not saying a word until the time warranted.

"KENNY, IT IS THAT BAD!" Shavonee screamed.

"Why do you think that?" He asked, trying to figure it all out. It was only a baby she was carrying. Shavonee had no way of going around it. It was necessary she kept it real, that's what she promised the nurse.

"IT IS THAT BAD KENNY, CUZ NOT ONLY AM I PREGNANT BUT I JUST FOUND OUT, I GOT THE MONKEY!"

"What?" Unnerved, he wobbled his head. "What is the monkey?" He asked her, hoping to God that it wasn't what he thought it was.

"Nigga, c'mon you've been in the streets longer than I have. The monkey is that bug, you know that HIV, AIDS and stuff." She continued to release the anger that built up in her for years.

"What?" Kenny asked startled.

"HIV, you've got to be kidding me." His heart started pounding extremely fast and the room started to close in on him. One nurse ran over to him, scared that he was going to pass out. She waived a small ammonia stick under his nose. His nose raced to get away from the strong smell.

Shavonee wouldn't stop talking. Kenny's breaths were getting shorter.

"You heard me right, I'm pregnant and HIV positive. I can't bring a baby in this world to battle this disease that I can't even face myself." Shavonee cried from the shock of the news. She internally focused on how she sounded and appeared to be relating to the ghastly news. Her goal was to act a certain way like she didn't care, but physically, her feelings couldn't be hidden, the grief was written all over her face.

"Shavonee, it's not that bad." One of the nurses pointed out.

"I know things seem a little dismal right now, but there are affordable medicines that can help control HIV."

"Shut the fuck up bitch! You are not the one with this fucking disease! Things are a little distant for me right now." She hollered. It was sad that even in this situation, Shavonee couldn't comprehend what the nurse was trying to tell her.

"With that attitude dear, you won't last a year with HIV." The nurse replied.

"I realize this is overwhelming for you right now, but it will absorb and make sense soon enough."

How the hell did she figure that? A young woman pregnant with HIV, unaware of the full comprehension of the disease and how she contracted it, how was she going to absorb that and live on?

Kenny's eyes were twitching. He wasn't sure what to say, what to do and what direction they were going. A nurse interjected between the crying from both, Shavonee and Kenny.

"Kenny, we bought you back here because Shavonee seems to think you may be at risk for the disease as well. Did you at anytime have unprotected sex with her?" She asked.

"Of course he did asshole, that's why I had you bring him back here!" Shavonee yelled at her.

The nurse was fed up with Shavonee. "I'm asking the questions now, not you. You've already answered what we need you to. Now if you would, please prepare the list we asked you for on all the partners you can remember you had unprotected sex with." She said sternly.

"Yes," Kenny responded. "On more than one occasion.

"Well, we need to ask you some simple questions and then we would like to administer the test afterwards. Is that okay with you?" She asked, but refused to take no for an answer. They were going to test him, whether he agreed or disagreed.

"Yes." He nodded.

"Good, please fill out this form and sign it giving us the consent to test you." She went down a number of questions asking him about his sexual behavior. Shavonee paid attention to the answers as he shared them with the nurse.

"Okay, have you ever encountered a same sex relationship?" She proceeded. Kenny paused.

"What do you mean same sex relationship?" He asked nervously. Shavonee's eyes beamed, wondering what the hell he meant by that. The nurse responded attentively.

"What that means is, have you ever had a sexual experience with a man?"

The room seemed to get real quiet and it seemed like the words bounced from wall to wall. Have you ever had a sexual experience with a man? With a man? With a man? That's all Kenny heard. The room started closing in again, and the nurse pulled open another small pack of ammonia to bring him back with them. The question drew knots in Kenny's stomach, and as hurtful as it would be to tell the truth, for the first time, he let it out of his system.

"Yes, I have." He answered, no longer afraid of the unspeakable reaction from them.

"*Oh my fuck'n God! Oh my fuck'n God!*" Shavonee bawled in disbelief.

"This nigga just confessed that he was gay! Why did you do this to me? Why?"

He looked at her with forgiving eyes, listening to the words coming from a woman with a cesspool of lies and deceit. "Don't look at me you faggot mothafucka! I HATE YOU! I HATE

YOU! YOU RUINED MY LIFE." He didn't have anything to say at first.

The nurse tried to calm her down.

"Hold on now Shavonee, the man hasn't even been tested yet. There's a possibility that he may be negative. If that's so, then what are you going to do? You've already informed us that there was a long list of others that you had sexual intercourse with without using a condom. There's a chance that you contracted this disease from someone else, please keep that in mind young lady."

"No, I didn't! None of them are faggots. You can only get this disease from a gay man and that's the gay mothafucka over there!" She was now out of reach. They knew nothing was going to stop her from acting a damn fool.

"Shavonee, just to set the record straight about HIV, homosexual encounters is not the only way to contract this disease. We have several pamphlets to explain what the disease is about and how you may have contracted it. We're going to set up an appointment with a counselor and have him or her explain everything in detail." Both nurses tried to remain professional. Shavonee was up out of the chair, pounding on the walls.

"I KNOW I CAN'T BRING A CHILD IN THIS WORLD THAT IS HIV POSITIVE, HAS A MOTHER THAT IS POSITIVE AND A FATHER THAT IS GAAAY!" She screamed, loud enough for other patients to hear them. In a matter of three days, their lives had been shattered.

"Shavonee, please." Kenny stated humbly.

"It wasn't my fault. I was raped in jail, please believe me. I don't need to ask you if you believe me because I'm confident enough that you do. I'm telling the truth, I expect you to believe me. I was tested several times in prison and each time the results came back negative. I never meant to hurt you."

All four of them, standing in the room, but not one of them looking Kenny directly in his eyes. He glanced at the floor, searching for more answers and looked back to see if they still avoided eye contact with him, they did. At that moment, he knew of the dislike they had for him. He tried to go over and hug Shavonee, thinking he'd get some sympathy from her. *What the hell did he do that for?* Like a bat out of hell, she charged at him punching and digging her fake nails deep into his skin. The two nurses couldn't control the room, they called for back up help.

Kenny let her relieve all the pain that she held on the inside until her strength turned to weakness. He held her tight and they both cried hard in that small, closed-in clinic room.

Chapter 11
On Bended Knees

Ms. Rhonda completed all that was required of her, her accomplishments alone still didn't satisfy her motherly instincts to find out the truth about her baby girl. She wanted to know more about what happened in the course of her daughter's journey. She was doing good, not picking up and using during her difficult days. She'd written down the return address from the package and died to know if this was the last place of residency for Mona. She didn't want Yatta in on this ordeal or her plans to find out if this were true. At the church she attended, she asked the Pastor's wife to get directions online from Mapquest.com. What lie ahead of her was unbelievable.

The two and a half hour drive put a strain on her. She hadn't driven this far in years. In fact, most of the time she went away, others drove for her. Driving, trying to precisely follow the directions, she thought she made a wrong turn when she pulled onto the estate. Looking at the outside of the house, she sat astonished. She glanced down at the paper again, yup, this indeed was the correct address. In fright for about ten minutes, she just sat there before she stepped out the car. Her legs wobbled as she walked up the steps from her nervousness. She pushed the bell and waited to see who would open the door. The butterflies in her stomach were going bananas. Granny peeked from the inside.

"Who is this?" She thought. She pushed the intercom button to speak to the visitor.

"Yes, may I help you?" She asked.

Ms. Rhonda cleared her raspy voice. "Hello, I'm sorry to bother you, but my name is Rhonda." She paused.

"Rhonda Foster, I believe my daughter's last place of residency was this address. May I come in? I'd like to ask you some questions, if I may."

Granny paused with uncertainty. She didn't know this woman from a can of paint. Cleary this was a mistake.

"I'm sorry Miss, nobody else resides with me, except my grands. You must be mistaken."

Ms. Rhonda pushed the button to speak, hoping this woman would hear her out.

"Please Ma'm, my daughter's name is Mona, Mona Foster. Does that name ring a bell to you?" She asked. Granny blinked her eyes. "Why yes, yes it does. I'm sorry." She let Ms. Rhonda in. When inside, Ms. Rhonda marveled over the beautiful threshold.

"I can see why my daughter fell in love with this place." She said to herself.

"You have a lovely place, Mrs.?" She said with a question.

"Just call me Granny, everyone else does. The kids, even Elders at the church call me that. Anyway, Roda." Granny began.

Ms. Rhonda impeded her thoughts. "No Granny, it's Rhonda, Rhonda Foster, is the name." It didn't bother Granny that she mispronounced her name.

"Well, Rhonda, how can I help you?" Ms. Rhonda began seeking answers. "I came all the way from Delaware to find out somethings about my daughter when she stayed here."

Granny asked, "Was that child a runaway? I told that boy not to let her stay in this house." She tried to keep her voice down, cause a few of the church mothers were in the kitchen playing cards.

"What is she up to now with her conniving ways?'

Ms. Rhonda immediately took offense. "My daughter was murdered, excuse you!" Granny sat up in her chair, "Murdered!" My Lord, my Lord!"

Ms. Rhonda brushed off Granny's fake concern. She was just talking ill about Mona. "Listen Granny, I'm here to get any information you may have, what you seen, heard, anything!"

Granny straight away put up her defense. Just as animals have rules for their territory, so did Granny. She was threatened by Rhonda taking her out of her comfort space, and attacked Rhonda with words.

"Oh, no you don't! You won't get me involved in that scandal. I don't know anything. In fact, the girl barely said two words to me." When the mothers of church heard all the commotion, they came out with their jackets and coats ready to leave.

"Granny, you need to pray for this sister." One of them said, very upset about the way

Granny was treating her visitor. The church family was hearing all kinds of rumors about the things Granny allowed to go on in her home but this, was the icing on the cake.

Granny tried to smile at her sisters in Christ. Her nose didn't spread, her cheeks didn't lift and they knew that smile didn't conceal the true feelings that she held within about the situation. She was extremely sad.

"Granny, don't do this to me. Please tell me the truth!" Rhonda begged.

"Look woman, she'd be up in that bedroom doing God knows what, melding mostly. Honestly, I didn't want her here. It wasn't my choice, it was..." Granny stopped talking and Ms. Rhonda finished where she left off.

"It was Cam's decision, right? What affiliation do you have with him?"

Granny quickly stated, "None"! I think that's enough questions for today. I'm sorry I couldn't be of help. Your daughter, well, she was a hot mess. She was a fresh young gale. Maybe you should have raised her with some decency."

Ms. Rhonda stood up facing Granny. She was humiliated enough. Here she was a grieving mother, and the only solution Granny could offer her was to raise her up with some decency. *How dare her talk about the dead like that!*

Ms. Rhonda gathered her bag, "How dare you talk about my child like that! There's no way in hell you can be a born again Christian. God is love and there's no love in this household. How you can sit there and fix your mouth to degrade a deceased person is ungodly! What a hypocrite you are! You didn't even know my daughter that well to be passing judgment."

Granny moved closer to her umbrella. In seconds she was going to hit Ms. Rhonda over the head, had she not left her house.

"You're standing too close, in my personal space, and I don't like it one bit. You listen to me woman, I knew enough about your daughter to know she was up to no good. I didn't say nothing to that boy when he found out some of his money was missing. It's so strange, that when the money disappeared, so did she. I could have led him to the little thief but I felt sorry for her homely behind. If she had to steal then, just maybe she learned it from her upbringing. You wouldn't by chance know what happened to the money would you Miss Holy Roller? How did you get my address anyway? Did you come to return what doesn't belong to you?" Granny asked, raising her umbrella at Rhonda.

Rhonda took steps closer to the entrance door. Granny was coming at her with the umbrella launched in the air.

"Yes." Ms. Rhonda cried. "I came to return something, your dignity!" When the tears fell this time, they fell in anger and anguish.

Granny swatted the umbrella at Rhonda, just narrowly missing her hand as she tried to shut the door behind her. Granny yelled out to her, "And, don't come back around here. The apple doesn't fall to far from the tree, that's why that girl was so messed up!"

Rhonda realized it was a substantial error on her part for showing up at Granny's, thinking she'd get some questions answered. It just wasn't going to happen, not if it had anything to do with Granny giving up the information. When inside the car, she cried, she cried like tomorrow was never going to come. If she'd had a pipe in the car with her this time, she would have sucked on it hard, but fortunately, she didn't have one. The way she was feeling, she had to call her son to tell him about her hideous experience at Granny's.

"Son." She tried to explain, with brutal tears of pain coming down her face. "I did something today that I'm not proud of." Yatta was scared that she'd relapsed with all the pressure of things.

"What did you do Mom?" He asked, with great concern.

"I went to that woman's house." She responded.

"What woman's house?" He asked, confused.

"Granny's, the house where Mona was staying last. That's where I went."

Yatta's antennas went up. Mona never gave up the red tape on Granny's house. She knew if she did, her brother would have somebody run up in there. For Mya's safety, she kept Granny's house a secret.

"Mom, where are you?" He asked her.

"I'm in Jersey, headed home now." She sniffled and tried to wipe the snot from her nose at the same time.

"What happened and explain to me who Granny is once more?" He wanted to be sure this was the house he thought it was.

"Granny is the woman who lives at the house; the address was on the package that Mona sent. I didn't want you to know. My curiosity led me to her house, hoping she would help me put all the pieces together. She was so mean and nasty to me. All the bad comments she made about your sister were extreme." Yatta really wasn't concerned about what her thoughts of Mona were, his only concern was trying to get the address from his mother.

"Mom calm down, you still have to get back home in one piece. Why would you risk your life like that? Let me handle this side of things. What's her address?" He waited patiently for his mother to let off of the information. She hesitated for a moment, but then spit it out. Yatta jotted it down. It was payback time.

"Okay   Mom,   drive   very   carefully. Everything is going to be all right. Call me once you get home. I love you, hear." He hurried up and disconnected the call from his mother to call El'san.

"Yo, I got the niggas address to the stash house. I got the niggas address to the stash house." He repeated, with much excitement.

"Supposedly, a woman by the name of Granny lives there. I figure it must be his grandmother with a name like Granny." El'san faced Sweetie with his thumbs up.

"Got one!" He told her and they gave each other some dap.

"Hit me off with his address, son," El'san informed him, "You stay put in Delaware, I don't want to fuck this up. I'll handle this on my end and I'll call you when it's done." He assured Yatta.

"I don't want you affiliated with this shit at all. It's about to get real ugly."

"That's what's up!" Yatta agreed. El'san contacted all those he wanted involved. They gathered together and were briefed about the hit. Later that evening, they would hit Granny's house.

Things were going as planned. Creeping like thieves in the night, they entered the estate, slightly hitting the outside lights one by one. Granny was a hard sleeper and had no idea what was about to transpire. Tone smashed one of the back windows with his jimmy. They hesitated before going inside, just in case an alarm system was activated. Too bad for Granny this night, she hadn't put it on. Andre climbed through the window and opened the back door for the others to follow behind him. By the full black attire, you couldn't discern who was who. The only feature visible was eyes and lips, even the nostrils were concealed.

They tiptoed in the house, searching for money and valuables. El'san glimpsed around for Granny. He knew they had to find her and wake her to find out where the real stash was. Granny must of sensed, in her spirit, that something was going wrong because she laid in position with her knees bending like she was in prayer.

"Get the fuck down, old lady!" El'san warned her. Granny looked up at him in dazed amazement with scary wide eyes. A big barrel shotgun was pointed right in her face. Two others stood on both sides of the bed. El'san jumped on the bed with the barrel faintly touching Granny's forehead. She was so scared she peed herself.

"Where the fuck is the money?" Butter questioned. Granny was speechless.

"I'm going to ask you one more goddamn time old lady, if I have to ask you again, I'm gonna blast on you woman. Where the fuck is the money at?"

The treatment Granny was getting was directed at Cam. Since he wasn't present, Granny would get the undeserving treatment. El'san pulled her out the bed by her hair. The wig she had on slipped through his fingers, pulling the bobby pins and strands of hair out.

"Oouull." Granny wailed. He threw her chubby body to the floor in her housecoat and had his boy wrap her hands, mouth and feet in duct tape. They carried her by her hands and feet like they had captured a wild animal. They pulled her out of the bedroom and slammed her body against the wall. Her old bones ached. She cried hard for all the times she withheld and suppressed Cam's irrational behavior. This was her pay back.

They rummaged through the house until they discovered the chest. Not even bothering to ask Granny for the keys to open it, each lock was blasted away. They cleared everythingout of it carefully. Fingerprints would never be an issue, for there would be none. Each man had a pair of black gloves on. Granny struggled to speak with the duct tape covering her mouth. Feeling a little empathy, El'san ripped the tape off of her mouth.

Granny gasped for air. "I can't breathe, I can't breathe." She finally spoke.

"My heart, my heart!" He watched her body spasm. Without second-guessing her problem, El'san knew she was having a heart attack. They hurriedly ran out of the house with all of Cam's money in that spot. In the midst of the hustle, El'san took a pit stop at a pay phone to call 911 for ambulance assistance to pick Granny up for medical attention. He didn't want to really hurt her, just scare the shit out of her. A heart attack was never expected.

Granny was in the hospital, half way dead, in the intensive care unit. The only contact information they had was Nikki's and the Pastor of her church, they called them both. The minute she heard about Granny's condition, she flew up to the hospital. Bad smell, tore up from the floor up and all, she was going up in the intensive care unit to see her grandmother. The Pastor was already there, praying with Granny, when Nikki walked in.

She watched her grandmother closely. It hurt but she couldn't shed one tear. She was pained on the inside but not one tear dropped from her possum looking eyes. Doubtlessly, she counterplayed if it was necessary to contact Cam. Indeed, she knew it had to be done. His outrage, nonetheless, would be directed at her. Officers asked question after question but didn't get one answer out of Nikki. She didn't know a damn thing.

They left her their card and proceeded on their way. She called Cam on his cell phone to let him know what happened. The conversation was less than pleasant.

"Where the fuck is Mya?" That was his first question.

"I don't know. Granny was home alone." Nikki pleaded.

"What the hell do you mean, she wasn't there?" That didn't sound logical to him, coming from her mother.

"All I know from what the officers said, was the house was burglarized and Granny had a heart attack. That's all I know." She yelled out of frustration. She knew that Prince took Mya away, but for Mya's and Prince's safety, she would never reveal the truth.

Cam hung up the phone in Nikki's ear. He arrived at the hospital in less than ten minutes. The Pastor left out to update some of the members of the church who were waiting nervously in the visiting area.

The ICU finally stabilized Granny's condition by giving her nitroglycerin. She still couldn't talk, only nod her head as a way of responsiveness. Cam yanked Nikki up by the collar.

"You dirty bitch! Where is my fucking daughter?" He smashed her head against the glass divider.

"I don't know, Cam!" Nikki said, grabbing his hands from her shirt. A nurse from the ICU caught a glimpse of what was going on and offered her assistance.

"Is there a problem?" She asked right confidently.

Nikki responded, "Everything is fine. This is a bad time for our family, that's all. No need for assistance."

Cam let loose of her collar. The woman left the room with a flustered face. She watched them from that point on.

"Who have you been talking to bitch?" Cam asked her.

"Have you been running your mouth over Kiesha's to any of those buster niggas? I've never had a problem with niggas running up in Granny's. Don't nobody even know about that spot. Just who the fuck have you been talking to?" Nikki convinced him that she hadn't uttered one word to anyone.

"What the fuck, do I seem that damn gone to you that I would give the address to where my only daughter rests? Give me some fucking credit! I may not be in the best shape, but I ain't doing that bad to do some shit like that!" Cam slapped the shit out of her.

"Exactly, bitch! That's why I know you had something to do with it. And, you claim you don't know where Mya is. One thing I know for sure, you know where your daughter is. Tell that shit to the next man." This time she knew if she went back to Kiesha's, her life would be over.

Cam stood over Granny hoping to get answers.

"Granny, I know you can't talk right now but nod baby to respond to the questions. I need to get some answers.

"Where is Mya?" He was trying to find out if she had been abducted, but nobody would give him the answer. Granny didn't respond.

"Was Mya at the house at the time of the robbery?" Granny didn't respond. Nikki knew she had to distract the attention before Granny revealed the truth. She was hoping this time she kept her mouth shut for Mya's sake. Cam continued the questioning.

"Did the robbers find the stash?"

"Yes." She nodded.

"Damn." Cam hit the side of the bed hard, pulling one of the heart monitors off, it started beeping.

Oblivious to the beeping sounds, Cam kept the questions coming.

"Did you recognize anyone?"

"No." She nodded.

"Was it Prince? Did Prince have anything to do with this?" Her head nodded no, wildly. He didn't want to believe she was nodding no.

"Come on Granny, you have to nod your head yes or no. It's important that you tell me these things. "Do you know who did this to us?" The nurse came running into the room. Granny's blood pressure reading had shot up.

"That's enough!" The nurse screamed, in disbelief. He was badgering a patient in the ICU division. *How selfish was that?*

Cam turned around to question Nikki, but realized she was gone. "That bitch! I know she had something to do with this."

Nikki sat in the nurse's station behind closed doors and asked them to call security for help. Her only outlet was to do as Prince mandated of her, admit herself into a rehabilitation center. The nurses felt sorry for Nikki and the condition she was in.

They immediately contacted the Social Worker on duty to find out if there were any beds available at a Rehabilitation Center in their jurisdiction. When the answer was no, Nikki was distressed, but when they said they had beds open in one of their sister properties in Delaware, the Crest Outreach Center, Nikki followed them while they shielded her from any harm, down the back entrance.

A car was waiting for her outside. She was on her way to a Delaware intense rehab center where she knew but a handful of people. This was the start to her new beginning. Security guards came through the ICU doors and Cam walked pass them, troublesome that no one seemed to know where Mya was and Nikki was gone.

Granny was sitting in the hospital from a massive heart attack, and to top that off, his stash had been taken. Add that to the information he received on Kenny, and you had a raving bull on your hands. He started to reflect on all those he had a beef with in the last few months. It was hard to tell. There was Jab, Prince, Nikki, Controversy, Yatta, Nee, Shavonee, El'san, Sweetie, and his own flesh and blood brother Kenny. Which one of them was involved in the heist? Did they all play a role? It was sad that he'd done so many people grimy. Maybe then he'd be able to pinpoint, at least, one suspect. Who was bold enough to come after him like that? It had to be Prince; he had more at stake than anyone. Yeah, he thought.

"I bet that's who has Mya." He called both of Prince's numbers, only to find out they were both disconnected. He couldn't believe shit was going down like this.

"What the fuck?" He asked of himself. He
went back home to sort out all his feelings. This
was the first time since his mother's passing that
he felt so alone. Kenny wasn't home and he was
glad, cause tonight, he was sure to confront him
on that punk shit. He looked out the living room
window looking up into Shavonee's apartment.
Without a doubt, it was near 2:00 in the morning.

The streets were filled with late night
cappers and the darkness peered misty like a film
of fog surrounded the area. The stench of rain
filled Cam's nostrils as he watched the scene in
Shavonee's window. It appeared that she was
having a physical altercation with someone. Cam
thought it to be Kenny whipping her ass. What
he didn't know, was that it was El'san and
Sweetie up in her apartment.

Settling all scores, El'san gave Sweetie the
red light to whip Shavonee's ghetto ass, cousin
and all. El'san was excited from all the work he
put in today. To go in was completely foolish,
why waste the energy that surged in his veins.
He made sure that all beefs were handled, cause
tomorrow would be the start of a new day.

El'san fooled Shavonee into letting him in
her place. He told her he needed a place to rest
for the night. El'san was her flesh and blood, she
didn't mind him crashing over her crib. She
didn't know Sweetie was right behind him.
Sweetie slid from behind him soon as the door
opened and proceeded to beat the shit out of her.
It didn't dawn on Sweetie that Shavonee didn't
attempt to fight back. Shavonee didn't seem to
mind her ass was getting a serious beat down.

She was hoping that from the beating, a miscarriage would follow.

Kenny pulled in front of the building, jumped out his vehicle and ran up in Shavonee's like someone stole something from him. He ran into Shavonee's apartment. Even though she didn't want any part of him anymore, he couldn't let her go out like that. He pushed through the door and was shocked to see these unfamiliar faces.

"What the fuck is going on? Who are these people Shavonee?" Kenny asked.

When El'san spoke the intendment rose. The voice was the same voice he heard after he was raped in prison. El'san didn't leave his mind to wonder.

"It's me nigga, your savior! Don't I sound familiar to you?" Kenny didn't know what to say.

"What's going on man?" Kenny asked him.

"What's gong on is your girl deserves this beat down for being dishonest and stealing from my lady. That's what's going down. Care to join in? Cause, I'm ready to knock a motherfucka out." He was hyped beyond principle.

"Look, my concern is that Shavonee is pregnant with my baby." Sweetie stopped pounding on her.

"What?" She said, very concerned. She knew getting an assault charge on a pregnant woman was double the penalty. Then if the baby died, her ass was in deep shit.

Shavonee said to Sweetie, "That's right bitch, keep it coming! I don't want this baby nohow. If I did bitch, I would whoop your ass like Ike did Tina. I'd rather live with the fact I lost a baby by fighting than to hold the weight on my shoulder of having an abortion."

Kenny frowned up his face. El'san pulled out his gun. He felt that he could kill two birds with one stone. He'd just hit up his brother. Why not hit him up too?

"Empty your pockets, nigga!" Shavonee yelled over to El'san, "Kill the mothafucka, I don't care!" El'san didn't give a damn what Shavonee said.

"Sit the fuck down Shavonee. You don't have nothing to do with this right here. You don't know shit about this punk nigga!" She moved closer to Kenny's side.

"Yes, I do El'san." She told him.

"I know about his past and his past has caught up to me." El'san cocked his gun. She didn't really know the truth, he thought.

"What? You don't know shit about this man, I'm telling you." He pointed the gun at Kenny with force.

"I said, empty your pockets man!" Kenny pulled out a knot of money and placed it on the table.

"That's all I have, man." He didn't put up a fuss. Kenny wasn't a fighter, no way.

"Let's go Sweetie, our job is finished here." They walked pass Kenny and Shavonee like they were over there for a friendly visit. Kenny's pride once again was shot down.

Outside, Cam sat on the steps watching the nightlife. Spotting him, El'san made Sweetie get down on her knees and crawl to safety.

"Crawl, do whatever you need to do to get out of reach. Take the car and meet be back over the 'Borough at your place. Now go!" He spoke with influence. An all out war was about to begin. Cam's six sense made him jump behind the Pathfinder that was in front of his house. El'san peered around the car.

"Man up, mothafucka!" El'san summoned.

"You got this coming to you." Cam let off the first shot. *Boom!!* The glass shattered from the car El'san hid behind.

Kenny heard the gunfire and ran out of Shavonee's apartment. It was two against one. El'san wasn't about to get out of this situation alive. He ran trying to get out of reach of Kenny. Kenny grabbed for his 45 that he put in his pants pockets. Good thing he left a piece in Shavonee's apartment. If Shavonee hadn't hid it, he would have had it sooner. Cam was concerned about his brother's welfare and the position he was in.

"Kenny." He yelled.

"El'san is to the left of you!" El'san fired another shot that came close to hitting Cam. *Boom!!* Cam dove down on the cement pavement. Coming up, he fired another shot at El'san.

"What are you doing man?" Cam asked Kenny. "Nigga, shoot the mothafucka!"

Kenny never tried to pull the trigger. El'san's target was Cam. Cam felt in his heart and knew Kenny wasn't going to do shit, not even shoot at this nigga that was trying to kill his own brother. Kenny felt he at least owed El'san that much. That's why he didn't put up a fight about the money, when he got robbed.

El'san had Cam in plain view. This would be the end of him, He attempted to pull the trigger when his hand locked on him, he couldn't move it. El'san had a clear shot at him. Cam, in turn, fired one last shot at El'san that plunged deep in his tissue. The shot burned, hitting his body in rapid motion. It felt like his body was on fire. He stumbled to the ground and ran before Cam could finish him off, trying to get back to the 'Borough to meet Sweetie. Cam didn't run after El'san, he wanted answers from his brother.

"Tell me that shit is not true." Cam declared to his brother.

Kenny walked closer to Cam's reach, "Can't we discuss in another setting? This is not the time."

Cam put the gun down to his side. "Nah man, explain that shit to me, right now! Is it true that you got duked in prison?"

Kenny spoke in a crackly voice finally trying to put all this behind him. His burden was heavy enough waiting for the results of the HIV test.

"Yes man, I was raped." He said in profound awkwardness.

How was Cam to feel? He was rumored to be a hard-hitting dude from BK, Brooklyn, with a punk for a brother. The little brother in him wanted to kill the man that stripped his big brother of his manhood, but the man in him wanted to beat his brother's ass for not fighting hard enough to keep his manhood. Kenny was the only person left in his family, and to live with the fact that his brother was punked, hurt him more than his heart could stand. He'd rather end his brother's misery than to allow him to live on.

Back inside her apartment, Shavonee called the police for help. She was bleeding liberally. It seemed her wish would come to pass. Her body was miscarrying. The sirens sound of the ambulance was getting louder and louder. Cam wiped off his gun from prints and threw it underneath a car several feet away. The police covered all angles of the street. Both Cam and Kenny looked at each other. This was it, Kenny knew he wasn't about to go back to jail.

One officer screamed, "Put your hands up in the air!" They both hesitated. With no defense, Cam put his hands up in the air and turned toward the officers. Kenny still didn't adhere. The cops warned them again.

Cam yelled to Kenny, "Put your hands up Kenny, and do as they say!" Kenny didn't bulge.

An easy route to end his misery could be made by one wrong movement and this movement he was willing to take.

Kenny lifted his gun with his hands and the officers thought he was aiming in their direction. Immediate fire blasted him in the chest, three, four times or more. First his knees buckled, then his mid-section caved in, lastly his face, sealed with a peaceful smile plummeted on the worn concrete. Kenny regurgitated blood, trying it's best to go down his esophagus, choking him as he tried desperately to make it come back up. Cam jumped to his brother's aid, racing to protect him. A shot rang out from one of the officer's hitting him in the back. His body jerked up in the air before it hit, lying him face flat in the middle of the street.

The ambulance left with two stretchers, one for Shavonee and the other for Cam. The coroner's office took Kenny's body away. When the attendant questioned Shavonee about the occurrence, she didn't tell them the truth. She lived by the street code, never ever get the authorities involved in a situation you can handle yourself. Sweetie was the one who had to live with what she'd done, killed an innocent seed.

Cam was taken to the trauma center, the same hospital Granny was in. At first, they listed Cam as John Doe until the Pastor from Granny's church identified him walking past Cam's room to Granny's.

Cam laid in trauma not able to feel any movement. All he could see was visions of his mother, his brothers and sisters and lastly, a vision of Mona Foster. All of them dancing around like they were having a grand time together. At that moment, Cam wanted to join them, to smile as they were smiling, to hug as they were hugging and to love as they expressed their love, but he couldn't.

The shot to Cam's back hit his spine and caused severe paralysis. Movement no longer would be an option for him, he would never walk again. He was paralyzed from the neck down. Somehow the bullet moved within his body and affected his vocal cords. Not only was he paralyzed, but also he was mute. The hospital called all the numbers listed in their computer system for the King family to inform them of Cam's condition. When a tall, dark man, medium build came up to identify he was kin to Cam, Cam shit in his pants. The mystery man was his stepfather Jab, his next of kin. Cam's torture was just beginning.

El'san made contact with Tone who picked him up just blocks away from the fury. In the car on the way back to the 'Borough, his shoulder bled dangerously. Blood engorged the grey cloth interior of Tone's Buick Regal. Tone kept looking back at El'san, hoping he'd make it. The constant kicking and shifting around in the back seat told him that things weren't looking too good. El'san was in serious pain, and though it was only his shoulder bleeding, the loss of blood increased by the cup full. Leaving El'san in the car, Tone banged on Sweetie's door crying for her help. The events of the night were all over the news. Sweetie panicked, she hoped it was El'san at the door. She rushed to the door and screamed when Tone barged in with his clothes full of bright red blood. Just the skim of touch left blood inside of her apartment.

"Let's go!" Tone yelled at her and she stood in disbelief. Sweetie was standing there not saying a word but completely traumatized. Tone tried to break her non-movement.

"Sweetie, if we don't hurry El'san is goin' to be dead. We have to get him to the hospital." He pulled her behind him to the car.

El'san had kicked a dent in door of the back seat. No way was Tone going to get the blood out that stained the inside of his car. While in the house, Tone grabbed some white towels.

"Here." He said to Sweetie. He ripped the towel in pieces.

"Take these and tie them real tight to try and control the bleeding." Sweetie grabbed them quickly and tied four pieces of towel around his shoulder. El'san screamed after she tied each one.

"I'm sorry baby. I'm so sorry but I had to do this to stop the bleeding." Blood was getting all over her clothes. She reached in her bag to pull out a painkiller. Good thing she always carried them with her at all times. Once the pain eased some, and the bleeding slowed down, El'san managed to escape from his lips, "Call Yatta for me." Sweetie's only concern was getting El'san safely to the hospital.

"Yatta can wait. I'll call him after we get to the hospital." Sweetie said, in response to him. She was happy that El'san made it back in one piece. This was her only time to supplicate the thoughts she was keeping in.

"El'san." She begged. "This has got to stop. Haven't we been through enough? I hope you realize that this war you're fighting is not *your* war to fight alone. You need a multitude of others that believe in your mission. It will never be addressed if you continue to rob the robbers. Honestly, we aren't any different. We both have a strong spiritual belief. Let's rely on our beliefs to take care of those going against the grain. The next time you won't be so lucky. It might be you next leaving in a body bag. Let's settle the commitment with Yatta and leave this shit alone. Hustlers aren't the only ones to blame for the rise in narcotics. You see the majority of hustler's are smart, mathematical geniuses. They control and triple their money better than most large corporations. If they could only be shown a legitimate way to flip their situations, they could make it work. Instead of beating them down, let's help them out. Are you with me?" She asked sincerely.

"Yes, baby I'm with you. Now can we get to the hospital before you let me bleed to death?" He responded to her, still in unbearable pain.

A few days went by and Yatta hadn't heard anything from El'san. He wondered how things went down. The pressure was on to fulfill his sister's last request, see to it that Cam gets his. When El'san contacted him, Yatta was over his mother's house with Nee, explaining to her that Kenya was her grandbaby. Rhonda asked for paperwork to verify it. She wanted the truth on paper, not by word of mouth. Her heart was tender. This was indeed her first grandbaby.

El'san let him know about Cam's condition that spread all over Brooklyn streets and how the police gunned down Kenny but that the job was taken care of. He even wanted Yatta to come and get a portion of the money. Yatta declined, sweet revenge is what he needed. With Cam being paralyzed that was enough for him. Cam would never conquer his new condition. He'd finally been defeated. To live with that was hellified torture. Yatta informed his mother and Nee word by word. They were all happy and finally had some closure. The grieving process had just begun. Rhonda openly admitted to her son and Pastor about her very close encounters of getting high. Both of them recommended that she attend an intense six-month, inpatient drug rehabilitation program at the Crest Outreach Center. She agreed, admitting herself the next day.

The Foster Foundation Group Home was underway and was operating smoothly, every bed in the house was occupied. The staff on board worked great together, Rhonda never had to oversee them. If she was gonna stay clean, she had to be clean, free from all the guilt and pain her issues handed her. At the center, she was made to share a bedroom with another recovering addict, Nikki was her roommate's name. Rhonda and Nikki would come to know each other real well in those six months, especially the common bond that they shared, Mona Foster. Nikki shared things with Rhonda that none of the other girls could. Nikki answered many of her unanswered questions.

Once El'san recuperated from his war wounds, he decided it was time for him and Sweetie to move up out of the 'Borough and move to the sunny lizard state, Florida. El'san's Mom was already living lovely down there and had just purchased another piece of property, this time a duplex, that El'san and Sweetie were going to live in. Before they left, they made it their business to go down to the Justice of Peace to make it official, get married. Everyone in the 'Borough was happy for them, including Pop.

Granny made way after six long weeks in the hospital, trying to get her limbs to cooperate with her mind. One of the mother's in the church asked Granny to sell her house and come live with her. Really, Granny didn't have a choice, she knew she wasn't going back to that house and she had nowhere else to go, so she accepted her offer. Besides, she needed someone there 'round the clock to care for her. She was still able to get around, but barely.

Jab took Cam from the hospital with him to a dirty, abandoned apartment he was staying in.

He tormented Cam by just looking at him. He knew how much Cam hated him. Cam couldn't say two words to him, but inside his heart was crying out. *What had he done so bad in his life that it had to end like this?* When Jab had enough of the insulting smell of Cam being around, shitty and stinky, he placed him in a nursing facility to live out the remainder of his life.

Prince stretched out on the back porch of his newly built, three-bedroom single family home in Charlotte, North Carolina. Mya ran around in the backyard with her white fluffy poodle chasing her, pigtails flopping, batting those beautiful deer eyes. Prince waved to her as she smiled with much happiness. He could never forget the day he told her the truth about being her father. It was her response that was even more unbelievable.

"I knew you were my Daddy a long time ago silly, but I knew if I told my other Daddy I knew the truth, I wouldn't see you no more, so I acted like I didn't know, but I knew the truth all the time Dad-dee. I luuuv you! I have one question though, is Mommy my real Mommy? Cuz, she sure don't act like it!" She *said, giving him a big kiss on the cheek.*

He looked at her and vowed never to underestimate a child's mentality, they know more than you think! All he needed now, was a good ole' southern woman to be his wife and a mother to his child.

Guess it is true, you reap what you sow, whether good seeds or bad. It may not come back the same way you dished it out, but it comes back in a way you least expect it, somehow as Karma would have it.

Lay Down Your Heavy Burdens

Pieces of your mind, pieces of your dream
Scattered all around but never unforeseen
Unfortunate for you that you just don't want to believe
That even in the midst of your mess
God is there to intervene
Yet you pass him by and continue on till the weight gets heavy
To heavy of a load for you to move on and carry
Your back, your shoulders, your arms and legs, can't seem to balance it out
It's the weight of the world that continues to turn you out
Don't rob, kill and steal to take the load away
Just lay down your heavy burdens
For it is HIM
That will help you peel those layers away!
Lay Down Your Heavy Burdens...
The End.

ORDER FORM

Triple Crown Publications
PO Box 247378
Columbus, OH 43219
1-800-Book-Log

NAME	
ADDRESS	
CITY	
STATE	
ZIP	

	TITLES	PRICE
	A Hood Legend	$15.00
	A Hustler's Son	$15.00
	A Hustler's Wife	$15.00
	A Project Chick	$15.00
	Always A Queen	$15.00
	Amongst Thieves	$15.00
	Betrayed	$15.00
	Bitch	$15.00
	Bitch Reloaded	$15.00
	Black	$15.00
	Black and Ugly	$15.00
	Blinded	$15.00
	Buffie the Body 2009 Calendar	$20.00
	Cash Money	$15.00
	Chances	$15.00
	Chyna Black	$15.00
	Contagious	$15.00
	Crack Head	$15.00
	Cream	$15.00

SHIPPING/HANDLING
1-3 books $5.00
4-9 books $9.00
$1.95 for each add'l book

TOTAL $_____

FORMS OF ACCEPTED PAYMENTS:
Postage Stamps, Personal or Institutional Checks &
Money Orders.
All mail-in orders take 5-7 business days to be delivered.

ORDER FORM
Triple Crown Publications
PO Box 247378
Columbus, OH 43219
1-800-Book-Log

NAME
ADDRESS
CITY
STATE
ZIP

TITLES	PRICE
Cut Throat	$15.00
Dangerous	$15.00
Dime Piece	$15.00
Dirty Red **Hardcover**	$20.00
Dirty Red **Paperback**	$15.00
Dirty South	$15.00
Diva	$15.00
Dollar Bill	$15.00
Down Chick	$15.00
Flipside of The Game	$15.00
For the Strength of You	$15.00
Game Over	$15.00
Gangsta	$15.00
Grimey	$15.00
Grindin' **Hardcover**	$10.00
Hold U Down	$15.00
Hoodwinked	$15.00
How to Succeed in the Publishing Game	$20.00
In Cahootz	$15.00
Keisha	$15.00

SHIPPING/HANDLING
1-3 books $5.00
4-9 books $9.00
$1.95 for each add'l book

TOTAL $_____

FORMS OF ACCEPTED PAYMENTS:
Postage Stamps, Personal or Institutional Checks & Money Orders.
All mail-in orders take 5-7 business days to be delivered.

ORDER FORM

Triple Crown Publications
PO Box 247378
Columbus, OH 43219
1-800-Book-Log

NAME	
ADDRESS	
CITY	
STATE	
ZIP	

	TITLES	PRICE
	Larceny	$15.00
	Let That Be the Reason	$15.00
	Life	$15.00
	Life's A Bitch	$15.00
	Love & Loyalty	$15.00
	Me & My Boyfriend	$15.00
	Menage's Way	$15.00
	Mina's Joint	$15.00
	Mistress of the Game	$15.00
	Queen	$15.00
	Rage Times Fury	$15.00
	Road Dawgz	$15.00
	Sheisty	$15.00
	Stacy	$15.00
	Still Dirty *Hardcover	$20.00
	Still Sheisty	$15.00
	Street Love	$15.00
	Sunshine & Rain	$15.00
	The Bitch is Back	$15.00

SHIPPING/HANDLING
1-3 books $5.00
4-9 books $9.00
$1.95 for each add'l book

TOTAL $_____

FORMS OF ACCEPTED PAYMENTS:
Postage Stamps, Personal or Institutional Checks &
Money Orders.
All mail-in orders take 5-7 business days to be delivered.

ORDER FORM
Triple Crown Publications
PO Box 247378
Columbus, OH 43219
1-800-Book-Log

NAME	
ADDRESS	
CITY	
STATE	
ZIP	

	TITLES	PRICE
	The Hood Rats	$15.00
	Betrayed	$15.00
	The Pink Palace	$15.00
	The Bitch is Back	$15.00
	Life's A Bitch	$15.00
	Still Dirty *Hardcover	$20.00
	Always A Queen	$15.00

SHIPPING/HANDLING
1-3 books $5.00
4-9 books $9.00
$1.95 for each add'l book

TOTAL $_____

FORMS OF ACCEPTED PAYMENTS:
Postage Stamps, Institutional Checks & Money
Orders, All mail in orders take 5-7 Business
days to be delivered